# THE BITTER PAST

1/24 (3)

# THE
# BITTER PAST

## BRUCE BORGOS

MINOTAUR
BOOKS
NEW YORK

First published in the United States by Minotaur Books, an imprint of St. Martin's Publishing Group

THE BITTER PAST. Copyright © 2023 by Bruce Borgos. All rights reserved. Printed in the United States of America. For information, address St. Martin's Publishing Group, 120 Broadway, New York, NY 10271.

www.minotaurbooks.com

The Library of Congress Cataloging-in-Publication Data is available upon request.

ISBN 978-1-250-84807-9 (hardcover)
ISBN 978-1-250-84808-6 (ebook)

Our books may be purchased in bulk for promotional, educational, or business use. Please contact your local bookseller or the Macmillan Corporate and Premium Sales Department at 1-800-221-7945, extension 5442, or by email at MacmillanSpecialMarkets@macmillan.com.

First Edition: 2023

10  9  8  7  6  5  4  3  2  1

To the Downwinders, for your sacrifice.

"A is for atom. B is for bomb. C is for cancer. D is for death."

J TRUMAN (DECEMBER 30, 1951–FEBRUARY 4, 2021)

ENTERPRISE, UTAH

# THE BITTER PAST

# CHAPTER 1

We don't have a lot of murder in Lincoln County. The long stretches of open road provide us with more than our share of high-speed vehicular deaths, the images of which can haunt your dreams, but there just isn't a lot of people killing other people on purpose. When we do encounter it, it's never like this. This is something from hell.

The crime scene is monstrous. The victim, retired FBI agent Ralph Atterbury, has been skinned, mostly on his arms and thighs, and strips of various lengths and thicknesses lay like lasagna noodles on the floor around the recliner to which his naked seventy-four-year-old corpse is bound by two blue ratchet tie-downs, like the ones people use to secure a new fridge in the bed of a pickup. The straps are as tight as they possibly can be, boa constrictors around tiny mice, feeling every last heartbeat of their prey.

His face, nose, and lips have been blowtorched, his nipples blackened like cinders. His fingers, all broken, are folded back in a horrible, twisted wreckage, and most of his teeth have been pulled and lie floating in a mug of cold coffee next to bloody pliers on a nearby end table. In this entire nightmare painting, it's the sight of the teeth that sends an icy shudder down my spine. Imagining the pain he endured and the horrific screams that must have followed is a little more than I can handle at the moment, so I will let those things come to me at night when I am alone.

The blood still smells of metal and is plentiful. It's all dried up now, even the purge that has oozed from what's left of the victim's mouth and nose, indicating he has been dead for a few days. He's also bloating from the gases that have leached out of his dead organs, and the smell of the sulfur in his body is especially over-whelming. The rate of human decomposition is fairly predictable but depends on temperature, moisture, pH, and oxygen. While it's cold and dry outside, as February tends to be here, the heat in the house is only speeding the rot. I check the thermostat on a nearby wall and see the furnace is on full blast. *Jesus, did the killer turn up the heat?*

It's a level of torture I've never witnessed, and that includes what I've seen the Taliban do. So, I have to ask, "Tuffy, until Mr. Atterbury here, what was our most violent murder?"

My best deputy suddenly drops to one knee, and I silently call on the Gods to keep her from retching again. The first time triggered a chain reaction around the room. Thankfully, she is genuflecting only to get a better angle on ex-agent Atterbury, her camera clicking every few seconds, occasionally firing off a quick flash followed by the little popping noise that invariably follows as it recharges.

Tuffy Scruggs is one of my twelve officers at the sheriff's de-partment and my lead sexual assault investigator. This looks like the furthest thing from any kind of sex crime, but everyone in the department wears a bunch of hats, and Tuffy is meticulous. She's built more like Dick Butkus than Dick Tracy, and from the back you would be hard-pressed to guess her gender, especially when she's in uniform like she is now.

I watch her deep in thought, in her crime scene booties and gloves, her thick, tightly wound sandy curls glistening from the sweat of her perspiring scalp in the overheated house that smells of burnt flesh and murder. Always über-efficient, she had the exterior of the residence taped off before most of the team arrived, not that anyone expects a lot of rubbernecking and foot traffic from the public way out here. Tuffy values good habits, which is the biggest reason I appreciate her.

"It was that domestic in Alamo in 2014," Wardell Spann finally answers for Tuffy. He's scanning the living-room carpet with his flashlight for more blood, as if that will somehow provide the clue to solving the case. "April, I believe. Old Mexican shot his wife three times and then hung her."

Wardell is my only lieutenant in the department, the product of an unhappy marriage of convenience, specifically the consolidation of the City of Caliente police with the county sheriff's department, a deal finalized last month. I know he feels like the unwanted stepchild in this arrangement, and I don't really begrudge the man his displeasure. As Caliente police chief, Wardell had ten years on me, a fact he shares with the rest of the county's electorate whenever he gets the chance.

I say to him, "He was Dominican, not Mexican." I don't consider myself particularly *woke,* as I understand the term, but still, calling someone Mexican just because he's brown is a bit tiresome. Wardell is a flat-out racist, and out in the high desert of eastern Nevada, where about two black people live at any given time, you might think he would be in good company, but not so much anymore. People here are pretty twenty-first century and generally accepting of others, which explains why Wardell will never be sheriff.

I pretend I don't notice him staring at me with death ray eyes. "Like there's a difference," he mutters, cracking his big knuckles. I let it go, as stepdads sometimes have to.

My attention makes its way back to the decedent. "Either of you know him very well?"

Tuffy shakes her head but doesn't look up from her work as she gets more close-up shots of the burns. "Met him a few times," Wardell says. "Thought he was a bit of a weirdo."

I can't stand the smell any longer. Bad smells trigger my stomach worse than anything you'd see in a Tarantino movie. "Have we processed the windows yet? We have to vent this place."

"Give me a sec, boss," Tuffy says, setting her camera down.

"Five will get you ten it's a robbery," says Wardell. "Addicts most likely."

I scan the interior of the house, wondering what on earth could possess him to think this is a robbery gone wrong. Yes, there are huge holes in the drywall and every room has been tossed. But the victim has been burned and skinned and . . . and then I see it. A box on the kitchen counter. About the size of a box of dishwasher detergent. Thallium salts. Very old. Not something you see every day. I flash on a memory from a previous life, gruesome pictures running through my brain.

For anyone else this would be a teaching moment. "That seems unlikely to me, Wardell. This was an ex–FBI agent tortured for what looks like hours. He was a man living on a pension, and while his killer appears to have been looking for something, it wasn't money. Look around, with all this damage, his guns are still in his cabinet in the corner there, his money and ID still in his wallet. It doesn't look like anything was actually stolen, does it?"

Wardell surveys the living room, scowling like one of the bad guys that gets killed at the end of every episode of *Bonanza* or *Gunsmoke*. "What do you think happened here, professor?" he asks.

I swear I'm looking forward to his retirement as eagerly as a nun getting ready to leave the convent. "Something . . . else."

I wander outside to check the exterior of the home. I recall seeing it under construction, wondering who would want a place this far out in the sticks, set in front of the vast Big Rocks Wilderness where the wind has two speeds, hard and harder, your immediate neighbors are rattlesnakes, and boulders the size of multistory office buildings line up like rows of soldiers guarding the high ground. To build out here, you're seeking one thing. Privacy. Hell, it's a four-mile dirt road just to get to where I'm standing. The house is completely off the grid. Solar panels on the roof provide the power, and internet and telephone are available only via satellite. There's no cell service this far off the highway.

The structure itself is nice, single story, Spanish tile roof, smooth stucco finish with a marbled color that blends nicely with the ancient formations behind it like a chameleon camouflaging itself on a branch. There is a little vegetation poking out of the snow, not much, mostly cactus and a few trees, all natural and not requiring any time or love come summer. The windows are intact, and none of the exterior doors have been jimmied or kicked in. A lot of people in this county don't lock their doors, but I envision a retired G-man to be naturally less trusting of strangers, which means he might have known the killer or decided to let him in for some reason. *Who would you let in that might end up torturing you?*

Back in the house, I watch as my deputies recover and impound as much evidence as possible, a process that will surely take the rest of the afternoon. My eyes find the many plaques attesting to Atterbury's days in law enforcement now strewn, broken and bloodstained on the floor. I take another look at his driver's license, my mind instantly recalling the times and places I've seen him. That's how my noggin works, cataloging faces, even when I don't want to. I can do it with words, too. Whatever I hear somehow gets logged into my memory banks like old pictures. It's a skill that served me well in the military but it makes it impossible to forget the details of life's painful moments, a blessing some days, a curse on others. While I had met Ralph just a couple of times, I had seen him around the county plenty, mostly driving in that forever dust-covered black Sierra of his. *What were you up to down here, Agent Atterbury?*

I ask New Guy Pete to go out and process Atterbury's truck. "You need help with that?" Pete was first on scene, the result of a welfare check requested by the dead man's daughter in Ohio who says she's been trying to get her dad on the phone since Wednesday. Today is Friday.

"I'm good, Sheriff," Pete says.

"It's Beck," I tell him. "You don't have to call me sheriff."

Pete Alexander seems like a decent guy. Ex–military police, early thirties, bright, handsome in that Ken doll sort of way, and the only one of us who hasn't tossed his lunch yet. I make a mental note: impervious to chain reactions. He has only been on the job about sixty days and is Wardell's hire, a not-so-subtle middle finger in my face. I had asked him to wait so that we could interview more candidates, but Wardell can be like an old dog with a bone pretending to be hearing impaired.

When my newest deputy exits the house, I remind Wardell that Pete still needs to go to the state academy up north, before he can be a permanent officer.

"Christ," Wardell grunts. "The guy's been a cop for ten years."

"Not here." I decide not to mention that Wardell is still wearing his Caliente police uniform, an entity that no longer exists. It seems petty when you're in the company of a mutilated corpse, plus there's the fact that my preferred uniform is blue jeans and a flannel jacket, a point Wardell would surely raise and I would have to counter by saying something about a sheriff's prerogative.

Wardell is a man who always has to have the last word, and accordingly walks over to Tuffy. "Addicts, I'm telling you," he says under his breath before turning those death rays on me again. "Probably *Dominicans*."

That would be a long shot. Yes, the drug problem in Lincoln County has been booming over the last few years, mostly heroin and other opioids, as they're cheap and easy to get, even in cow counties like mine. And it is an incredibly violent world. But when I look down at poor ex-agent Atterbury again, I'm certain his death is not a product of that world. Addicts would have taken something. Televisions, computers, something they could turn into quick money on the street. And those wounds were delivered with a steady hand, probably not what you'd find on a junkie looking to score. This was the work of someone with a purpose.

I say to Tuffy, "Best call down to the Vegas FBI office and let them know one of their retirees has been murdered. Maybe they want to send someone up here. And loop in our friends at Metro."

"Sure, Beck."

It's what everyone calls me. Nobody but my family and my signature uses my first name, which is Porter.

I ask, "Who's working next of kin?"

"Let's have Pete do it," Tuffy says. "He took the daughter's call."

"Good. Neighbor canvass?"

Collecting dried flecks of blood off the carpet and scraping them into a sterile container, Wardell grunts again but with more disdain this time. "Well, I don't hear anyone volunteering, so I guess that's me." He drops the container into an evidence bag.

"Excellent. Thanks, Wardell." When we use the term *neigh-*

*bors* here, nobody means a two-block radius. People are spread out. By area, Lincoln County is the seventh largest county in the nation, roughly the size of Maryland, and neighbors are anyone living within twenty miles. And out here at the base of Big Rocks Wilderness, it might be forty miles.

That box on the kitchen island turns my head again. I walk back in and take a longer look at it. Thallium. "And Tuffy, make sure we recover this and process it for prints." When I give instructions like this, it sounds like I really know my crime scene stuff. It's not so much from my experience as sheriff. As I mentioned, we just don't see crimes up here like this. But I've been around the darker side of the world. And I remember it all.

She's bagging the decedent's hands to preserve any possible trace evidence. "Will do."

"And let's ask the coroner's office to get some swabs of Mr. Atterbury's mouth and throat."

"Yes, boss."

*Please be wrong,* I think. Please be wrong.

# CHAPTER 2

I'm deep in thought, staring down at the pictures of the tortured body of Ralph Atterbury, and don't see her walk into my office, which is not exactly expansive. Her words don't register either, and I can understand why that might set someone off. I'm just lost in my own world sometimes.

"I'm sorry. Are you *not* Sheriff Beck?"

The question finally reaches the hamster in my brain—currently on a smoke break apparently—in charge of processing incoming messages, causing my head to lift slowly from the desk. "Why do you say it that way?"

She is striking. Mid-thirties, by my almost-always-accurate age calculator. Long black hair parted in the center of a perfect Middle Eastern head. Dark eyes to go with her olive skin, an annoyed look on her slightly red lips. "Pardon?" she asks.

"You said, 'Are you *not* Sheriff Beck?'" I'm still examining her, making mental notes, certain she knows I'm contemplating where our wedding should take place. She's in a tan leather jacket that stops at her waist, too light for this weather—so she is definitely from out of state. Gray scarf draped around her long neck that falls nicely onto her white T-shirt, beneath which I can see the product of a lot of core training and hot yoga. She's several inches shorter than me, about five foot eight and maybe all of a hundred and twenty-five pounds with her clothes on. Zero body fat, a BMI built for a BMW. Right off a New York runway if she were so inclined. Yes, the results are in, she's a good match for me.

The lady ignores the question and pulls out her ID, her badge bright and shiny just like she is, sticking it in my face. "Sana Locke, FBI. How do you do?"

*Sana.* The name falls like a little steel ball through my mental pachinko machine. Arabic, meaning mountaintop, splendid, brilliant. Yes, I agree. Her mountaintop is truly splendid and brilliant. I detect a trace of East Coast upper crust in her voice, maybe Brown University, possibly Wellesley. "Good meeting you, Sana. I was kind of expecting someone from the Bureau yesterday. Did you walk up here from Vegas?"

When she responds with only a muscle twitch in her jaw, I feel compelled to restart the conversation minus any snide editorials. "Uh, I was just reviewing some of the crime scene photos."

She nods. "I'd like to see it, please."

"The photos?"

Her eyes close, her exhalation controlled, like she is just finishing a meditation session and has pushed every thought of backwater law enforcement types out of her serene mind. "The crime scene, Sheriff. The crime scene."

I start to wonder if I am losing my touch. My contacts with the fairer sex are somewhat limited out here, like Robinson Crusoe if I'm being bitterly honest, and I don't get a lot of practice. Oh well, namaste anyway. "Sure," I say, retrieving my Glock .40 from the desk drawer. "It's a bit of a drive, I'm afraid."

She is already turning toward the door. "Isn't everything here?"

Seriously, I am Robinson Crusoe. Like the famous castaway,

I left home against the wishes of my father, had a tumultuous journey—the military in my case—and ultimately wrecked my ship on the shores of the Moscow River.

I follow the alluring Special Agent Sana Locke out of my office. At least the outer office is teeming with activity, as this always impresses visitors. There are a handful people doing various things in a facility I imagine might be a tenth the size of the lunch room at FBI headquarters.

"Busy day, Sheriff?" asks Agent Locke as I grab my ultra-warm Duluth jacket and we exit the building.

"Yep, somebody reported a kitten stuck in a tree, so we've got the full task force working it." I flash her the smile my mom left me and am happy to see it seems to take her breath. Or is that the cold?

The early morning sun reflects off the patches of snow on the surrounding hillsides as well as the parking lot, making the world appear almost black and white. I drop my aviator sunglasses over my eyes real subtle like and motion her to my black-and-white police pickup at the far end of the lot.

When we get to the truck, Agent Locke looks up, scanning the perimeter. "What's with the razor wire?"

She climbs in and I start the engine, mistakenly cranking the air conditioner. Sometimes I get confused over the blue and red on the temperature control. "Well, you know we're just due east of Area 51 here."

She rubs her upper arms vigorously, trying to shake the cold. "And?"

"Little known fact," I say, stepping on the gas, "aliens hate razor wire."

She isn't quite sure what to make of that, or me for that matter. "You mean illegal aliens."

I pull onto the highway that stretches more than three hundred miles through landscapes that look the same today as they must have to the Shoshone when they first found it, much of it still pristine wilderness. "Nope, and we call them undocumented persons out here, Agent Locke. I mean the aliens from space."

Her eyebrows suddenly knit together, her head cocking slightly. "Oh," she says, and I'm sure she's wondering how many cards shy of a full deck I am.

I let the awkward silence play out until she peeks over at me like a hitchhiker in a horror movie. "The razor wire surrounds our detention facility. We house more than a hundred prisoners at any one time, mostly from Clark County and North Vegas."

The air explodes from her lungs. "Shit, I thought you were serious."

That keeps me smiling almost the entire sixty miles to the victim's house. About two miles into the dirt road leading to Big Rocks, she blurts out, "Where the hell are we going?"

I give her my best blank stare, which is Oscar-worthy by the way. "We are going to Agent Atterbury's house. The crime scene. I thought we covered this already."

She's had just about enough of me, and that's fine. The road gets a little nasty now, the snow turning to slush and making my tires do the tango. We hit enough large rocks—by accident, mind you—to make Agent Locke think she's riding a bull at the National Finals Rodeo. Finally, we arrive at the house.

"You are fucking kidding me," she says, staring at the single structure set against a backdrop of giant stones.

I take a deep, clean breath into my lungs. "I know, it's wonderful, isn't it?" There are places up there in those rocks that no man has ever set foot, and that thought always fills me with a sense of awe.

Johnny or Jimmy Green, I'm not sure which one, is standing post just outside the front door. Whichever one he is, he's half the matched set we refer to as the Twin Peaks, identical twin deputies out of our main station sixty miles to the north in Pioche, both six and a half feet tall and good-natured young men, a trait which has earned them a second nickname, the Jolly Greens. They were my first two hires when I took this job, so you would think by now I could tell them apart, but like I said, they're identical.

"Johnny, meet Agent Locke, FBI."

"It's Jimmy, Sheriff," he says with a wince.

"It was worth a shot. Jimmy, meet Agent Locke."

Sana Locke walks right by him, lifting the yellow crime scene tape over her head. "You're very tall."

"Yes, ma'am," he says.

She looks back at me. "Booties and gloves, Sheriff?"

The question catches me off guard, coming from a seasoned FBI agent. She's aware we found the body yesterday, so is she thinking we've somehow left everything in place for her? "The scene is fully processed. You're good. Careful, though, we're staging for an open house later today."

Just out of spite, I guess, Locke pulls a pair of gloves out of her coat and puts them on, giving me that look that federal agents display whenever they have to lower themselves to work with Neanderthals.

We enter the home, and I notice the stench of death is not as prominent today, though it hasn't completely abated. I lay out the photos in the appropriate places to give her the best possible sense of what we found and how we found it. She spends a lot of time looking over the ones of Atterbury himself, and I can see her body shudder as if suddenly hit by the icy wind of my air conditioner again.

"My God."

My gut tells me she has some experience with murder, but I can't tell how much. "Not your run-of-the-mill home invasion," I say.

She turns away from me, slowly but methodically moving around the living room, examining the photos of evidence and the relation each has to where the body itself was. "Not your run-of-the-mill anything." Her gaze lingers on the damage to the walls in various places. I watch her canvass the rest of the house, equally as abused by the killer but without the blood, while she periodically references the report Tuffy compiled.

"Are you thinking one suspect?" she asks.

I have a theory but am not willing to share it just yet. "Difficult to say. We found no prints, other than the victim's and a couple of local handymen, both of whom have solid alibis. No trace evidence. Very clean for a killing that appears to have been performed with this much . . . anger."

Locke shoots me a quick, inquisitive glance as we enter Atterbury's ransacked office. "You think he was angry. That's interesting."

"I said *appears* to have been angry."

She's on the floor now, rifling through some of the papers emptied from the four-drawer filing cabinet. She's looking for something but isn't finding it. She looks up at me. "Do you have a theory?"

My eyes are the perfect shade of noncommittal, and Locke doesn't wait for me to respond, as if she has just asked a silverback gorilla what he thinks about the price of eggs. My department has a number of cases every year that necessitate calling in the feds, mostly drug-related, and I've learned to be careful about sharing ideas too quickly.

When we finally make it to the kitchen, Agent Locke doesn't find anything interesting in the cupboards or refrigerator. She almost completely passes over item #32, the photo of the box of thallium salts I placed on the island.

"What's this?"

"Thallium salts. Old rat poison. Not readily available anymore." She stares at the photo too long. "Something?"

Sana Locke shakes her head. "Nope. Just not familiar with it. I'd like to see the body now."

I give her a quick nod. "It's a bit of a drive."

"I wish I had known the body was in Las Vegas before I made the drive to Upper Butt Crack, Sheriff. You could have saved me a few hours."

Agent Locke is not happy. Even the coffee I pick up at Lou's in Alamo, literally the best for fifty miles in any direction, the only actually, doesn't seem to be helping her mood. I try unsuccessfully to stifle my amusement by letting the coffee burn my upper lip. "I assumed that you would know that out here in the sticks we don't have the facilities or expertise for an autopsy, so we utilize the Clark County coroner's office. I thought everyone in the Las Vegas field office of the FBI was aware of that."

She doesn't say anything. Mostly because she's not from the Las Vegas field office, and now she knows that I know that. It's a good two-hour drive, so we have some time to chat. "You're from D.C., I take it." Not a question.

She looks over at me, feigning surprise. "What makes you say that?"

Okay, if we have to play that game, let's play. "If you were from Vegas, you would have been in my office yesterday."

"Not necessarily."

"So, someone figured Atterbury's killing was a big deal. We called you guys about twenty-four hours ago. That means Vegas called D.C., a decision was made by someone pretty high up on the food chain, and someone had to track you down and get you out here. By the time you were ready to go, it would have been too late to catch a commercial flight, except a red-eye. You didn't take a red-eye because you look like you just came from a photo shoot and don't have any sleep in your eyes, which means, in all likelihood, you flew out on one of those DOJ Gulfstreams and got plenty of sleep."

Her eyes light up. "You think I look like I just came from a photo shoot?"

That was poor execution on my part. Now she knows I find her attractive. I attempt to distract her by adding, "And the SUV you drove up in is a rental car. Vegas and Reno feds use their own vehicles when they come here and get reimbursed for the mileage."

Agent Locke turns back to me, not a cursory examination this time but a much deeper one. "Well, I never said I was with the field office in Las Vegas, but impressive powers of deduction all the same." She swivels in her seat so that she's fully facing me now. "What else?"

I'm about to ask why FBI headquarters thought it necessary to take this case, but the radio crackles to life and Arshal Jessup at the Alamo substation interrupts me.

"Beck, it's Arshal. You copy?"

Arshal is somewhere in his late sixties, I'm not quite sure where exactly, and his voice sounds like he's swallowed most of the gravel on Lincoln County roads in his forty-plus years on the job. That's because he's had three separate bouts with thyroid cancer, not uncommon for people who grew up downwind of the test site in the 1950s when we were setting off atomic bombs like firecrackers. Arshal was one of those kids who were given radiation badges to wear on their clothes so the Atomic Energy Commission could swing by later and collect them to compile data on the dangers of splitting the atom in the open air. My mom was one of them, too.

He's had two sisters die from cancer already, one from leukemia and another from bladder cancer, but you won't hear him complain about it. He's had a good life by most measures and lives with a daughter that dotes on him like roses on a loamy soil.

Arshal is also the best Jack Mormon I know, which means aside from drinking Pepsi and working on Sunday, he would give you the shirt off his back and his last penny if he thought it would help.

I pull the radio from the console. "Yes, sir." This is my military training coming out. Even though Arshal works for me, he's earned the respect.

"Ayup. Just an FYI for now, Beck, but I got a call from the people over at the cemetery this morning outside Rachel. Seems there was a bit of vandalism last night." *Ayup,* so you know, is not a Paiute greeting, just Arshal's way of saying *yeah*.

I catch Agent Locke's grin out of the corner of my eye. "Big case," she whispers.

At this point, I have no choice but to shoot her in the head with my loaded finger gun. "What sort of vandalism, Arshal?"

"Couple three graves got dug up, looks like."

"How many is a couple three?" Agent Locke asks me with a giggle.

I hold up four fingers and key the mic. "Dug up?"

"Ayup, that's affirmative. Four caskets opened."

"Vandalism to the remains?"

A few long seconds tick by. "Well, here comes the odd part," Arshal says. "I don't think there was anything in those caskets to vandalize."

Agent Locke starts humming the theme from *The Twilight Zone,* and I give her a gentle shove on her nicely toned shoulder to shut her up. This is known as law enforcement foreplay.

"Say again, Arshal?"

"I went out and checked them myself, Beck. If anything had been rotting in there, it hasn't been for a good long time. Maybe never. And the caretaker said the same graves were dug up a few years back."

None of this makes much sense. "Whose graves were they, Arshal?"

"Unknown. They were unmarked."

I honestly don't know what to say to that. The radio chirps again. "Beck, you there?"

"Okay, keep me posted. I'm headed to the coroner's office. Might catch you on the way back." I replace the radio in its holder, but something is nagging in my brain, so I pull it off the console again. "Arshal, how old were those graves?"

"Best we can figure by their placement, they go way back," he says. "To the 1950s."

I see Agent Locke whip out her cell phone. "Who are you calling?"

She looks at me with deadpan eyes. "Ghostbusters."

Wonderful.

# THE PAST

Freddie had only been in town for ten days when he first set eyes on Katherine Ellison. It was late March 1955, and he was on duty at the newly opened Dunes Hotel and Casino, a magnificent, neon-sparkling oasis in the middle of the Mohave Desert and the fast-growing city of Las Vegas. He had applied to be a dealer in one of the games because he heard the tips were good, but those jobs had been filled already, and the hiring manager told him his job would be to attract gamblers to the tables as a shill.

"You're not half bad in the looks department," the man told him. "We want guys like you throwing dice and playing cards."

In fact, Freddie Meyer knew he was considerably better than half bad, with soft blue eyes and champagne-colored hair that crested just over the six-foot mark. And playing with house money, it was easy to lure other gamblers to the games. Blackjack, roulette, craps, it didn't matter. It was easy work, though not entirely on the up-and-up in Freddie's Presbyterian mind. It was only the second night on the job when he saw Kitty. She was in the Helps Hall where the employees ate their meals, with a group of other young women. She wasn't the most striking, wore little makeup compared with her friends, and with her black cat-eye glasses and conservative clothes, had suppressed any semblance of glamour. She looked like a math teacher with her butterscotch hair perpetually tied efficiently behind her head, not alluring like the cigarette and cocktail girls in the casino, and it seemed appropriate to Freddie that she worked in the count room. Her friends seemed shocked when Freddie approached them and asked for her name rather than one of theirs.

Their first date followed a week later, dinner and Frank Sinatra. Freddie spent his entire paycheck to impress the bookish girl from Chicago, and it worked. They saw each other as often as possible over the next few weeks, on shift and off. They were a couple. Kitty and Freddie. A bit of an odd pairing, some thought. The couple themselves seemed oblivious to their differences and were continually surprised at what they had in common, which culminated on a night in mid-May when Freddie started talking about the composition of the cosmos under a million stars at the magnificent red sandstone formations known as Valley of Fire about fifty miles north of the city.

"I took physics in high school and a year of it at Penn. But then my mom got sick, and I had to leave." He told her the story that eventually left him alone in the world and finally led him to the desert.

"I lost my mom, too," she said. "Three years ago. Polio."

Freddie shook his head. "And now I hear we have a vaccine for it. I'm sorry."

"The future is up there," she said as they lay on a Navajo blanket on a large slab of limestone that in the darkness looked like a strawberry-vanilla swirl. "In those galaxies that look like clouds, and the ever-expanding universe. Just like Hubble described it."

Freddie's pupils flared. "You know physics!"

She laughed. "I studied physics at the University of Chicago."

He thrust his hands in the air. "How did I not know that?"

She looked at him, lowering her glasses down the steep incline of her nose. "A lot of boys would find that intimidating."

Freddie shook his head. "I don't understand. Why are you here? Why are you working in a casino?"

Kitty drew in a long breath and released it slowly. "Not easy for a woman to get a job in the sciences. And my father wanted me to be here with him. He was alone my last couple years at school."

Freddie raised up on one elbow and faced her, taking her hand. "Tell me about him."

She curled upward to him, undoing her ponytail and letting her hair fall naturally. "He's a physicist and one of the leading scientists at the atomic testing site not far from here." She rolled her eyes. "He's going to flip when he meets you."

Seconds before 4 A.M., Kitty kissed him deeply. And then the sky lit up like it was the middle of the day, illuminating their faces. They looked up at the same time.

"My God," Freddie said in awe. They could see the multicolored mushroom spiraling into the heavens.

"Not God," Kitty said. "That's my dad."

A few weeks later, she asked him home for dinner. It was a nice house with a tan brick exterior and just about a mile west of the center of the rapidly expanding city, its population now close to 45,000 by recent estimates. Opportunities abounded in the desert.

Kitty showed Freddie into her father's study and introduced him. Roger Ellison was a tall, big-bellied man in his late forties, a good three or four inches taller than Freddie, and he had long slender hands, one of which seemed to be always around his pipe. Soft hands, Freddie thought as they shook. The hands of a scientist. His dark brown eyes were like those of a hawk, widely set on his oval face and not missing anything. Freddie felt they could see right through him. They made small talk for a few minutes over drinks until Freddie caught sight of the chessboard on a small table along the exterior wall. It was the pieces that actually caught his eye.

The three of them crossed the room and Freddie picked up one of the finely crafted ivory pieces, an elephant. "This is beautiful."

"Do you play?" Dr. Ellison asked.

He answered by beating Kitty's father in eleven moves.

"I don't meet a lot of people who understand the game so well," Dr. Ellison told Freddie over a nice ham and mashed potatoes a few minutes later. "Especially your age. Where did you learn?"

Freddie was still chewing, so he politely held his hand in front of his mouth. "In school mostly. During the winter, we didn't go outside that much, so a lot of us learned chess."

Kitty winked at him. "Daddy's impressed with you." And to her father, "He's a physics buff, too, Daddy."

Ellison dropped his fork on his plate and sat straight up. "My God, son, is this true?"

Freddie nodded. "Yes, sir. I only have a year of college, but I read whatever I can get my hands on. I'm fascinated by the work Kitty tells me you're doing out there at the Proving Grounds."

"Are you now?"

"Atomic testing," Freddie said excitedly. "It's the cutting edge of science."

Ellison was almost breathless in his enthusiasm. "It's a race, I tell you, Freddie. A very important race to this country. And to the world."

Freddie happily agreed, and before long the scientist mentioned the government was looking for security guards to man their rapidly expanding operations.

"You should apply," he told Freddie. "I have to believe it would be substantially more than you're making at the casino, and I could put in a word for you."

Freddie didn't know what to say. In physics, motion describes how an object changes its position over time. He was in motion.

"You've been recommended by Dr. Ellison, I see," said the man in the black suit. "He thinks highly of you." Then the questions began.

Freddie was sweating profusely, and not from nerves. It was 105 degrees outside, and he had waited forty-five minutes in line just to reach the air-conditioned interior of Federal Services Incorporated at the corner of Second and Bonanza. Then it had been an hour of documenting his life on paper, followed by fingerprinting. If he could land this job as a security guard, he could buy better clothes, maybe a better car. The pay was supposed to be twice what he was making as a shill at the casino.

As the man in black lit one Camel after another and smoke billowed in the room, Freddie got a lot of questions about his political leanings, a grilling that was a by-product of the McCarthy hearings and the paranoia about communism and the Soviet Union and its reach into the United States. Freddie answered them all with confidence.

"Well, presuming your background check doesn't turn anything up, your Q clearance could be granted within five months. For now, go back to work. We'll be in touch."

It only took three months. One morning Freddie saw the letter under his door at the Lamplight Motel. He had a job in security in the Land of the Tall Mushrooms. His reporting date was in ten days on September 30th at 8 A.M.

Kitty was elated for him. After a celebratory dinner, he dropped her at home in the navy blue '51 Ford Crestliner he had bought earlier in the day and drove up Stewart Avenue to the Las Vegas Federal Courthouse and Post Office. It was late, well past closing hours. Freddie went inside, extracted a key from his pocket and opened box 188, which he rented for fifty cents a month. After inserting the letter and relocking the box, he left the building and returned to his room at the Lamplight. The September evening seemed just as warm inside as outside, and Freddie wondered if the temperature would ever drop below ninety. He extracted a can of Krueger beer from the small fridge and punched two quick holes in the top. Crossing the room, he took a long pull and raised the window shade to the three-quarter position. Then he sat down on the bed and stared at the window. Now there was nothing to do but wait.

They were taken in buses. Not as nice as the one he hopped to Las Vegas back in the spring, but comfortable. Through the pall of cigarette smoke, Freddie counted forty-three men, and he estimated there were similar numbers on each of the other buses that were making their way north on the two-lane highway to the Nevada Proving Ground and Camp Mercury. Some were new security guards like him, in their tan uniforms with the star patch on the shoulders that identified them as employees of Federal Services, Inc. Most of the occupants, however, were dressed in civilian clothes. By the look of them, Freddie guessed many were construction workers while others surely held more important jobs, their pressed slacks and shiny shoes indicating a higher level of education and training. Since he was in the security business now, he would make a point to get to know all the men from his morning bus stop. He would befriend them. He would learn all he could about them.

It was his first journey this far out into the vast Nevada desert, and for miles there was nothing but scrub and dirt and the constant smell of diesel exhaust inhaled by his bus from the one in front of it. More than an hour passed, and then gradually he saw signs of life. Signs along the thin strip of road warned about the importance of security and secrecy. Behind his blank expression, Freddie grinned, but it evaporated quickly when he saw the warning that trespassers could face imprisonment and even risked being shot.

He was moving from the high-stakes games at the casino to the highest stakes of all, and he wondered how he would perform when it was his time. If the sweat beading up inside his shirt and trousers was any indication, he wouldn't make it through his first day of training.

"You okay?" asked the man seated next to him. "You're breathing like you just ran a mile."

Freddie managed a half smile, commanding his heart to slow down. "Fine," he said. "New job is all."

"Nerves," the man said with a nod, returning to his newspaper. "You'll do fine."

The sign at the main security gate at the entrance to Mercury still said Nevada Proving Ground, but it appeared to Freddie that they were replacing it with one that said Nevada Testing Site. Once off the bus, he and seven other similarly uniformed men were escorted into the main annex for FSI employees. After their credentials were thoroughly examined, the men were ushered into a long rectangular wooden building that said FSI 3 above the single door. There were several rooms, and as they passed, Freddie could see each contained six to eight beds with small metal frames and a thin mattress. There was a washroom as well, and he was surprised by its abundance: six wash basins, four lavatories, and six showers. There had been long periods in his relatively short life where he would have killed for accommodations like this.

They were issued three uniforms each from measurements previously supplied. There was a camp laundry facility, but each man was required to do his own. Finally, Freddie and the other new recruits were led into another room and told to deposit their duffel bags on a bunk and to take a seat. A tall, lanky man named Lon Greaves introduced himself as their sergeant. "Listen up," he said in a voice as dry as the desert, "there are only four things you need to know here. One, everything here is classified. Everything means everything. What you do here, what you eat for breakfast, where you take a piss. Classified. You don't talk to people about this place. *Capisce?*" The recruits glanced nervously at one another. "Two, your family and friends are not exempt from this rule. That includes your dog and your goldfish. Outside these gates, you do not engage in conversation with anyone about what goes on inside these gates. Three, there are many different levels of security clearances here. Not all of them are created equal." Greaves pointed to the badge on his uniform shirt. It had three different colors. "Your job is to ensure everyone has the proper clearance for entering the areas you will be posted to. You will arrest, detain, or kill, if you have to, any person not adhering to this rule. Understood?"

Freddie eyed the other men. Most nodded confidently. These were the men with military training. Some would have served in the Korean War.

"Four," the sergeant bellowed, "any breach of any of the aforementioned rules is grounds for termination and possible imprisonment. Or, if I catch you, death."

And that's when the realization hit him: *I'm working at America's most secret scientific facility!*

They were asked to sign a document pledging their allegiance to the United States and essentially surrendering their constitutional rights so long as they remained in their employment in the Nevada desert.

Next, it was out to the range for marksmanship training. Each man was outfitted with a .38 Special Smith & Wesson pistol and a Thompson M1A1 submachine gun. When the range master, a small, stout man whose name tag read Irby, handed Freddie the Thompson, he asked, "Name?"

He answered immediately. "Freddie Meyer, sir."

"Ever shoot before, Freddie Meyer?"

Though he preferred to hold a book, guns were not unfamiliar to him. "I used to hunt a lot as a kid." It was the truth. His first real use of a rifle had come twelve years earlier when he was just a boy. He had killed a man on a hillside not far from his home. After that, his proficiency with weapons grew quickly and out of necessity.

"Well," said Irby. "Shooting at little animals is one thing. Shooting people is another thing altogether. I shot plenty of them all over the Pacific and in Korea. Let's hope you never have to."

*Yes, let's hope.*

He excelled on the pistol range, missing his target only enough to maintain the illusion he had no military training. He took to the disciplined structure that FSI insisted upon like a duck to water, memorizing all fifty-eight radio codes by his second day on the job, dismaying his superiors, some of whom still could not remember them all. He raced through every manual they gave him and found himself the unofficial tutor to his fellow recruits. It was hardly a demanding regimen, at least not compared with the training of his youth. In their downtime at the test site, Freddie and the other men competed in bowling and darts. He was amazed at the comforts test site employees were afforded. The camp cafeteria had a turnstile at its entrance, much like the ones he had seen in his brief time in the subways of New York just a year ago. The difference here was the turnstile required a silver dollar, and when you dropped it in, you could eat all you wanted. He had never seen such enormous bounty.

By day, he absorbed as much information as he could, given that his movements at the site were restricted to his training areas and the main social facilities at Camp Mercury. And despite his success at getting through the vetting process and making his way onto the FSI payroll, he had his sights firmly set on learning as much as he could about the science of atomic testing.

At night, lying on his bunk, he missed Kitty. He missed discussing the stars and the properties of matter, but mostly he just missed the dulcet tones of her voice and how they warmed his insides like whiskey. So much of what would come, he knew, depended on his relationship with Kitty, and by extension, her father.

At the end of his fourth and final week of training, Private Freddie Meyer took the wheel and drove out with his sergeant to a new, extremely secret operations area of the site, a place they were calling Delta. Because he had excelled in every aspect of training, he was told he was one of only five men chosen to guard the base just over the hill from Yucca Flat, and the only new man selected. On the long drive north, he was not surprised the dirt road was the only indication of civilization. The West was a huge place, much of it inhabited only by animals. In fact, he had learned that prior to becoming the optimal location to detonate atomic bombs, much of this land had been a wildlife preserve. Their driver was part tour guide and historian, telling Freddie and Sergeant Greaves that, in addition to the bighorn sheep, mountain lions, rattlesnakes, and other assorted creatures, Native Americans had once resided in the mountain caves of the area and that there were plenty of paintings and petroglyphs that could still be seen on their walls.

*And the people who made them? Wiped out.*

As the jeep pulled up to the west-facing gate, Greaves got out and spoke to a man in civilian clothes who was armed with a machine gun. A man in civilian clothes, Freddie knew, was likely to be CIA. He felt the hair on his arms and neck rise. Greaves and the man conversed and then approached the vehicle.

"Badge, please," the man said to Freddie. Freddie handed him his badge, which had recently changed color. FSI and the military were hypersensitive to security, and they had done a good job of compartmentalizing the entire test site. Only those with the required clearance could access particular areas.

The CIA man matched Freddie's badge information to what was on his clipboard and then motioned to another man in a small booth to raise the gate.

Greaves then informed him, "End of the line for me, Private. I don't have Delta clearance. This man will take you the rest of the way."

"Slide over, Private," the man said, climbing in behind the wheel.

As they drove into Delta, the man introduced himself as John Anderson. The corners of Freddie's mouth turned up. "Is that your real name?" Anderson just grinned.

Freddie immediately noticed that the Delta site was much like the barren desert he had just driven through. There wasn't much here. He saw a single airstrip, a large airplane hangar, and a small wooden building Anderson said would be his post. Nothing else but miles of barbed wire as far as the eye could see. Fear slithered its way into his brain. He hadn't come all this way only to be confined to an area where there was no scientific activity. "Exactly what am I guarding?"

Anderson glared at him. "You don't need to know that, do you, Private? You're security. You will secure this site and its perimeter. No one without Delta clearance will come through any entry point, and that includes God himself. Do you understand that?"

Freddie lowered his eyes. "Yes, sir." *And do you understand that before I'm done I will know everything?*

"You were handpicked for this job, son," the man said. "Start acting like it."

After four weeks at the test site, Freddie returned to Las Vegas and immediately picked up his mail from the post office, which included his first utility bills, a copy of the latest *Scientific Amer-*

*ican,* and a large package from Aunt Sally in Hershey, Pennsylvania.

Entering his new apartment, he tossed his duffel bag on the ugly blue carpet and sat down with his mail on the lumpy sofa that came with the small coffee table that came with the rent. Everything had his name on it, and seeing it gave Freddie a sense of confidence. He opened the magazine first, the cover of which showed a tree branch with some beautiful fall leaves. The table of contents listed the major articles for the November 1955 edition, and Freddie's eyes quickly found the ones he knew would contain important information. The first was "Radiation and Human Mutation," and the second was "Empty Space," a look into the vast reaches of the galaxy. Both titles contained a tiny red dot in the first letter, almost imperceptible to the naked eye, and placed there by someone other than the publisher. In truth, he was more excited to read the articles for their scientific value, but his light reading would have to come later.

He pulled out his pocketknife and cut the twine from the box from Aunt Sally. Carefully, he removed the brown mailing paper, knowing there may be some additional message on the underside, written in disappearing ink called thymolphthalein. He rose from the sofa and retrieved a small spray bottle from under the kitchen sink. Laying the mailing paper on his small dining table, he lightly sprayed it with the solution. Nothing appeared. Returning to the sofa, he opened the box and found a shiny black lunch box. Inside, next to the large thermos, were some cookies wrapped in wax paper and a note written in a woman's handwriting. *Good luck with the new job. Love you, bub. Aunt Sally.*

He extracted one of the chocolate chips and placed it his mouth. "Thank you, Aunt Sally," he mumbled. Freddie pulled the thermos out and examined its exterior carefully. The bottom third of the insulated container had a tiny separation from the upper part. He placed one hand on the bottom and rotated it counter-clockwise. It moved easily. Inside, he found a camera, much like the one he had practiced with during training. It was just over seven centimeters long and two and a half centimeters tall. He looked into the tiny viewfinder. *Brilliant.*

The camera was everything. It would allow Freddie, whose real name was Lieutenant Georgiy Dudko of the Committee for State Security, also known as the KGB, to document everything he saw.

# CHAPTER 3

The Clark County coroner's office is located conveniently in the heart of Las Vegas, and more important, only a few blocks from the Omelet House. Since our appointment is at noon, I thought it best to do some carb-loading before seeing dead ex-agent Atterbury's corpse a second time.

"Is that wise?" Agent Locke asks as I lay a portion of my Denver omelet on top of my toast with the same care I used when removing the heart in that kids' game *Operation*.

"Probably not. The eggs sometime roll off right before they reach my mouth." Sure enough, Humpty Dumpty takes a big fall back onto my plate. "See?"

She shakes her head and takes a sip of coffee. "I mean eating before an autopsy. Aren't you afraid of regurgitating it all?"

I'm not. I seriously doubt I'm going to see anything worse than what I encountered yesterday. "Otto—Dr. Weezard—has probably already completed the autopsy. We're just going for the post-game wrap-up."

She puts her coffee down. "I need to see the body, Sheriff."

"It's Beck, okay? And see the body you shall, Sana. Can I start calling you Sana?"

She rolls those beautiful, dark-roasted eyes. "Very well . . . Beck."

"It's just that Special Agent Locke is a mouthful, you know? I mean it's a little weird, don't you think, all you special agents calling each other special agent this and special agent that?"

Sana laughs. "We don't really do that, and I think you know that, Beck."

Hearing her say my name makes me warm inside. "You don't have to say my name in every sentence. If you do, it will be awkward." Our eyes lock, and I feel the magnetism growing between us, hoping it's not the repulsive kind.

"You're not at all what I was expecting in a sheriff out . . . here," she says.

"Oh, boy," I say, setting my fork on the plate. "All right, fire away."

"Well, to start with, other than that star on your belt, you don't wear a uniform."

I relax into my seat. "Hey, it's casual Friday."

"Today is Saturday."

"Right. Casual Saturday. What else?"

Sana studies me. "You don't wear a uniform because it wouldn't go well with that two-day stubble and your nice wavy hair that is a little too long, I think, for a Nevada sheriff. I think you have a problem with authority."

I shake my head. "I spent almost twenty years in the Army, lady. Of course I have a problem with authority."

"And you have a quick wit and don't take yourself too seriously."

I smirk and slide my sunglasses back on. "Ma'am, I'm afraid you'll have to come with me now."

She laughs. "See, you're not like that, and that's . . . unexpected."

I let my smile do the talking for a long moment as we watch each other. "That's pretty good, Sana. Okay, my turn."

She looks away. Interesting, I think. Not comfortable under the spotlight. I lean closer across the small table, mapping her features with my eyes, cataloging the data. "You are obviously of Middle Eastern descent. This is on your mother's side, of course." My head tilts a bit to the right like I'm studying the brushstrokes on a painting. "I would say . . . Jordanian, possibly some Egyptian mixed in."

Sana turns back, her eyes widening. "There you go surprising me again. Not many people would be able to be so . . . specific. My mother is Jordanian, but our lineage stretches across the Red Sea. How could you possibly know this?"

"It's my superpower," I say, pulling back out of my trance. "I've spent some time in the region. But Locke, obviously your father's name, is English. I'm guessing your old man is a scholar of some sort, not in law enforcement like his daughter."

Sana holds a hand up. "Stop. Is this a magic trick? You just met me."

"It's your elocution," I tell her. "Dead giveaway for a life spent in books. Let me guess, he's a literature professor?"

"Oh, fucking hell," Sana says loudly, half the Omelet House suddenly watching. "You are not real." She composes herself by reaching out with her fork and taking the last bite of my eggs, which I find incredibly seductive.

My job is done here. I've made her laugh and piqued her interest. I plop some cash down on the table and wink at her. "We're off to see the Weezard."

Otto has the body fully draped when we enter the examination suite, where the air is heavily scented with ammonia and which looks like a showroom for all things stainless steel. Faucets, sinks, the tables where the dead are opened. Gadgets of every kind are mounted to the ceiling, cameras, lights, things that look a lot like special drills. The place gives me the heebie-jeebies, much like Otto Weezard himself. Though not stainless steel, his rail-thin body sports a grayish hue that under these lights would render him practically invisible if it weren't for his white lab coat.

"You're punching above your weight, Beck," Otto tells me as his assistant lifts the sheet over Atterbury's head and chest. "This kind of mutilation is something I've honestly never seen." He pauses a second. "And I've seen some cartel shit that made me think twice about my chosen profession."

I'm not looking at the body. I've already seen the body. I'm looking at Sana who is studying the body. No flinching. No revulsion. No visceral reaction whatsoever. Impressive.

"Show me the rest of him, please," she tells Otto.

Otto looks to me, and I give him the nod. "She's already seen the photos."

He peels back the sheet to uncover the rest of the body. Cleaned up and laid out as he is under the bright lights, Atterbury's wounds are even more pronounced now.

Sana walks slowly around the table, leaning in here and there to better examine the long, almost perfectly rectangular patches of removed skin. "What kind of tool peels skin like this?"

Otto nods. "A grafting tool called a dermatome. Nothing else could do that so precisely."

Sana moves up to the shoulders and face. "And the burns?"

"Acetylene torch. Most likely small, like what a plumber would carry around for soldering pipes."

I say, "We found one at the house."

She crosses over to a sink and splashes some cold water on

her face, her fingers gripping the counter tightly. "Took his time, didn't he?"

Otto glances at me again. "Give her all of it, Otto."

"Well over an hour, I'd say. Kept him awake with adrenaline."

I step to the table. "Cause of death?"

Sana spins around from the sink, drying her hands and face with a paper towel. "Seriously? The man was flayed and set fire to. Do we need to know more?"

My eyes are trained on hers like truth detectors. "Otto, do we need to know more?"

"Well," he says, "likely heart failure from everything you see here. But there is one more thing. Something odd. If he hadn't been tortured, his cause of death would have been poisoning."

I'm still watching her. "You don't say?"

"Yes." Otto crosses the room, removing a plastic container from a refrigerator. "Thallium." He opens the container and shows Sana, then me. "Forced them down his throat. Some even made their way into his stomach."

Sana folds her arms over her chest. "The rat poison."

"Yes and no," Otto says. "It was a rat poison a long time ago. Not legal to buy now in most countries, including the U.S. Too toxic."

I touch her on the shoulder so she'll look up at me. "We don't have a rat problem in my county."

She pulls her eyes from mine. "So?"

Otto continues. "So, you've already pretty much killed the guy. But you go to the trouble of feeding him thallium salts? Why on earth would you do that? It would take days, maybe longer for him to die from that."

"Symptoms?" I ask, entirely for Sana's benefit. I know the symptoms.

"Of thallium ingestion?" Otto shakes his head. "More torture really. Quite agonizing in its own right. Arrhythmia, difficulty breathing, large swings in blood pressure, violent vomiting, pain. Lots of pain."

I gaze down at the poor man. "But pain he probably never felt, I'm guessing."

Otto nods. "Correct. It would have taken a few hours for the symptoms to hit. This was . . . this was purely an afterthought. Overkill."

I have to ask. "Symbolic? A signature perhaps?"

Sana pulls the sheet back over Atterbury's body. "With respect, Beck, I think you're overthinking this. The man was brutalized to death, end of story."

She's what I always imagined Helen of Troy must have looked like. Men would go to war over her. But her dismissiveness has a five-alarm fire starting in my amygdala. "Otto, anything you can surmise about the killer, or killers?"

Dr. Weezard picks up a file from the counter and opens it. "It's difficult to say if there was more than one. What I can tell you is that the person who inflicted these wounds is likely male and right-handed."

Sana is suddenly interested again. "That's it, no other DNA? Nothing?"

Her question seems strange. DNA is a very specific thing to ask about. I think she means "any trace evidence," which could be in multiple forms like fibers, hair, essentially anything that can be transferred between people. "This isn't like the *CSI* you see on television, Sana," I say. "It takes a few days to process everything."

She ignores me. "Thank you, Doctor. This was helpful. I trust his family has been contacted and arrangements will be made for the body?"

Otto gives her the details and we leave. Outside in the truck, she's waiting for me to start the engine. But it's time for some answers.

"You have to turn the key," she says.

"Should I drop you at the airport?"

She's nervous now. "Excuse me, are we done with this investigation?"

I take a long look out the window. "Well, I'm certainly not done with it. But it's a murder investigation, and your agent was retired. Is there some reason for you to stick around?"

She takes a moment to calculate her response. "The Bureau looks after its own. I would like to get a better sense of what happened before heading back, if that's okay."

"So, you would like to work together?"

She bats those beautiful lashes at me. "Yes."

"That would be great, but I'm not really feeling like we're on a team here. If we were doing this together, you'd be sharing what you already know."

Sana makes a poor attempt at bewilderment. "Like what, for instance?"

"Like why a retired agent's murder is big enough to get you out here. Was he really retired? What was he working on, Sana?"

She swivels around and leans her head back against the passenger window. "I told you. We look after our own. And yes, he was retired."

Bullshit always makes my nose crinkle. "You can call an Uber or taxi from here. I'll have one of my people drive your rental car back."

She laughs. "And I'll have thirty agents in your office within six hours. Would you like that?"

Still crinkling, I don't budge. "Wow. Thirty agents. That's a lot of attention for one guy." We just stare at each other for a few minutes. Or an hour. Finally, she looks out her window. "All right. What do you want to know?"

Now we're getting somewhere. "Oh, there's quite a bit, but let's start with why the Russian Foreign Intelligence Service came all the way to my county to kill a man who hasn't been in the FBI for almost twenty years."

# CHAPTER 4

"Who said anything about Russians?" My mention of the SVR, the Russian Foreign Intelligence Service, has thrown Special Agent Sana Locke into a bit of a tizzy.

I'm in a tizzy of my own, not because I hate driving in Vegas but because the perfume she's wearing has just the slightest hint of jasmine mixed with jelly donuts, a combination I find difficult to resist. I brake the truck as if a toddler has just run into the road, and Sana's seat belt locks painfully into place on her hips and chest. "I'm going to save us both some time, Sana, so that you don't have to pretend with me. A good deal of my career in the Army, I was a foreign area officer. Do you know what that is?"

I can tell she's considering lying again, but then she looks at me and just nods.

"My area of specialty was Russia. I spent five years in Russia. I know the SVR much better than I'd like to, and I know that their predecessor's choice of poison for a long time was thallium. It's slow-acting, colorless, tasteless, and odorless. The SVR was suspected of using it as recently as 2006 when they whacked a dissident named Litvinenko in London." History lesson aside, I have a much more personal reason for a state of high anxiety when it comes to the SVR, and already my blood is pumping.

"My, my," says Sana. "We are not in Kansas anymore, are we, Dorothy?"

"Toto."

"Pardon?"

"The line is: 'Toto, I have a feeling we're not in Kansas anymore.'" See, I literally cannot forget things.

Sana is properly annoyed with my smugness, which kind of makes us even. We pull onto the interstate and I mash the gas pedal. In seconds, we're flying by other vehicles at an increasing rate, my heart rate matching the truck's speed, and I have an uncomfortable feeling forming in my gut that is not my Denver omelet. "Atterbury was ex-FBI. He was an old man living in retirement in relative obscurity and was savagely tortured before his killer shoved thallium down his throat, which in addition to being a poison is also radiological, an interesting coincidence since my county is located right next door to the Nevada Test Site. In my experience, you only torture someone because you want information on someone or something. Atterbury's house was ripped apart, which tells me the killer was looking for a thing. Now, why don't you tell me what it was?"

Sana puts her hands on the dash. "In your experience?"

"Yes, but not relevant to our discussion, and you're avoiding my question."

"Could you slow down, please?"

Being a reasonable guy, I decelerate and pull into the slow lane. Sana takes a moment. "This is going to sound a bit preposterous."

"Lady, I live right next door to where we park the UFOs. I can do preposterous."

She starts to speak, then stops, then starts again. "You are not cleared for this."

I wait, and smell her again. Jesus.

"I could lose my job just for telling you."

I swerve back into the fast lane.

"Okay, okay!" she yells. "Okay."

I can almost see the gears turning in her head. "Sometime in the 1950s, '55 or '56 we think, a Russian KGB agent came to Nevada to spy on the atomic testing program located, as you say, right next door to your county."

"Makes sense," I reply. "It was an arms race, especially with the advent of the hydrogen bomb. I'm sure the Sovs were crawling all over the place."

"Exactly. We didn't know he was here. We never caught him. We didn't find out about him until the early sixties, when he contacted the Bureau."

I take my eyes from the highway and peer over at her, and because my libido seems to be at DEFCON 1 today, my first thought is that she's even more beautiful when she's being honest. "He contacted us?"

Sana nods, drawing her feet up to the dash like a little girl. "Yes. Over a period of years, he fed us information on the Soviet spy apparatus in the U.S. Little gems about how the illegal program worked, to establish his bona fides, and then a lot of specific information about what the Soviets knew and didn't know about the American nuclear program."

Russia was my specialty in the Army, so I know quite a bit about the KGB—the SVR's predecessor—and its Directorate S, which coordinated the training and planting of Soviet spies in the U.S. to gather what we refer to as "illegal" intelligence. I know these were people trained to look and speak like Americans and were provided deep cover identities that allowed them to perform espionage against this country for long periods of time while living next door to their unsuspecting American neighbors. "Why? Why did he reveal that?"

"He said he was sorry for the part he played in it all. He wanted to make amends."

Something isn't quite adding up. "And the connection to Atterbury? Wait, was he the illegal's contact at the Bureau?"

She pauses. "One of them. There were several over the years. Atterbury was the last of them."

"So, what's the punch line?"

The corners of her mouth drop, and I know the bad news is coming. "The punch line, Beck, is that eight months ago a source our government has in Russian intelligence tells us that the SVR has turned someone on our side, and that the leaked information could have catastrophic consequences for us across the board."

Now I know why she's here and not some local G-man. "Well," I say, "that seems to happen every other week now. And you're speaking in generalities again. What's the impact on this story?"

Sana hesitates a second. "Some portion of the information leaked indicates everything I just told you as well as material suggesting this illegal is still alive." Before I can jump in with the ten or twelve thoughts I've just had, Sana continues. "It's a huge loss for us. Tons of classified stuff. Think Robert Hanssen but bigger. We started losing sources. And like with Hanssen, a lot of people got rounded up and shot, we think."

"And one of those files also had the names of the illegal's FBI handlers."

"Precisely," she says. "Atterbury included."

"You're suggesting the Russians have come looking for the illegal now? If he was still alive, he'd be in his eighties, maybe ninety by now. Why risk it after sixty years?"

She shrugs. "We don't know. But when you called us to report Atterbury's murder, we knew it was possible they had sent someone."

We drive in silence for a few minutes, me with the knot still in my intestines and her watching me as I digest the information she has just shared. "How is it you never found the illegal?"

Sana's hands go up in surrender. "We tried for years, Atterbury especially. It became a bit of an obsession for him. Like someone looking for lost treasure. Based on some of the information he provided, we believed the illegal had been in Nevada at least some of the time we were in contact. Of course, he never revealed where he was. And he was very good at hiding. We did get enough to believe he had been here at the height of aboveground atomic testing."

This was an era I know a lot about. My mother died at a young age from cancer, and Lincoln County and half of Utah are littered with the dead and dying resulting from the Cold War's radioactive winds that blew eastward from those detonations in the Nevada desert.

Sana's tongue is getting looser by the minute, which conjures another mental image I'm forced to stifle. "We knew that Atterbury had continued his search for the illegal into retirement, but honestly, most of the counterintelligence guys thought he was a bit cuckoo."

"He thought the illegal was still in Nevada? Like recently?"

"He did. We didn't. We scoured the country for years looking for this man. We went back and looked at everyone who worked at the test site or had contact with people who worked there during those years. We tore their lives apart. Nothing."

"Well, Atterbury had something or thought he did. We don't get a lot of people coming to Lincoln County to retire. We're more of a way station than a destination."

"I don't know," Sana says. "But you were right, Beck. Atterbury's killer was looking for someone. The illegal."

It hits me like a lightning strike, every nerve in my body suddenly on fire. "Yes, but . . ."

"But?"

"Atterbury's killer had access to the intelligence leaked to the SVR, intelligence which told him our government still didn't know who the illegal was. That's why he ripped Atterbury's house apart. He was looking for Atterbury's case notes, his files."

Sana's head drops solemnly. "Well, based on what he put the poor man through, I'm guessing he found them."

I flip on the light bar and toggle the siren switch, jumping back to the fast lane. "I don't think he did. He tortured Atterbury to death to get him to tell him where those files were. The only reason to rip up the house like that is because Atterbury wouldn't tell him."

Sana takes a peek at the speedometer, which has just passed 120. She grabs onto the bitch bar above her door, as if it will somehow help her survive in the event I hit something at this speed. "How can you be sure he didn't find them?"

"Because the man lived out in the boonies. You've been there. Nobody around for miles. The killer would have gone through anything he found on-site. He would have left the files there after combing through them. It's years of work, right? Research. Tons of paper, probably. Our guy wasn't in a hurry. He would go through it all right there, not cart it all out to his car."

Sana looks at me in a kind of horror. "The files are still there?"

"Yep," I say, as my truck tops 130.

# CHAPTER 5

It's mostly a barren stretch of two-lane highway and a steady climb in elevation back to Big Rocks, but on a lazy Saturday afternoon, I'm covering the distance at a personal speed record, Agent Sana Locke hanging on for dear life the whole way. It isn't like I'm being reckless, and the few cars we pass are all humming along at ninety-plus, well above the posted limit. As I explain to my terrified passenger, "This is Nevada. Fast is relative."

"How can you stand it out here?" she asks. "It's so . . . barren."

It's not an unfair question. I thought long and hard on it before coming back here after getting a medical retirement from the Army. When you've been all over the world, Lincoln County, Nevada, is typically not going to make your Top Ten List of Places to Live. In my case, my father was ailing, and there are times in life you just have to do the right thing. And while there are no big cities out here, there are bright lights like you've never seen anywhere else. They belong to the Milky Way, and they are truly something to behold in the high desert. Also, life here is of a more honest nature. People are pretty much what they seem, a far cry from my life in the military-industrial complex. There's something to be said for that.

Sana and I are not at the point in our relationship where I would feel comfortable sharing all that, so I just say, "Barren? How do you figure?"

Arriving back at Atterbury's, the house is still a crime scene, still taped off, but none of my deputies are standing post any longer. "We simply don't have the manpower," I tell her as we pull up. "We're covering 11,000 square miles with a combined force about the size of a Boy Scout troop." It's probably a good thing anyway, I think, because that pit in my stomach is still there, and while my people are excellent at local law enforcement, they are not trained to deal with Russian assassins, so I'm happy it's just me and the FBI handling this part of the investigation for now.

My pulse is pumping in my ears, though. This happens a lot when you're a cop, of course, especially when you respond to a domestic disturbance or a call that is emotionally charged in some way. But the kind of edginess I'm feeling right now I haven't felt since my days in Moscow when I was frequently trying to meet with potential Russian military or intelligence sources without being arrested by the Federal Security Service, their version of the FBI. As we approach the house, I realize it's been five years since I've had this sense that everything is about to go terribly wrong. Hopefully, I'm overthinking this whole thing.

"I still think you might be overthinking this whole thing," Sana says on cue, seeing me draw my Glock as we enter the house. "It's pretty obvious there's no one here."

My eyes sweep the front room. "That's not clear to me at all." She's rolling her eyes behind me, I'm sure, but as we enter the hallway that leads to the bedrooms, I'm relieved to see she has her gun out and ready. It's barely bigger than her hand, but I'm not complaining. That's why God made extra magazines.

As it turns out, she's right. The house is empty, and everything appears as we left it earlier in the day. We holster our sidearms and end up in Atterbury's den, the only room in the house where it appears the man kept any important papers. In my gut, which is where I keep all my important stuff, I know the answer is right in front of me. "Come on," I say to Atterbury's ghost, "where would you have kept these files?"

"Why are you assuming he would have hidden them?" Sana asks.

"It's the logical conclusion, isn't it?"

"How so? You said it yourself, the guy lived out here in the middle of nowhere."

"Because they're not here, and there is no sign of them." I crouch down, leafing through the items littering the floor. Bank and retirement statements, utility and medical bills, old correspondence, nothing related to his FBI days. "Let's assume the files were here. This is the only room in the house where there are any papers, right?"

Sana nods. "Okay."

"And based on everything you've told me so far, finding the illegal was something of an obsession for Agent Atterbury, correct?"

Sana takes a seat at Atterbury's desk. "Correct."

"So, he's collected everything he can. He's got copies of phone transcripts he and the other handlers had with the illegal over the years. He has operational reports perhaps of the Bureau's search for this guy. He's got information on the people who worked at the test site and people who had access to them. Photos, personnel files probably. We're talking a lot of paper here."

She runs a hand through her splendid hair. "You're losing me again."

"If those files were here and the killer found them and took them with him, he leaves not one single scrap behind?"

Sana bends down from her chair close to me, smiling. "Maybe they were in nice file boxes and he just loaded them up."

*Exactly.* "Shit, that's it."

"What?"

"File boxes. There aren't any."

She looks confused again. "Hence my point. He loads them up and drives away."

My head is already shaking before she finishes. "Nope, nope, nope. Again, if they had been lying around in file boxes, there would have been no need to rip up the house like this."

I stand and look at the west wall of the room where there is a bookcase and a comfortable recliner for reading. The bookcase has been largely emptied, and Atterbury's books are scattered on the floor. My head cocks automatically.

"What is it?"

"Follow me, please." I move quickly through the house to the dining room and out the sliding glass door that opens onto an expansive redwood deck. The sun is setting and we only have a few minutes of decent light left. We move around the house until we're on the west side. "What would you say the width of Atterbury's office is?"

I can see her visualizing the room in her head. "Ten feet maybe."

"Yeah, that would be my guess, too."

"But?"

"But," I say, pacing off the exterior from where the bathroom ends to the edge of the house, "it's at least fifteen feet on the outside of the house."

Sana's eyes go big. "Shit."

"And did you notice where the window was in that room?" Her eyes say no. "Too close to the east wall. Not centered like most windows." We race back into the house. I scan the west wall of the office again from left to right. "Notice anything?"

Sana shakes her head.

I turn on the light switch to illuminate my point. "What about now?"

She studies the wall again and then the rest of the room. "Paint is newer on that wall."

I nod like a teacher who has just found his pet student. "Yes," I say and start tapping the drywall with a closed fist. "If this were an exterior wall like it should be, the sound would be denser. This sounds hollow."

"The bookcase," Sana says.

We examine the long, heavy shelving unit that could easily hold 150 books. It's more than five feet in height and made of good, sturdy pine that is firmly attached to the wall.

Sana asks, "Why secure this to the wall?"

"There's only one reason," I say. I try unsuccessfully to pull it away from the wall and then run my fingers along the top and sides, feeling for a switch. "Hmm, nothing." I step back, nearly tripping in the pile of books on the floor.

"Careful," Sana says, catching me by the arm.

I look around the room again and then back at the west wall, where my eyes land on an electrical outlet just up from the baseboard a few feet away from the bookcase. "Hello."

"It's an electrical outlet," Sana says.

"No, it's an electrical outlet with a GFCI."

"A GFCI?"

"A ground fault circuit interrupter," I answer, dropping to my knees on the carpet.

"So?"

"So GFCIs are normally placed in the vicinity of water lines.

They're designed to prevent someone from receiving an electrical shock caused by faults in devices we use around the house, and they're installed in places where there might be water or moisture because water conducts electricity and makes a shock much more dangerous."

"Thanks for the science lesson."

"My point is this little baby is not serving any practical purpose." I take a shot and push the red reset button on the outlet. *Click*. The right side of bookcase disconnects from its mooring to the wall and swings slightly open.

Sana and I stare at each other. "Well, Aunt Gladys in a blender," she says as only the well-educated can. "How about that?"

I get back to my feet and Sana approaches slowly. I stop just as I'm about to pull it open farther, knowing what has to be on the other side. "So Atterbury knew of the intelligence leak, I'm assuming?"

Sana nods. "We told him as soon as we found out. We told everyone who was named in any of the files. Standard procedure. Just in case."

"He had reason to think someone might come to look for the illegal."

"I have no idea. We told him, that's all I know."

I sense that's not completely true. But I understand need-to-know, and right now I'm more interested in seeing what's on the other side of the wall. I pull on the bookcase and it moves easily.

"Eureka," I say, entering the small hidden office. It's as I expected, about five feet wide and running the full length of the real office. There's a light switch on the near wall, and Sana flips it. A fluorescent light zaps to life. Three large four-drawer file cabinets line the west wall, but that's not the most interesting thing.

"Christ, look at this," Sana says.

I turn around and see dozens of photographs taped and stapled to the other three walls. Most are pictures of men, but there are a few shots of women, too. Most are old photos, very old, I think. Fifty years plus probably. "A bit of an obsession was right."

Sana moves to the filing cabinets. They're not locked. She thumbs through some of the files while I take a seat at the small desk. I have to assume those are FBI files and no doubt contain sensitive information I'm not cleared for. Sana nods appreciatively. I'm nothing if not discreet. She takes out her cell phone and begins taking pictures.

"Jesus, he has copies of very sensitive documents here. A lot of this stuff has no business being outside FBI headquarters."

I notice she's not dialing any numbers. "You're not calling this in?"

She replaces some of the files and closes the cabinet drawer, turning to me. "We haven't identified the source of the leak to the Russians yet. If I call in the cavalry now, this might land on the wrong person's desk. I can't risk that."

"Good. First rule of intelligence work. Trust no one. What do you want to do?"

She shrugs. "Your instincts have been spot-on so far. What would you do?"

*Sure, ask me tough questions while I'm staring at your beautiful face.* I rise from the little rolling chair. "Well, the killer didn't get what he wanted, right? We know that because we just found it, and it hasn't been disturbed."

Sana slides along the west wall, examining the photos. "No question about it," she purrs, deep in concentration.

"So, if I were him—"

"Or them," she says.

"Or them. I would keep my eyes on this house to see if anyone else might find what I was looking for."

She stops cold, whipping her head around. Before our eyes can meet, I see her face lock on the back of the bookcase as it swings farther away from the wall, freezing her. I don't wait to see what's coming because my instincts have already told me. I take one step and dive toward her, drawing my Glock at the same time. In midair, I see a tall man with silver hair standing in the adjacent room raising a handgun. It all happens in a microsecond, but in my mind, everything turns in slow motion. Silver hair fires, the bullets pass over my back, the noise suppressed, and I return fire, three loud rounds into the drywall left of where the shooter is standing. Was standing. Sana and I roll to our knees, her Walther coming out while I empty the rest of my magazine into the wall, hoping a round or two catches the guy on his way out.

Sana is on her feet, firing into the bookcase and into the drywall on the right in case he's moved the other way.

I slam another magazine. "Moving!" I yell, feeling her just behind me, the small room now filled with smoke and the smell of fired gunpowder. We clear the bookcase into the original room, but the shooter is gone.

"Blood," I say, gun fixed on the door to the hallway where I see a red smear on the wall.

Sana passes me on the left. "Where the hell did that guy come from?"

Down the hallway we go. The back sliding door is open and the blood trail leads outside. We approach the door from opposite sides, and when I do a quick peek outside, the glass explodes, pieces impacting my neck and face. We dive to the floor.

"Are you hit?" Sana yells.

"Just glass. You?"

Sana expels a lungful of air. "Not yet."

No more than sixty feet from the back of Atterbury's deck is the Big Rocks Wilderness and the first group of boulders. Beyond that is a forest of giant rocks that stretches for miles. Plenty of places to hide. Sana pumps a few rounds into the first group, figuring our attacker couldn't have gotten much beyond them yet. Smart. She's hoping he'll fire back which will give away his location. I'm already on my cell calling for backup. It's not really a cell phone. There is no signal this far out, so our phones all transmit via satellite. And while we've solved the communications problem, the only problem out here is that backup is rarely close by. When Tuffy answers, I give her a quick recap and some instructions for sealing off 13,000 acres of land in the dark.

Hugging the back wall of the dining room, Sana looks over at me. "Ready?"

"No."

"Why are we waiting?"

I'm pulling glass shards out of my neck. "Because he has the high ground and knows exactly where we are. And because we have what he wants, so let's see if he'll come to us."

She rises to her feet. "You're forgetting he's wounded. He has no shot at getting those files now, and he knows it. He's running." She turns toward the opening again, crouched and ready to fire.

"Hold up there, sis," I say. "We're not betting our lives on that. We don't know if I nicked him or something worse. And it's almost completely dark now. Neither of us is wearing a vest. We wait for backup."

"Christ, man. You're the sheriff, aren't you? You are my backup."

I shake my head.

"I can't wait for you. At least cover me."

I jump to her side of the six-foot opening and push her farther back inside the house, knocking her to the ground. "Listen to me. I know this ground. We need daylight and more people. It's cold outside. You'll be hypothermic in thirty minutes out there dressed like that."

Sana is on her feet again. "Stay if you want. I'm going."

I grab her by the arm. "This guy is a professional killer."

She does some sort of jujitsu move on me, cranking my wrist so painfully that I'm suddenly on my knees. "So am I," she says. Before I can stop her, she's out the door and firing blindly.

# THE PAST

As the weeks passed at the Nevada Testing Site, Georgiy Dudko settled in at his new job, posing as Freddie Meyer and spending the three to midnight shift mostly confined to the small admin building at Delta and answering the phone that seldom rang. So far, he had learned nothing from answering the phone. What he had witnessed was just how secure all operations were here. Badges, gate after gate after gate manned by men and machine guns. It had been easy getting in. Kitty, her father, the Q clearance, all of it easy. Now he wondered if, when circumstances dictated, he would be able to get out.

When he wasn't in the admin building, he rotated to one of three other sentry posts. His job was to prevent any unauthorized people gaining access, and that included high-level, overly curious military types who wanted to know what the CIA was doing out here. He wanted to tell them there was nothing to see at Delta because there truly was nothing to see. Not once had he seen the large airplane hangar doors open. Not once had he seen any plane land or takeoff.

"We need you in America now," his KGB commander at the American School in Vinnytsia told him. "In the heart of their scientific community." They called it Coca-Cola City, the American town in the Ukraine, and they drove American cars and watched American movies. They learned the language and how to gather and communicate intelligence, to detect and elude surveillance, all of which often took five years or more to graduate. Georgiy was rushed through in less than three. He would go to America and

learn their atomic secrets, perhaps study under their most brilliant scientists. Now, a year later, he was guarding an empty field.

And while getting the camera concealed in his thermos past the main security at the Mercury gate proved to be no issue, he had seen nothing worth photographing. He began to worry that the men running Directorate S would think him unproductive.

As 1955 ended, Georgiy got even worse news: there would be no more aboveground tests until 1957. An entire year. He was crushed.

Off work, he traded coded messages with his handler, someone he had never met and probably never would. Face-to-face meetings were only to be used in case of emergency, to pass along extensive instructions or documents, and only after certain recognition signals and passcodes had been exchanged. After conducting a thorough surveillance detection through the heart of Las Vegas, Georgiy would place his operational updates inside a used oil can which he would bury at the base of a chain-link fence bordering the fifth hole at the Desert Inn golf course. Then he would drive back to the apartment he had rented downtown and draw a short vertical line on a telephone pole in the rear of the complex with a piece of chalk. By the next day, he would see a horizontal line intersecting the one he drew, indicating the message had been received. If there were two lines crossing his, it meant there was an incoming message ready to be picked up.

"Be patient," one message read. "The struggle is long."

Those words reverberated in his head whenever he lay down to sleep on his skinny dormitory bunk at the test site. Much like the snores of the other men, they kept him awake. When he wasn't thinking about how to get transferred to a more active area on the site, he was worrying about America blowing his sweet homeland into radioactive dust, much like what they had done in Japan only a dozen years earlier.

The lack of sleep, the fear, and the boredom wore on him.

But on a freezing, blustery February evening, the sun sinking in the west, everything changed. Georgiy was standing post on top of the water tower when the runway lights came on, illuminating the surrounding landing strip and the black desert around it. This had never happened in his almost four months at Delta. And seconds later, he heard a high-pitched whine cut through the icy air, growing closer and closer. And then what looked to Georgiy to be a giant shadow dropped out of the sky. The plane was pure black, and through his binoculars, Georgiy guessed the wingspan to be at least thirty meters. Not more than a couple of feet above the long runway, the enormous black aircraft seemed to stall, falling almost, as if unstable in landing. When it smacked the black pavement, two jeeps appeared on either side, swooping in as the plane slowed and finally stopped. They took a position under the tip of each of the enormous wings and two men inserted what appeared to be a temporary and removable landing gear, as if to keep the wings from falling to the ground.

Georgiy was mesmerized. He had been trained to recognize all manner of American strategic and tactical aircraft, but he had never seen one like this. This was new.

He was elated. *Finally some actual intelligence!*

In just a few days' time, he would learn this new plane was called the U-2. The irony was not wasted on Georgiy. He would now be protecting a top-secret airplane managed by America's spy agency. He was *lisa v kuryatnike*, the fox in the henhouse.

On an early spring morning, Kitty Ellison opened the front door and jumped into the arms of the man she knew as Freddie Meyer, kissing him feverishly. "You're back!"

"In the flesh," Georgiy said, brightening. "Radioactive flesh, I'll grant you, but still mine."

Kitty giggled. "Beggars can't be choosers. You'll do." A minute later they were in the car.

Happy to be driving anywhere but around the test site, where everything was brown and dry and, most recently, smelled of jet fuel, Georgiy reached across the seat and took Kitty's hand. The windows were down, and he loved how the cool air blew through his hair, invigorating him. He chided himself silently for his growing attraction. Kitty was a target, a useful mark for the larger mission, a means to an end. And he had been warned about it repeatedly while training at the spy school. "If you find yourself getting too close," his sex instructor told him, "remember that the object of your affection wants to blow your country off the world map. Your love must be for the *rodina,* first and foremost." And yet, despite this caution, Georgiy found himself hiding the truth about Kitty on his operational updates to Moscow.

The drive to the southern Utah mountains wasn't long, but with every passing mile, he was amazed at the striking differences between the two states. Utah was everything the Nevada desert wasn't, its brilliant red cliffs towered to the sky and it had vast stretches of grassland for sheep and cattle. Touring Zion National Park, Georgiy was sure it was the most incredible piece of earth he would ever see. The wildlife was as abundant as the colors Mother Nature had painted into the landscape. Deer were everywhere. They saw coyotes and wild horses, too. Mustangs, they called them here. They passed a few sheep operations, and Georgiy wondered for the briefest moment what it might be like to disappear into this vast expanse and operate a livestock collective like his grandfather had back home. As he was daydreaming, he noticed an older man in blue overalls and three younger boys tending to some sheep in rickety wooden enclosures behind a rusty fence.

He pulled the car off into the dirt, and Kitty looked at him with concern. "Freddie, what is it?"

"Spring lambing," he said with a grin. "Come on."

They climbed out of the car and walked up a short dirt path. "We don't know these people, Freddie."

Georgiy shook his head. "Doesn't matter. These people are the same all over the world." He knew immediately he should have said *country* instead of world, but he didn't much care.

"Afternoon," the man said to them, tipping his baseball cap. He looked to be in his seventies, about the age Georgiy's own grandfather would be now had he survived the war.

"Afternoon," Georgiy said. "I'm Freddie and this is Kitty. We were just driving through and saw your operation here." Georgiy peered over the fencing. There were about forty ewes in the enclosure and five or six young lambs. "Lambing season, I see."

One of the boys was pulling a baby right out of its mother by the front legs onto a bed of straw. The lamb was coated in a yellowish, green slime, and Kitty had to turn away to keep from getting sick.

"Yuck," she said.

"That's just normal, miss," the man told her, laughing. "They all look like that when they pop out." Another of the boys reached down and with gloved hands cleared the newborn's mouth. The lamb was still.

"See if you can get it going," the man instructed the boys. Then he extended his hand to Georgiy. "Rance Preston. And this motley crew is Hagen, Waylon, and Heath. We're happy to meet you."

While Georgiy was shaking Preston's hand, he noticed that some of the adult ewes had scabs on their mouths, noses, and ears, and many had patches of wool instead of a full new coat coming in. "Looks like some of these are sick," Georgiy said.

Preston nodded. "They are. These are the lucky ones that survived all those bombs going off out in that desert where you folks are from. Saw the plates on your car."

Kitty was taken aback. "Why would you say that?"

The oldest boy, who couldn't have been more than ten, looked at his grandfather and shook his head. "Shit, Gramps. Another one. Stillborn."

"Watch that mouth, boy," Preston snapped. Turning to Kitty, he said, "I say it because it's true, miss. Those damn bombs already killed off half the sheep in this area. The worst one for us was that one they called Turk—yeah, they name them—just about a year ago. We winter our sheep on the Nevada range, just east of the proving ground, and one day at the crack of dawn we're out there sitting in our wagon, and the sky lights up like nothing you ever seen. And then that dust and smoke seemed to rise up to the heavens and spread out in all kinds of colors. We come out the next day after that cloud passed over and more than half our herd was dead. And we weren't the only ones. Everybody who uses that range had the same." Preston snapped his cracked, swollen fingers. "Twenty-five hundred sheep. Gone just like that."

Kitty was shaking her head. "Well, there must be another reason, sir. A virus of some kind perhaps. The government monitors radiation exposure and has determined there hasn't been any negative effects for livestock or people in this area."

Preston offered a friendly smile and nodded toward the dead lamb. "I've heard much the same, miss. But this is the seventh stillbirth we've had this week. You can see that a lot of these ewes don't have a full coat of wool. Some of the babies are born without any wool at all. Now I've been doing this all my life. I've seen every kind of sickness that life can visit on these animals. My people have been here sheep ranching since the 1860s, and I ain't ever seen anything the likes of this."

Georgiy felt for the man. He could see the pain in his face. "My grandfather raised sheep," he said solemnly. "I'm sorry for your losses, sir."

Preston nodded. "There's a war on with Russia. We get that. Everybody has to sacrifice. We're trying not to complain, but this is our livelihood, and it just ain't right." He lowered his voice so the boys couldn't hear. "It's not just the sheep or cattle, either. That dust is killin' people, too. We had thirteen women who were pregnant here when that cloud rolled through. Every single one of them miscarried."

Kitty was stricken. "Oh my God, I'm so sorry."

The old man's expression softened. "Well, it's not like you're the one who's doing it. 'Sides, God has a plan for everything. That's what we believe."

They said their goodbyes and returned to the car. Kitty couldn't stop crying. Georgiy took her hand and wondered if the sheep rancher could be right. Yes, radiation was deadly. People had known that since Marie Curie had died from her own experiments with it. Certainly, the Americans' use of the atom bomb in Japan demonstrated the horror of being in the blast radius. But two hundred miles away? Was this the reality of the nuclear age?

As they drove away from the small village, Georgiy remembered something else the man said. It is a war, and everybody has to sacrifice.

*Better the Americans than the good Soviet people.*

They returned to Las Vegas in time for dinner at Kitty's house, and Dr. Ellison already had the table set.

"I hope you like lamb, Freddie," he said as they sat down. "It's a specialty of mine."

Before he could answer, Kitty began sobbing.

"My goodness, dear. What is it? What's the matter?"

Georgiy handed her his handkerchief. "We visited a small town across the border on our drive today and spoke to a sheep rancher who believes the atomic tests are making his sheep sick."

"And killing them," Kitty said loudly. "And not just the sheep."

Dr. Ellison nodded. "I see."

Kitty dried her tears. "Is it true, Daddy? Is the radiation making them sick?"

While considering his answer, Ellison helped himself to some lamb and passed the plate to Georgiy. "Now Kitty, you know the Atomic Energy Commission has done numerous tests on this, as well as the military, and none of those tests conclude that there is any real danger to either animals or people."

Georgiy didn't know quite what to do. He was staring at the plate of lamb, wondering whether he could eat it. He knew well the effects of radiation poisoning and wondered where this meat had come from. The sheep he saw at Preston's had sores and scabs on their mouths and noses, probably from grazing on contaminated foliage. Suddenly, his appetite was gone.

Kitty shook her head vigorously. "Then the AEC and the military should get out to Cedar City and test those sheep. And while they're at it, they should test everybody's blood who lives out there."

They sat in awkward silence for a few moments. Eventually, Georgiy set down the plate of lamb.

Ellison folded his hands in front of him. "Kitty, this country is in a race for the future of this planet. The Soviets are developing their own thermonuclear weapons, and we are the only thing standing between them and a communist world, the only thing stopping them from blowing everything to bits. Some losses, a few sheep, are acceptable *if* they were caused by our efforts to keep up, and that hasn't been proven, mind you. Yes, there are risks, and we do everything we can to mitigate those risks, but we cannot afford to lose. Do you understand?"

Georgiy had been told the Americans believed this, so he wasn't shocked that Ellison espoused such lunacy. His days at the test site were spent in the company of similarly brainwashed men. He knew the truth, however. His country was a peaceful nation. Marx himself had taught them that wars result from capitalism, a competition for resources between great and imperialist powers. Yes, the communist ideal advocated for a proletarian world revolution but through peaceful means.

Kitty looked at the plate of lamb and erupted into tears once more. "I'm sorry. I can't eat this. Excuse me." She ran up the stairs to her room.

After a minute, Ellison rose from his chair. "Please excuse me, Freddie. I should go talk to my daughter."

Georgiy nodded. "Of course, sir. Take your time."

As soon as Ellison had left the room, Georgiy was on his feet. He bounded to the door to Ellison's study, pausing at the bottom of the stairs to hear Kitty still crying and her father trying to calm her.

The door was unlocked. Quickly, Georgiy moved into the office, quietly closing the door behind him and extracting the tiny camera from his trouser pocket. The office was immaculate, every book in its place on the shelf and a desktop clean of everything but a lamp, a pen, and two sharpened pencils, laid out like a silverware setting. The desk was locked, of course. Georgiy expected nothing less, and it was a good sign. It meant that, in all likelihood, there was something important inside. He examined the lock type, one that he had seen many times in his training. From his belt, he removed two elongated pieces of metal and inserted them into the lock. Three seconds later he felt it click.

The top drawer seemingly held nothing of value but Georgiy photographed it anyway. He was keenly aware that his inexperience might make him overlook something. He then went directly to the bottom drawer on the left. It held files, neatly organized in hanging expandable folders. One by one, he removed the files and photographed each page. There was no time to read the material. Let the experts determine what's important, he told himself. When he was done with the desk, Georgiy took a quick look around the study. He removed a few of Ellison's books from their place on the shelves and studied them quickly. He took pictures of the bindings, noting the titles. If he could get copies or even summaries of the books from Moscow, he would have more to talk about with the scientist. Common interests would help gain his trust even further.

Crossing the room to leave, Georgiy felt a slight depression in the floor and heard a creak. Peeling back the corner of the rug, he found a small floor safe. He took a picture of it.

The combination lock appeared quite common, certainly like the others he had practiced on in training. Georgiy retreated to Ellison's desk, picked the lock once more, and opened the top drawer, looking for the combination. Nothing. A quick search of the room had the same result. *It's in his head.* He returned to the safe and tried Kitty's birthdate, 11–13–32, but that combination didn't work. He tried the numbers in reverse, and the lock tumbled.

Georgiy couldn't believe his luck. He paused and listened for Kitty and her father. She was still crying and he was still talking. Georgiy pulled the door open and was immediately disappointed. The safe contained only one item, a thin three-ring binder which he extracted. He examined the cover on which was printed in small block letters only two words: PROJECT 57.

He opened the binder and noticed there were only fifteen to

twenty pages of single-spaced text, along with some charts, which he quickly scanned. They seemed to project the spread of plutonium isotopes across a geographic area. *Plutonium.* Georgiy knew he had something vital to his country's interests here, and he worked his camera quickly, photographing each page.

He had three pages to go when he heard Kitty's door open. As fast and quietly as he could manage, Georgiy snapped the remaining pages, replaced the binder in the safe, and closed the door and relocked it. Kitty and her father were coming down the stairs. They would see instantly that he was not at the dinner table, and they would see the light was on in the office.

"Freddie?" Ellison's voice was loud and filled with concern. A moment later, he entered the office, Kitty behind him. "What are you doing in . . ."

Georgiy stood over Ellison's chessboard, deep in thought. "Hope you don't mind, Doctor. I was checking out your latest move."

# CHAPTER 6

**G**od *damn it.* I do my best to cover Sana as she sprints out of Atterbury's house after the silver-haired assassin, firing blindly across the rocks above her. The response is immediate. Four rounds slam into the stucco exterior wall next to me, and my keen auditory memory tells me they came from a Makarov, possibly a Yarygin, not that the type of Russian pistol used to kill me is especially important right now. Then I hear Sana's gun answering and take a quick peek outside, barely catching the muzzle flashes and her position below me to the right at what must be the bottom of the deck stairs. She's twenty feet away. I reach up and kill the lights inside. Better late than never.

Again, the Russian doesn't hesitate. Another burst of four chipping away at the redwood railing close to her. *That's it,* I silently command him. *Burn up your ammo.*

Even if it wasn't dark out, this approach would be madness. He controls the high ground and has us completely pinned down. "Uh, say there, Sana," I call out. "How's it going so far?"

"Eleven o'clock!" she yells, firing again. "Feel free to move at any time."

"I'm going to give you some more covering fire. You're going to use that opportunity to scoot that exquisite butt of yours back in here. Have I made myself abundantly clear?"

"Will you actually be aiming at anything this time?"

I pop in a fresh magazine. "Go!" I shout and begin shooting at what I sincerely hope is well above her beautiful head. By the time I'm empty, she's back inside, hunkered up against the wall on the opposite end of the slider. "Nippy out there tonight," I say as she catches her breath. "We should stay in for a while. Maybe crack open some wine. I saw a few bottles above the kitchen cabinets. What do you think?"

"I think you must be blind. Do you ever qualify with that gun, or is it just for show?"

It's a fair point. For it is nighttime, inside and out, and I cannot see in the dark.

Well, I can see a little, my central vision is decent, but once the sun goes down, it narrows dramatically like I'm looking through a long tube. It's a condition called retinitis pigmentosa, and it's been getting progressively worse. Caused by a gene mutation, it's passed from mother to son. I've often wondered if, in addition to the cancer she probably got from being a Downwinder, my mom had some chromosomal damage from all that bomb fallout which caused me to get RP. My ophthalmologist, a top-notch guy down in Vegas, assures me RP cannot be caused by exposure to radiation, but like many of the people who grew up in an area that is like living next door to Chernobyl, I have my doubts about what is and what is not possible.

At any rate, this night blindness thing is a real bugger. It caused me to leave the Army before I wanted to, and it's not the best medical condition to have when you're a cop. And yes, I'm cognizant of the fact I haven't shared the details of this affliction with anyone in my department or my constituency, mostly because when I took the job it wasn't this pronounced and I thought I could treat it with massive doses of vitamin A. So, when I have to run out of a house in the dark of night shooting at something, I'm very lucky if I don't stumble and shoot myself, or in this case, Special Agent Sana Locke.

Thankfully, Sana quickly comes around to my way of thinking, and we decide to wait for backup. And the sun. We need light. What I can do now is dispatch some of my crew to patrol the highway from Hiko, about twenty miles to the west, as well as the dirt road that abuts the west side of Big Rocks itself. Our shooter is on foot, which means he's up in those rocks and has nowhere to go, especially in the dark. He's got one hell of a hike in front of him if he wants to escape. Which makes me wonder how he got to Atterbury's in the first place. Was he camping out up there and watching the house on the off chance we would find what he couldn't?

I can generally get a fixed wing Civil Air Patrol plane to help with a search and rescue, but not to help run down a fugitive, and as I suspected, we're too far south for the Bureau of Land Management's helicopter to be of use, but that's okay. Our shooter is up there somewhere, wounded and hiding no doubt under a very big rock. Sometimes my county's geography works to my benefit.

In the next few hours, I have a full posse on site, literally just like you see in the movies. It's mostly support personnel for manning the command post and making sure the search team has what it needs, but inevitably word gets out about things like this and the Good Samaritans start arriving, some with their horses. We can always use the extra manpower and often enlist the locals to help us search for lost hikers or the occasional mountain lion that is terrorizing some of the county's sheep or cattle. But as I explain to Sana, "This isn't a search and rescue. It's a search and arrest. It may be a search and destroy. We'll see." I send the Samaritans home with my thanks. It pays to have good neighbors.

Our base of operations is Atterbury's house, and everyone takes caution to stay out of any line of fire from the rocky hills above. I formally introduce Agent Locke to my team and let them know that I believe we are chasing a Russian intelligence operative who is a trained killer, at which point Sana interjects. "This is highly sensitive information. I can't emphasize enough the repercussions that will follow should this get out."

Wardell shows her his middle finger, which makes everyone laugh. We pass the night drinking coffee and fighting to stay awake, looking at a map of the area and discussing the best way to drive the fugitive, as Isaiah said, like a peg into a firm place. We've also carefully moved Atterbury's files from the secret room to one of our trucks, which is now on its way back to the main station in Pioche.

"Too bad you didn't keep the horses," Sana says with a tremendous yawn, as the sun breaks over the earth's curve, its earliest rays dancing on the rooftops of Big Rocks and incrementally returning that which is stolen from me each night. It's all of twenty degrees out here, and the stiff wind from the northwest makes it feel more like ten.

"We'll have to wait for another time to give you the full western experience," I tell her, handing her an extra down camo jacket I keep in my truck. Tuffy passes out radios to everyone, and I'm happy to take every advantage I can get, thank you very much.

Sana laughs, stuffing her cold hands inside the big pockets and pulling out a knit hat and some gloves. "I knew you were a cowboy."

"I prefer a motorcycle, but you'd be surprised where a horse can take you that nothing else can. You ride?"

"Does a pony on my eighth birthday count?" Sana motions to the toy hauler and some four-wheelers and more snowmobiles inside. "Are we taking those?"

I point north to the mineral skyscrapers that pepper the land as far as a good pair of eyes can see. "The four-wheelers will secure the western edge of this place like a picket line. Where we're going, it's on foot or nothing, I'm afraid."

"No helicopters?"

She's not crazy about hiking in, and I don't blame her. "Too far out. They'd have to turn right back as soon as they got here or run out of fuel. If you prefer, you can stay here."

"Oh, hell no. I'm going with you."

Wardell and New Guy Pete are fully decked out in camos and are already armed with AR-15s and a .308 Remington respectively. They also are strapping on small packs, as we never know how long we will be out on a hunt like this, so it's food and water for everyone, an emergency blanket, and plenty of extra ammunition. I continue to hope the cold is wearing on Ivan the Terrible up there in the rocks.

Sana checks her Walther has a full magazine. "Got another AR?"

I yell over to Tuffy to grab the one out of my truck. When she brings it over, I hand it to Sana. "I imagine you've used this before."

"Once or twice," she says, looking down the sight.

"Uh-huh, well, we're likely to get spread out a bit up there. If you have to shoot, don't shoot the guys wearing what we're wearing. The guy we're hunting was wearing a gray pullover last time I saw him."

"Hey," Sana says. "I can't promise anything."

Since this will be New Guy Pete's first manhunt with the team, I ask him if he's comfortable carrying the .308.

Wardell answers for him. "He's checked out on it, Beck. Jesus."

I like New Guy Pete. He's growing on me. Wardell, not so much. I send Johnny and Jimmy Green, along with a couple friends from the Forest Service, out on the Commander ATVs north on the narrow road to the west. "Keep line of sight with each other, about a quarter mile distance," I tell the Twin Peaks. "You're the wall. Don't let him past you."

They reply in unison, of course. "Yes, sir."

"Are we ready?" Sana asks.

Just as I'm about to say that we are still waiting for the dog, Tom Harker pulls up in his truck and climbs out, along with Bugsy, a basset hound with the longest ears and most pitiful face you've ever seen.

"What the hell is this?" Sana asks.

I scratch Bugsy behind the ears. "This is the best damn blood tracker in the county," I tell her. "Aren't you, Bugs?"

Sana looks at me in disbelief as Bugsy lifts his head and gives me a big, slobbery kiss.

Tom Harker looks over at Sana. "He's not fast, ma'am, but if this boy's bleeding, he'll find him. He can track a wounded deer or mountain lion to hell and back." Hopefully, we're not going that far.

Tom is a good man, like most people here. A solid citizen and a great hunter. He runs a taxidermy shop in Caliente, and the inside of his home looks like a hunting lodge with the heads of every big game animal he's ever killed mounted on the walls.

I place a gentle hand on his shoulder. "Tom, we're after a pretty dangerous guy here. Why don't you let me take Bugsy?"

"He won't go unless I do, Beck," says Tom, scratching at his gray beard. "I'll be fine."

In accordance with my authority, I deputize him on the spot, which consists of the old tracker raising his right hand and agreeing to a round of beers after this whole thing is over. If Tom were to get injured or killed, he would be considered a county employee and he or his family would be able to collect benefits. I don't like putting a civilian in the line of fire, but I don't have much choice right now.

"You got some blood for us?" Tom asks.

I take a handkerchief from my jacket and hand it to Tom. It's got the shooter's blood from inside Atterbury's office. Tom puts the cloth up to Bugsy's snout, and the dog takes a few good whiffs.

"He's ready," Tom says.

"It's your show, Tom. We'll cover you the whole way."

We start out, coming around to the back of Atterbury's house and moving quickly to the huge rocks above. Bugsy, like the Russian, is likely to follow any number of game trails, which will take us into the jumbled boulders known as Mecca to the rock climbers who frequent the area. With the first real morning light, I can see the posse stretching out along the road to the west. If our Russian is just waking up, he's not going to like his odds in that direction.

I hear Tuffy in my earpiece. "Base to Jolly Greens. Base to Jolly Greens. Our party is headed into Big Rocks. Report any sightings, please, and look for any squirters coming your way."

In no time, the team begins spreading out a bit. New Guy Pete is on point, and then Tom and Bugsy, followed by Wardell and Sana, who sweep back and forth with their ARs. I have the rear. The light snow cover on the ground adds a little caution to our steps, but it's not enough to slow our ascent. And even now, twelve hours since this bastard almost killed me, I can see his red blood trail speckled over the cold ground every few feet. Maybe he's already dead, I think. That would be nice.

Feeling cocky about my vision now—I can actually make out shapes and sizes and colors—I move closer to Sana, reaching to my throat and switching off my radio mic. "How we doing?"

She never takes her eyes from the rifle sight. "Beautiful morning for a walk," she answers. A minute later, "I guess I haven't thanked you yet. You know, for saving me back there. The guy had me cold."

"Gave me a chance to jump you," I say. "Though I normally like it to last a bit longer than that."

"Hmm," she says. "I'll give that some thought."

After thirty minutes, we're in the heart of Mecca, slipping carefully down steep rock faces and climbing narrow cracks through the boulder field. My eyes are suddenly drawn to Bugsy whose tail is wagging at the speed of sound. He lets out a low whine and sits, a signal I've seen a few times. "How close?" I ask Tom quietly.

"Best guess, no more than a few hundred yards."

Bugsy's talent is leading Tom to a deer that's been shot, so this isn't much different. On a search and rescue where someone is bleeding, he'll take you right to them. But I don't want to risk him or Tom on this track, so I find a nice rock for them nearby and plant them there.

Pete and Wardell fold back, and the team takes cover for a moment. "Shooter close by," I whisper to everyone." I give the same message to the Twin Peaks on the radio and then motion Pete to the left and Sana up the middle. I tell Wardell I'm going right and he's staying back with Tom and Bugsy.

"The hell I am," he says, taking a step around me.

I put a hand on his arm. "Yes, you are, Wardell. If he gets past us somehow, you need to get Tom out of here. I can't leave that to anyone else.

"We want him alive, if possible," I tell them all. Everyone has their sunglasses over their eyes to cut the glare except Wardell. Old guy sees like an owl. Another reason not to like him.

We fan out. Five minutes later, Sana radios she's found a stash of clothing, a sleeping bag, and some empty freeze-dried food containers along with a pair of binoculars. "And there's some medical gauze soaked with blood. He was camping out here, Beck, watching the house."

I ask her how long, based on the blood she's seeing.

"Minutes," she says. "Minutes."

"I've got the suspect," one of the Twin Peaks says over the radio. "Two hundred yards from your location, heading northwest and hurting, by the look of him."

*Shit.* That's Pete's direction. "Pete, he may be heading your way. Sana and I will head north. Move farther west if you can. Let's see if we can pinch him."

I can't see any of them at the moment, but I know they're doing what I'm doing, moving cautiously from cover to cover behind the giant rocks. This guy is committed, I think. Camping out, patient, and apparently not dead.

I make my way west, looking for any kind of movement, my eyes picking up Pete moving like a spider over the rocks maybe a quarter mile away, but there's no sign of the others. Suddenly, there's movement in front of me about fifty yards out. I stand and take aim. Catching him in my scope, I see it's just a deer. But something spooked him.

I don't have time to consider what that might be because a bullet whizzes by my left ear just then and blows up a patch of snow a few feet away. The sound is unmistakable.

"Rifle," Sana says, taking cover next to me.

I nod and speak into the mic, whispering. "He's due west of me, Pete. Not far. He's got a rifle. If you have a shot, take it. Say again, if you have a shot, take it."

Sana tugs at my arm. "We need him alive."

I give her a quick nod. "He knows that."

She looks back at me with imploring eyes.

"Again, Pete, wound if possible. We would really like to question this guy."

I'm scanning the boulders to the north, looking for any movement. Nothing. Sana and I pick up the pace, darting from rock to rock, our breath steaming out of our mouths and noses in the cold like dragons.

"Well, he's either pretty banged up or not a great shot," I tell her.

"Yeah, if he was on his game, I'm guessing that shot would have gone through your head."

"Can't plan for everything, I guess. He wasn't planning on a gunfight out here."

My earpiece crackles again. "Sheriff, it's Pete. I have him below me about two hundred yards. I have a shot."

I wonder how the hell he got ahead of the guy. Sana looks at me with a final plea, but I shake my head and key the mic. "Pete, did you copy my last? Can you put one in an arm or leg?"

"I can only see his head."

"Copy. We're coming. Stand by."

Just as Sana and I move, I hear the crack of the Russian's rifle again, and simultaneously, the bullet hitting the rock just above our heads. We dive to the ground. A second later, there's the distinct sound of the .308, and New Guy Pete confirms over the radio, "Suspect down."

"Copy, Pete. Toss some smoke down there if you can. Wardell, you can come up. Approach with caution."

Sana takes off at a sprint. "He might still be alive."

When we work our way up to him, Pete is sitting on a rock a few feet from the body, his face ashen. From the side, the dead man appears to be in his late twenties or early thirties, and is wearing a thick coat now. I carefully slide the wool beanie from the top of his cratered head and see the same silver hair I glimpsed in Atterbury's den. His rifle lies next to him, an AS Val, a Russian assault rifle I've seen once or twice. So, the good news is we appear to have bagged the right guy.

Wardell arrives a few minutes later, huffing and puffing. The back of the shooter's skull is caved in from the round it took, and what remains of it and the light snow around it is covered in red Russian blood. He is, most definitely, dead. Sana checks for a pulse anyway and then turns him over on his back. His forehead is gone as well, and his blood hit the rocks in front of him like it had been tossed from a bucket. I open his jacket and find another wound between his left third and fourth ribs, bandaged and soaked with blood.

"He wouldn't have made it much longer," Wardell tells me, photographing the torso with his phone camera. "You plugged the bastard good."

Sana checks the Russian's pockets. "Nothing to tell us who he is."

"Not even a library card?" I gaze over at Pete. He looks numb, a picture I have seen many times over a long military career. I walk over to him. "You all right?"

He nods.

"What was your location when you took the shot?"

Pete stands and wheels in his boots and points north and west to a grouping of boulders. "He was lining up on you again, boss. I had to take the head shot."

"You really hauled ass, didn't you?"

He manages to meet my gaze. "Yes, sir."

"Let me have that rifle, son." Pete hands me the .308. "Was that your first?" He looks at me and nods, processing that he has taken a life. All his time in the military he was spared the trauma of killing another human being. "We'll put you on a desk for a while. Or you can stay off duty. Technically, you're on administrative leave until we clear you on the shooting."

"Hell," Wardell rejoices, "that won't take any time at all. Clean shoot all the way."

*Yeehaw, you moron.* "Paid time off, if you want it, Pete."

Pete nods and walks away. "Get him out of here, Wardell. Start the paperwork."

When they're gone, I bend down next to Sana in the snow.

"We'll process his campsite as well. See if we can find anything that might help us identify him."

She looks up at me. "He's a ghost."

She's probably right, and I'm almost sorry about it. "I guess you'll be heading back to Washington now. Job well done and all, catching your Russian."

"Job's not finished," she says. "There's still a Russian here somewhere. The one Atterbury was looking for. We just have to find him."

# CHAPTER 7

B y late morning, we're all running on fumes. Sana in my office trying to ID the dead man, my staff at work completing all the paperwork that's required whenever you whack a Russian out at Big Rocks, and me trying to re-create Atterbury's hidden room inside one of the empty jail cells in my detention center, the photos previously on the FBI man's walls now on mine. Atterbury's files have a methodology I can relate to, well-ordered, chronological accounts of each person's life and career, but there is a mountain of them. *He was a good cop.*

Just as I'm having that thought, Sana walks in with two cups of coffee. "Impressive reconstruction."

I take a big whiff of coffee smell into my nostrils while I stare at a group of the photographs on the wall, mostly of young men, a few women. All have names printed at the bottom. They are predominately black-and-white and look like headshots from employment records. Some are blowups of driver's licenses or other government-issued ID. Then there are the Polaroids, which probably means the 1970s, and still others are much more recent, digital snaps of people taken from a distance. Surveillance photographs, most of them not very clear. "Yeah, I figured if we kept everything pretty much the same, we might be able to get into his head a little bit. Any luck on a name for our dead Russian?"

She yawns and hands me a coffee. "Not yet. Facial reconstruction is a bit challenging, seeing as we blew up that part of his body."

"Yeah, sorry about that. Anything else that might help you?"

Sana takes a seat on the floor and rests her back up against the bars. "Well, very quietly we're reaching out to our asset in Moscow to see what he can find out, but we have to be extremely careful. You know what I mean?"

I do know. Once upon a time I had my own asset in Moscow, and I know what happens if you're not careful. "Right, because you still don't know who leaked the information about Atterbury's illegal still being alive."

"*Possibly* alive. Yes."

Tuffy wheels in a dolly with several more boxes of Atterbury's files. "Where do you want them?"

I point to an open spot on the floor. "I'm afraid we have another problem, Sana."

She looks up at me. "Will it require me staying awake any longer?"

"It might. The guy we killed this morning is not the person who killed Atterbury."

That's enough to get her to her feet. "Please tell me you're joking."

I can't seem to drag my tired eyes away from some of the pictures I tacked to the walls. "Our shooter yesterday was left-handed."

"How do you know that?"

"Little things."

"Like?"

"He was using his left hand when he shot at us."

"You remember that?"

"Like it was yesterday."

"It was yesterday, you dope."

"Oh, yeah. Anyway, he was definitely shooting at us with his left hand."

"So?"

"So, the coroner said the guy who killed Atterbury was right-handed."

"I believe his exact words were *likely* right-handed."

"No," I say, recalling Otto's words in my head like the lyrics to a favorite song. "His exact words were 'likely male and right-handed.'" I remove some of the more recent pictures and some of the government ID enlargements. All of them are of old men. I tack them to a different wall. "Which we will assume is the gospel truth until proven otherwise."

Tuffy looks at me. "Which means this isn't over."

Sana kicks the wall. "Shit."

I nod. "Which means this isn't over. Whoever killed Atterbury still hasn't found his agent."

Sana runs a hand through her hair. "His *traitor,* at least in his mind. Why are you moving those, Beck?"

I finish my reassembly. "Okay, look here on the right. These are the ones I think Atterbury took. They're relatively recent, and I recognize some of the men in them and some of the names." I pull Tuffy closer to the wall. "Look, Tuff, these are from Lincoln County. Atterbury was surveilling these men."

Tuffy examines them one by one. "Definitely from around here, but he wasn't very good with a camera. A lot of side shots, and his focus wasn't very good."

"Right, he snapped them quickly, probably on the move.

Problem with surveilling someone here is there's nowhere to hide while you're doing it. We know that from our own experience."

"And these?" Sana asks, pointing to the driver's license photos.

I raise a hand to my now three-day-stubbled chin. "Now these are interesting. A lot of them are from other states, and most have the red X on them."

"He ruled them out," says Sana.

"Yep, I agree. But we're going to look at them all anyway. I'm hoping we'll find a file for each of them in those file cabinets or these boxes."

"Or," Tuffy adds, "the X means they're dead already."

"Extremely likely," I say. "Either way, Atterbury hadn't been here long. He didn't know the people here like we do, so he might have ruled some out prematurely. Now, figure a Soviet spy comes here in, say, '54 or '55. He's probably in his mid-twenties, minimum. Add sixty-two years to that. If he's still around, he is one old goober."

"Can't be too many of those left," Sana says, moving back to the other wall where most of the photos remain. "So, do you recognize some of these faces?"

"Not from the old batch. But people change a lot over sixty years. Plus, most of these folks probably settled elsewhere. Big cities, other states. Our first order of business, then, is matching the photos to the files Atterbury compiled on them and determining who they are and where they currently reside."

Tuffy takes notes. "Copy. Including final resting places."

"Including final resting places." I turn to Sana. "I wonder why Atterbury never came to us for assistance. We might have been able to help him narrow his search."

She looks at me in disbelief. "Someone needs a nap. See this stuff, Beck? These photos, these files? It was illegal for him to have this. He couldn't ask anyone for help."

I can feel it in my shoulders and back especially, the need to hit the rack. All of us have been up for about thirty hours or more. But in my brain, I know the grains of sand are trickling through the hourglass. Time is literally running out. "I suppose that's another reason why he had the secret room. Didn't want to get caught with any of it. Might screw up his pension."

Sana says, "It definitely would have."

Tuffy tells us there are more files she still has to bring in and excuses herself. When it's just the two of us again, Sana says, "Maybe he did locate the illegal."

"No, he didn't," I reply.

"How can you be sure?"

"When you finish a jigsaw puzzle, what do you do?"

She scans the jail cell again, all the pictures, all the files. "You put the pieces back in the box."

"Yep, and Atterbury didn't do that. He was still working the problem."

Sana pulls a photo off the wall, one that has the big X across the face. "I'm not sure any of this will help us. As soon as the Bureau found out about the illegal, as soon as he contacted us—I think this was 1962 or '63, our agents went back through every single employee at the test site and revetted them. Interviewed them exhaustively. Dug into their personal lives, their pasts. Polygraphed them all. The illegal we're after wasn't an employee."

I take the picture from her and look at it. "Maybe he had reason to disagree with that conclusion, or maybe the illegal was just someone who had contact with people working at the site. Maybe that's how he got his intelligence."

A quick head bob. "That's been our working theory ever since."

"Right, we look at everyone who was in the area at that time, regardless of whether they were test site employees, and we focus on people who still live here."

"And are still alive," Sana adds.

I laugh. "Yes, people who still live here who are not dead."

"Sorry, I'm punchy."

I hand her my coffee. "Keep the caffeine going." I look at the photos on the wall again. "Our problem is one of geography. The county is big but only has about six thousand residents. It's a lot of ground, a lot of little nooks and crannies and people living off the grid. People like ex-agent Atterbury. Some of them are hiding from something, escaping from something, so while we know most people here, we don't know them all. Especially me, I've been back a few years but was gone for almost twenty-five."

An older man enters the cell. A few inches over six feet, even taller with the yellow straw Stetson that appears molded to his angular head, he is slender, with silver hair and a mustache that trails over the sides of his mouth to his rugged jawline. He is not in uniform but has a star on his blue denim shirt and a .45 strapped to his belt. His arms are folded, and if looks could kill . . .

I hold up my hands in self-defense. "Don't be pissed at me, Arshal."

"What the hell, Beck?" The man's voice sounds like a scratchy vinyl. "You go hunting a man in my area and you don't call me?"

I bob and weave like Muhammad Ali over to Sana. "Special Agent Sana Locke, this crusty old bird is Sergeant Arshal Jessup. Arshal was here when the dinosaurs roamed the earth."

"Piss on you, Beck. The old man would never have done that to me."

Sana hesitantly extends her hand. "Sergeant. I recognize the voice."

Arshal takes it. "Ma'am."

"I was with the sheriff when you radioed in about those graves being dug up."

Arshal nods politely but turns to me, red-faced with a nice vein bulging in his neck. "How could you do that to me?"

I treasure the man but will never admit it. Instead, I raise a finger in the air. "First, it was late, and I figured you were probably asleep." Another finger joins the first. "Second, I promised LaThella I would keep you out of harm's way when I could, Arshal, and I'm more scared of her than I am of you." I shift my attention to Sana. "That's Arshal's daughter. And third, Pop has told me the same. 'You can't afford to lose Arshal.'"

Arshal removes his hat and bangs it against the cell door. "That is such horseshit, Beck. Please excuse my language, ma'am."

"Certainly, Sergeant."

His feathers still ruffled, I say, "I'm glad you're here, Arshal. We can use your help." I motion them both out of the cell but turn back to the man I first met when I was a kid. "Why are you here, anyway? Did you dig something up on that grave situation?"

Arshal sighs heavily. "Oh good, we're having puns for breakfast."

"Seriously. Is there something going on, or did you come up here just to kick my ass?"

The older man looks down at his boots. "Got a call from Amon."

"Uh-oh." Arshal and his brother generally despise each other and hardly ever speak. Whatever comes next won't be good.

Arshal nods, fiddling nervously with his mustache. "Girl ran off apparently."

"Ran off? How old?"

"I don't know. I was trying very hard not to listen. Amon swears she's been kidnapped."

"What did you say to that?"

Arshal looks away, clearly frustrated. "What the hell do you think I said?"

I shouldn't have asked. "So now Amon wants to talk to me."

"Ayup."

"Okay, Agent Locke and I will go see Amon if you'll stick around here and help Tuffy sort through all of this."

"We will?" asks Sana.

Arshal looks around the cell. "Oh, wonderful. Paperwork."

I clap him on the shoulder. "Or you could go see Amon."

"Fine," Arshal says, crossing his arms again.


As we drive north out of Pioche, Sana asks, "Why am I going with you? More to the point, why are you going? Last time I looked we were hunting a killer and looking for a spy."

I crank the heater up another notch or two. "Well, you've pretty much seen my department. I don't have a bunch of officers I can dispatch to these kinds of calls. And we don't get a lot of people who go missing here, so I can use the help."

"But shouldn't I have stayed back to go through those files? After all, they kind of belong to me."

I shake my head. "Technically, they're evidence in a murder investigation. So, they belong to me now."

Sana reclines in the seat. "You know I can change that with a phone call, right?"

I wonder who might pick up on the other end of that call. "Yeah, but then you would risk alerting your mole. Plus, you're sort of impressed with my instincts and abilities, so you'd rather let this play out a little longer."

She thinks about that for a few seconds. "In truth, I'm sort of impressed with your instincts and abilities, so I think I would like to see this play out a bit longer."

I flash my momma's smile. "Good choice."

Sana's dark eyes stay locked on me. "What's the story with Arshal and this Amon guy, and before you answer, does everyone up here have weird names?"

"I'm sorry, weird names?"

"Arshal, Wardell, Tuffy, Amon, Porter. It's like the Bible meets Zane Grey."

Wow, I think. She knows who Zane Grey was. We should definitely start planning our wedding. I muster my best backwoods accent. "These are the names we was given, ma'am."

She laughs. "Arshal doesn't seem to care for this Amon fellow."

I take a deep breath and release it slowly. "Arshal and Amon are brothers. Amon is a year older, I think, and he's the head of the FLDS up here."

Sana sits up straight. "The polygamist sect? That FLDS?"

I turn on the wipers as the snow starts to fall and reach in the back seat, grabbing my down jacket, handing it to Sana. "One and the same. They're not crazy, at least not as much as the ones you've heard about down in Colorado City or other places. They operate some farms a few miles north of here, and they're very good at it."

"Polygamist farmers."

"Correct. Hey, do you know what the penalty is for polygamy?" Before she can answer, I do. "Two mothers-in-law."

Sana snickers. "Okay, that's a little bit funny. But why the tension between the brothers?"

"When they were teenagers, they left the church and the farm. Just walked out. After about a year, Amon returned to the compound. Arshal didn't. Eventually Amon rose to the top position, and Arshal never forgave him for going back to that."

"To that?"

"To a place where young girls are . . . persuaded to marry much older men."

Sana looks like her skin is crawling. "And older men persuade themselves it's okay."

I nod. "Yep."

"Can't you shut the place down? I mean, we did that in Texas and sent that lunatic to prison."

"Not the same thing here. They're good neighbors, run a productive business. They don't force anyone to stay. They don't force anyone to marry."

"Says who? The horny old lechers?"

I turn off the highway onto a back road. "You'll see."

Sana massages the back of her neck. "Okay," she says just before the light switch in her head goes out. She needs the sleep.


Thirty minutes later, I pull into the Mill Valley farming community. In the warmer months, there would be as many as forty large circular pivots, those waterwheel circular irrigation tracts, clearly visible from the road, growing everything from potatoes to melons to beans and a whole lot of hay. Green everywhere for miles. In February, everything up to the horizon is largely covered in white. I drive into the Mill Valley Produce parking lot, where the snow is falling slightly heavier, swirled about in the wind blender that is eastern Nevada, and where I know Amon Jessup will be waiting inside. I leave Sana in the truck, closing the door lightly to avoid waking her. She startles awake anyway and motions for me to wait.

"Sorry, you looked like you were crashing pretty hard."

"I'm okay. It's this coat," she says, patting the puffy arms. "It's like a cozy sleeping bag."

Just in front of us, a number of FLDS women exit the main building, their puffed-sleeved pastel dresses and long hair swept up or held in long braids down the back. None of them are wearing jackets, so we feel pretty wimpy.

Sana isn't prepared for the visual. "Like stepping back into the nineteenth century," she whispers to me as we enter.

"They don't cut their hair, because they believe they will use it to wash Christ's feet during the Second Coming."

"Get the fuck out," she says instinctively, the words catching everyone's ears in the huge warehouse.

"Language please, Sana," I say, smiling at her obvious discomfort and nodding toward a group of men in dark suits approaching from the back of the building, which contains a full grocery store and a warehouse stacked high with pallets of produce. Sana picks out Amon Jessup immediately. He looks just like his brother, only heavier and clean-shaven. The men around him are mostly younger, all clean-shaven as well.

I extend my hand. "Amon."

"Sheriff, thank you for coming. How is your father?"

We shake for a long time, Amon's way of trying to transfer some small portion of his God into me. "Right as rain, Amon. I'll tell him you asked about him. This is Special Agent Sana Locke of the FBI."

Sana produces her badge. "Very nice to meet you, sir. I'm not here in any official capacity."

Amon looks questioningly at me. "She's here on another matter, but Arshal said you feared one of your members had been kidnapped, so I thought I would bring Agent Locke along."

The old man is clearly uncomfortable with a woman in authority unless it's over a chicken in a pot. "You'll have to forgive us, Sheriff. We're on our way to services." Most of the men exit the building, and Amon instructs all but one man to continue without them. "This is Clem Edwards, Sheriff. He is the husband of Michaela Edwards, the missing woman."

I see Sana sizing him up. Clem is in his early forties, about my height, as round as a bowling ball, his suit coat squeezed tightly over his large frame, his neck bulging above the top button of his white shirt and his dark tie like a tight noose.

"Sure, I know Clem. I'm sorry for your troubles, Clem. What can you tell us?"

Clem looks back at Amon. Like most people here, he doesn't trust outsiders. "Like brother Jessup said, someone took Michaela, my wife."

I nod sympathetically and pull an official Lincoln County Sheriff's Department notepad from my jacket pocket, the same one I've somehow been using since I started this job. "Can you tell me when this happened, to the best of your knowledge?"

"Two days ago. She took some vegetables over to the Pony Springs Fire Station and never came back."

"About what time was that?"

"Just before lunch, I guess," Clem answers. "She holds those men in high regard, as we all do, for protecting us from those wildfires."

"Was she driving your truck, Clem?"

Clem snarls. "She was on one of the bicycles."

*Of course, because heaven forbid you should allow them to drive.* I do the distance calculation in my head. Half hour each way on a bicycle. Maybe forty minutes with the wind blowing that day. Out here, the wind blows every day. "You looked for her, I take it?"

Clem's big cheeks fill with air and disapproval. "Yes, we all looked for her, and no, she didn't run off."

I glance at Amon. "Not saying she did, Clem."

"Didn't have to. We know what you think about us."

I take a small step toward Clem and lower my voice, as a number of the women huddle nearby, staring. "Listen, Clem. I'm here to help, but to do my job I have to cover all the bases. Okay?"

"Whatever you need, Sheriff," Amon says. "Ask your questions."

I give Amon an appreciative head bow and continue. "How old is Michaela?"

"Seventeen."

Sana groans and rolls her eyes. "Jesus." All three men glare at her. "Sorry," she says.

"Description?"

"Red hair, brown eyes, about this tall," Clem answers, holding a hand up to the middle of his chest.

"You said she was on a bicycle. It's a ways to Pony Springs. Could the bike have broken down?"

"Could have. We thought that might have happened, but we didn't find it either, and we searched both sides of that road the whole way." Clem's fingers curl into angry fists. "I'm telling you, someone grabbed her."

He seems pretty adamant, and he has to know that if I find her and she did run away that I wouldn't just bring her back. "Did she make it to the fire station?"

"Yep, the men there said she left about one o'clock."

I make a note in my book to have the BLM fire guys interviewed and jot down, *Special relationship with one of them?* "They say she seemed okay?"

"Okay how?"

"Normal, friendly, not distressed in any way?"

Amon answers for him. "We didn't ask them that, Sheriff. We know when she left here she was her normal self."

I look into Clem's round hazel eyes for a few moments. "Clem, any problems between you and Michaela? I have to ask."

Stuffing his big hands into his pants pockets, he says, "No, damn you. I know you think she run off, but she didn't. We don't force people to marry here."

The cold air is thick and heavy with tension, so I dial it back. "Okay, Clem. I was married once, and there were times I thought I knew her mind, and it turned out I was wrong. Is there some place Michaela might go if she were angry, maybe a friend if she needed some time away?"

"Sheriff," Amon interjects, "Michaela has lived here her entire life. We are the only friends she has, and she loves her life here."

I sense I've gotten everything of use from the interview, and I'm inclined to believe Amon. He's like his brother, and you can tell when he believes what he says because, otherwise, he doesn't speak. "Okay, then. Just a couple more things. Do you have a picture of Michaela my deputies can use, and can you tell me what she was wearing when she left? I mean, was she wearing a jacket, gloves, a hat?"

Again, Amon answers for Clem. "Blue dress, gray jacket, tan deerskin gloves. I already told my brother this."

I make another note. I don't need to. I don't forget things, even when I would like to, but writing it down assures them I've got it and, hopefully, that I care. "And the photo?"

"We will email it to you," Amon says. I see Sana covering a smirk and know exactly what she's thinking. *They actually have email?*

I lower my voice again and look Amon straight in the eyes. "Appreciate that, Amon. Now we are going to do everything we can to find Michaela. When we do, if I determine she has been abused in any way or tells me some horror story about her life out here, I'm going to come back, and I'm going to have arrest warrants, and I'm going to bring Agent Locke and a bunch more FBI folks. Am I making myself clear?"

Leaving Mill Valley, I phone Tuffy at the office, our voices playing through the truck's speakers. After getting the rundown on Michaela Edwards, Tuffy asks how best to split the team.

"Pete is on a desk until he clears the shooting board, so keep him with you and Arshal on Atterbury's files. He's an ex-MP, so let's put his investigative skills to work. Send Wardell and the Jolly Greens out to interview people up here near Mill Valley. And see if we can get the BLM's chopper up there to search the desert. God help her if she's out there."

Tuffy doesn't immediately answer.

"Tuffy? Did you get that?"

"Well, Wardell outranks me, boss. You sure I should be the one telling him?"

I tap the wheel a few times, thinking. If and when I ever retire, Tuffy is the most qualified candidate for sheriff, so I find it useful to occasionally give her the opportunity to play the part. "If he gives you grief, call me. He'll probably head home anyway. Better for us."

"You should head home too," she tells me. "You guys have been up nearly two days. I'll call if something breaks on either case."

On either case. A Russian assassin on the loose and a missing young woman. Why, I wonder, am I more worried about Michaela Edwards? When I hang up, Sana asks, "What do you think? Runaway bride?"

My head rocks back and forth. "It's entirely possible, and we'll do a thorough canvass of this part of the county, people outside the community she might have had regular contact with. But I think it's more likely someone took her."

The tiny lines in her forehead lift up. "Based on what?"

"Based on the fact she was on a bicycle and wearing a dress on a cold day. Based on it being forty miles to Pioche. This is a lonely highway, as you can see, Sana. If those men searched both sides of the road and didn't find her or the bike, where did she go?"

"If it were me, I would have arranged for someone to meet me. Someone with a car. Make it look like I had vanished."

"If you were running away."

"Christ, Beck. She's seventeen and her husband is at least forty. These teenage brides have their own underground railroad out of these very special versions of hell."

Yeah, I say to myself, but not here. "It's possible."

"But?"

"But I've never seen that happen here. Hey, have you read that book *Living in Polygamy*?"

Sana shakes her head. "No, why would I—"

"It's by Sharon Peters."

She gives me a blank stare.

"Sharing Peters?"

"I'm not following," she says.

"Really?" I ask, turning to her. "That's such a good joke."

She peers into my eyes. "You're a very silly man, aren't you, Porter Beck? And sort of cute."

"And you are sort of beautiful for an FBI agent."

When people of Arab descent blush, it can be hard to tell, but I'm sure her face is turning red. "Well, kidnapping or runaway, this is a distraction we don't need right now." She pauses a second. "So, you were married once?"

"No, I made that up. Came close, but no."

She nods approvingly. "Good interview technique. Show empathy."

I don't respond. I'm thinking about what she just said. Yes, it certainly is a distraction.

# CHAPTER 8

I pull slowly to a stop outside the massive log entrance gate, waking Sana from another nap. The sign hanging from the top says LOST MEADOWS. Behind it, an orange dirt drive winds its way through a large meadow surrounded by tall green conifers on both sides.

"Christ, where are we now?" Sana asks with a wipe of her eyes.

"My dad's place. Mine too, I guess."

"It's beautiful. It must be extraordinary in the summer."

"I need to pick his brain about something. Plus, I always have Sunday dinner with the old man, so we might get stuck for a while. Can you manage to stay awake? I promise to get you to the hotel in town in an hour or so."

She laughs. "Wow, you're already taking me home to meet the parents."

"Just Pop, my mom's gone. But he'll get a kick out of you. Pop is the ex-sheriff here."

"Ah, the old man Arshal was referring to."

"The very same."

We drive through the meadow and over a hill that empties into a sprawling valley, checkered with snow and patches of winter brown here and there. In the distance sits a modest house and detached barn. Several horses are in the adjacent corrals supping on their hay.

Sana's face lights up. "Wow. Will Little Joe and Hoss be here as well?"

"Well, Little Joe for sure, but you never know who might show up for Sunday dinner." I brake to let a dozen or so sheep cross the road.

"Is he a sheep farmer now?" she asks.

"You mean rancher."

"Huh?"

"You don't farm sheep."

Sana reaches over and pinches my thigh. "Good to know. Is he a sheep *rancher* now?"

I pull into the gravel drive, stopping in front of the house. "Nope, he just likes having them around." Something big and brown and furry rises from the wooden porch right outside Sana's window. It is easily 150 pounds and thirty inches high with brown and black hair that surrounds its massive head like a lion's mane.

"My God, what is that?"

Loving surprises, I say. "That's Little Joe, Pop's dog."

She's reluctant to open her door. "That is not a dog. I've seen dogs. That is not a dog."

I laugh. "He's a Leonberger. I brought him home from Germany. Come on. He doesn't bite."

Sana slowly opens her door. "He doesn't have to bite. He just swallows."

I take her up on the deck and sink my hands deep into the dog's thick mane. "Hey, LJ, this is Sana." Little Joe groans deeply and nudges Sana's leg with his head.

"Can I pet him?"

"I believe that's the proper greeting, yes."

Sana drops slowly to one knee and strokes Little Joe's giant back. He is instantly in love, returning the affection by licking her face with his giant tongue.

"Some guys have all the fun," I say. "Come on inside, Sana."

The inside of my family home is as modest as the outside, not large and with furnishings mostly from an earlier time. The living room has a large oval rug on top of which sits a low coffee table that has the standard four legs and then the two from my dad who is snoozing in the brown recliner next to a large leather couch. There is a small fire in the wood stove in the corner, giving the entire lower level a cozy warmth and the pleasant smell of juniper.

"That's Pop," I say quietly. He's a shade taller than me, in his early eighties with a horrible half-moon scar on his right cheek that stretches to his ear. "He's got a problem with short-term memory, so if he asks you the same question over and over, just pretend it's the first time." Little Joe curls up next to the old man and falls instantly to sleep.

I lean down and swat my dad's big boots. "Pop, wake up. Time to eat."

Joe Beck's heavy eyelids open on Sana, his face brightening immediately. "Pop, this is Special Agent Sana Locke with the FBI. Sana, my father, Joe Beck."

"Fed, huh?" he asks.

Sana nods. "Afraid so. It's nice to meet you, sir."

"Trust me," he says with a leer. "It's nicer meeting you."

We adjourn to the kitchen where Pop removes a steaming meat loaf from the oven. "That smells heavenly," Sana says.

"My wife's recipe," he replies. "So, that's appropriate."

She looks at me. "Did your mom pass recently?"

"When I was still a kid. Lymphoma. She was a Downwinder."

"I'm sorry. I can't imagine what that must have been like."

Pop answers for me. "Let me tell you what it was like. It was like snow falling from the sky. She used to tell me that the day after a blast, she and the other kids would go outside and draw pictures with their fingers on the dust that landed on car windows."

Sana places a hand over her mouth. "My God, they had no idea."

"None at all," I say with a catch in my throat. "I'm not sure anybody did."

Pop goes about the last-minute preparations and asks me to set the table. Inside the dining room, Sana sidles up next to me, lowering her voice. "That's a heck of a scar he has. Work-related?"

I shake my head. "Not to being sheriff. He's had it since he was a kid. Was helping his grandfather with some sheet metal and his face got in the way."

"Amazing my Delia fancied me at all," Pop says, coming through the swinging door from the kitchen. "Scared the heck out of every other girl I met." He sets the meat loaf on the table, along with some potatoes.

"I'm sorry," Sana says. "I didn't mean to—"

Pop waves her off. "No worries here. My mind might be going, but I can still hear as well as a barn owl."

I grab some salad and open some wine for the three of us. Just as we are sitting down, the barn owl turns an ear toward the window. "Somebody coming." I turn around, taking a gander out through the shutters and spotting an SUV coming down the road. "Oh, boy."

I look at Pop. "Brin." Then to Sana, apologetically, "She's my sister."

A minute later, Brinley comes through the door carrying two large open duffel bags practically spilling with guns and ammunition, an automatic rifle slung over each shoulder in a very

Rambo-esque kind of way. "Am I late? Is that meat loaf I'm smelling?" she yells from the doorway, stripping off her jacket. She drops the bags on the floor and unslings the rifles, laying them on the couch. Little Joe rises from his slumber and jumps on her, putting his two front paws on her shoulders. On his hind legs, they are easily the same height. "Hey, baby boy." She gives him a big kiss.

Sana watches in fascination. Brinley is no more than five foot three, with sleek, taut muscles showing under her black sleeveless T-shirt and long caramel-colored hair extending almost to her waist. She is absolutely beautiful. Stunning, especially those eyes, which even from fifteen feet away, you can see are a sparkling emerald green. Behind those eyes, however, there are demons waging an unending war against a kind, gentle heart, demons that occasionally have kept Brin and me from getting along. The technical term for it is cyclothymia, a milder form of bipolar disorder. It's strained our relationship over the years, mostly because I care so much about her that I can't seem to keep from harassing her about her meds.

"Just in time, I see," she says, giving Pop a hug. "Hey, Pop."

"Sana Locke," I say, "Brinley Cummings."

Brinley wipes her hands on her trousers and reaches across the table eagerly, taking Sana's hand. "Very nice to meet you, Sana." She glares at me.

"I'll get you a plate," Pop says, getting up.

An awkward silence hangs in the meat loaf aroma until I say, "I didn't know you were back."

Brinley's sculpted eyebrows squish together. "Just now."

It's been a couple of months, and as I rise from my chair, she walks around the table and plants a kiss on my lips, her hands gently caressing the back of my neck and head. I catch Sana turning away in embarrassment while I pry Brinley's arms from me. "How are you, Brin?"

She grins like the devil. I can tell when she's having a manic episode, and she's soaring right now. "Absolutely perfect. Let me wash up. Be right back." In an instant, she has bounded up the stairs.

"Sister?" Sana whispers.

I take a sip of wine. "Long story." When I start cutting into the meat loaf, Pop stops me.

"Let's wait for her."

"Oh, by all means. Let's. While we're waiting, Pop, I need to talk shop with you for a few minutes."

"Shoot." He looks at Sana. "Sorry, figure of speech."

"I need to cover this first point with you, quickly, before Brin comes back down. Have you ever known of any young women from the FLDS compound to go missing, missing on purpose, I mean?"

Pop falls back into his chair. "Married or not married?"

"Just married," I reply. I can tell he's searching what is left of his memory, and I wonder when that will happen to me.

"I don't think so. They're not like that bunch in Colorado City or some of those other places. Amon doesn't force any of those girls to marry. I take it one went missing?"

I nod. "Two days now."

"Who's the husband?"

"Clem Edwards."

Pop looks confused. "Don't know him. Is he new up there?"

I glance nervously at Sana. "No, Pop. Clem has been there as long as most of them. He was born there."

He grins. "Just kidding. Of course I know him. Known him since he was a boy." Turning to Sana, he says, "My son thinks I'm losing my marbles."

"Geez, Pop," I say. "Don't do that to me."

He winks at me. "You think somebody grabbed her? That's

more likely, I think." Suddenly his face goes blank and he asks Sana her name. She looks at me, wondering as I am if he's pretending again.

"Pop, are you with us?" But he's not. He's faded for real this time.

Sana reaches out her hand. "I'm Sana, Joe. And thanks for having me to dinner."

"You and Porter dating?"

"Official business," she says. "I'm with the FBI."

Pop looks impressed this time around. "Fed, huh? What are you doing all the way out here?"

I prop myself on both elbows and join my hands. "That's the second thing I need to talk to you about."

With that, Brinley flies down the stairs and takes a seat next to Pop. How she could have made herself more attractive in three minutes I don't know, but she did. Now she's in a white sheer T-shirt and skintight faded blue jeans.

Brinley asks, "What are we talking about? Did you tell Pop about your big shoot-out this morning?"

I let go a mighty blast of air, lowering my head into my hands. "Damn it, Brin."

Brinley covers her mouth, pretending to hide her amusement. "Sorry. Is that a secret?"

"How did you hear?" I ask, though I don't really want to know.

Brinley stabs a piece of meat loaf. "Stopped in at the office on the way. Tuffy filled me in. Who was he?"

So Tuffy hasn't told her everything. "Unknown," I answer.

Brinley helps herself to some potatoes. "What's your connection to this, Sana?"

"I'm with the FBI. Just up here doing some liaison work with Beck. Pretty standard stuff."

"Oh, I heard you were looking for a Russian." She rubs her nose with her middle finger extended at me so Pop can't see. "That was Arshal, not Tuffy, so don't you be mad at her. Arshal is very upset with you, by the way."

Pop stops chewing his food. "Why are you looking for a Russian?"

I have been unable to take a bite so far, my silverware suspended indefinitely over the plate. "I'm not sure we are, Pop, but maybe you can help. How much do you remember about the '50s when all the aboveground testing was going on?"

Pop takes a long drink of wine and dabs at his mouth with a napkin. "Well, I wasn't here until '63, and by that time everything was being done underground, but I remember everything your mom told me. What do you want to know?"

"I'm not sure, honestly."

He looks up and to the right, as people do when trying to recall something. "I can tell you everyone here knew the fallout was bad, even if the government wouldn't admit it. It was killing a lot of the livestock, sheep and cows especially, or making them deformed. Started showing up in people later. Cancers, birth defects, and the like." He pauses a moment. "It was a different time, to hear your mom tell it. Even when they knew people were getting sick from it, they also knew we were trying to stop the Reds from planting their flag in every place on earth and trying to keep them from blowing everyone up. Believe it or not, back then we thought a nuclear war was winnable."

It was nothing I didn't already know. "I might bring some photos by for you to look at, if you're up for it. See if you recognize anyone."

Pop is suddenly perplexed. "Photos of who? You got a big case going on?"

He's starting to sundown, that late-day confusion people suffering from dementia often get in the evening. Brinley reaches across the table and takes Pop's hand in hers.

"It's not important, Pop," she says. "So, Porter, did you hear who I was dating?"

I am so thankful for the change in subject. "No, Brin. Who are you dating?"

"Michael B. Jordan." She looks for a sign, the slightest clench in my jaw that says I'm impressed.

"Wow, the basketball player? Thought he was married. Or does that matter?"

"No, stupid. Not the basketball player. The actor. Michael Jordan the basketball player is like sixty now. Why would I be dating somebody that old?"

My turn to have some fun. "You do get around, Brin."

"I always loved watching that guy play," Pop says.

Sana has to laugh. Brinley slams the table with her fist. "You know who I'm talking about. I know you do."

I try not to laugh but can't help myself. Turning to Sana, I say, "Brinley is a firearms expert. She trains celebrities how to hold a gun properly so they don't look silly when they're on TV."

"Asshole!" Brinley yells. "I train people to handle weapons safely to protect themselves and their families and get paid a lot more than you do, by the way. Celebrities just happen to be willing to pay top dollar for the privilege of my expert instruction."

"It's true," I tell Sana. "Brinley does know more about guns than any person I have ever met, and she gets paid a lot of money from people who like to look at her shooting a gun."

"I'll keep that in mind," Sana says, as Brinley glares at her.

We eat in relative silence after that, with Pop asking every few minutes what Sana's name is or what I'm working on. When we're finished, Sana says her goodbyes, and I walk her out into the frigid night.

"I like your dad," she says. "You seem to have a good relationship."

I laugh. "You'd never know we went for many years without talking."

"That surprises me," she says. "What happened?"

A great question, and one I don't have an answer for. The truth is I never really understood it myself. He seemed to resent me leaving Lincoln County for the Army. It was as if he was done with me at that point, I don't know. "Doesn't matter," I tell Sana. "We're past it now."

She nods. "Well, he's fairly lucid when talking about ancient history. Might be worth it to show him some of Atterbury's photos."

I nod agreement and bring my finger under her chin. "Look up."

She tilts her head toward the sky. "Oh my God. Look at the stars."

I wish I could. "Pretty amazing, huh?"

"I've never seen so many. They're so bright, so beautiful."

I lower my face to hers and kiss her. We linger there for a long moment, staring into each other, lips barely touching, feeling each other's breath. It has been a while for me, which my wide eyes surely betray, so I kiss her again. Finally, we both take a step back. I lead her by the hand to my truck and open the driver's door, motioning for her to get in.

"Me?"

"Would you mind? You got a little sack time earlier. I haven't had any. I'm afraid I might run us off the road." That last part was true, but of course it's the witching hour for me, the time of day when my eyesight dwindles to a small ray of light in the center and big, blurry clouds on the edges, not a secret I'm ready to share.

She takes the keys from my hand. "You okay? I could just take it to the hotel and pick you up in the morning."

I move around to the passenger side and get in. "Then I would be deprived of the pleasure of walking you to your door."

"So, Brinley," Sana says when we're heading out of Lost Meadows toward the highway. "What's the story there? Obviously not your real sister."

I crank the heater up high. "She's been with us since she was ten. Pop found her in a trailer up in the mountains. She was half-starved and beaten by her drunk shit of a father, chained like a dog to the bedpost. Mother had skipped out long before. Anyway, the guy saw Pop first and jumped him, and Pop killed him and brought Brinley home. I think he missed having a girl around the house after my mom died. Anyway, she was almost feral. Had never been to school, never really known anybody else."

Sana's mouth falls open. "Dear God."

"Yeah. Pop got temporary custody of her. Hell, the state didn't know what to do with her. But she adjusted to both of us pretty quick. We got her in school, and she's smart as a whip, as you can see. When she was twelve, Pop was able to adopt her."

"And the firearms thing?"

We reach the highway and I point a finger to the right. "Honestly, I think that came from all the trauma she went through. One day, she asked Pop to teach her to shoot, and she went at it like I've never seen anybody go after something. I think she was intent on never letting anyone hurt her like that again. She knows every fact about every gun ever made, and she shoots better than some of the snipers I served with in the Army. With a rifle, she's almost as good as Pop. She has a degree in forensic science. I've begged her to join the department a million times, but she likes the money she's getting and the travel, I guess. These Hollywood guys get infatuated watching a woman who can handle a pistol or teach them how to hold an M-16 for their movie shots."

It's not adding up for Sana. "But she still lives here. Like you. What is she doing here?"

A smile tugs at my lips as I think about Brin. "She'll never leave Pop. He's her foundation. She comes and goes, but this is home."

"You're here," Sana notes. "She'll never leave you."

That makes me laugh. "Hell, we fight all the time. She's not here for me."

"Well, that's good to know," she says. "Now, are you really going to just drop me at my door?"

Another great question, and I would like to say I'm considering it carefully, but since I can't see, I won't be driving home tonight. "Well, we still have an SVR agent out there somewhere."

"And a very old Russian spy," Sana adds.

"And a very old Russian spy. We're both out of gas, and we're going to need to sleep at some point to have any chance at catching them."

She reaches over, caressing my neck. "At some point."

# THE PAST

As the stiff winds of the spring of 1956 calmed into summer breezes, Georgiy learned a lot about the U-2. It would be America's premier spy plane. Delta, or Area 51 as it was also now called, was building up fast as the base for the aircraft they were referring to as the Dragon Lady. Georgiy had befriended a few of the pilots—*drivers* as they referred to themselves—that now resided in the many trailers placed in neat rows in the desert behind the high fences and, despite all the secrecy, had learned that the plane could go as high as 77,000 feet, an altitude he struggled to fathom and which was practically in space. His country had nothing comparable. The drivers wore flight suits that had multiple hoses protruding from them and large helmets, unlike anything Georgiy had ever seen in his own military. More surprising was the fact that the U-2 was apparently not a military aircraft at all. It belonged to the CIA. Georgiy and his fellow guards were forever turning back curious colonels and generals from Delta's gates. Here he was, a Soviet agent pointing his machine gun at some of the highest-ranking people in America's military, guarding their most secret airplane.

While those encounters raised the excitement level at work, Georgiy wanted to do more. So far, he had been unable to utilize his knowledge and love of physics to provide any intelligence to the analysts inside the Lubyanka. It would be another six months before the next series of tests really kicked off, and Georgiy knew he needed to find a way to get out of Delta, where there was nothing but the U-2, the pictures of which he had taken from too far away and were undoubtedly of little use to Moscow.

He offered to work overtime shifts, to show his superiors at FSI that he was ready and willing to take on any new work, any assignment. And work he did. Leaving the test site one early Tuesday morning, after three straight weeks on the job, Georgiy felt like he could sleep for three more. He pulled off the Widowmaker, the lonely stretch of two-lane highway connecting the test site to Las Vegas, into tiny Indian Springs to fill up his tank as he usually did. Thunderbird Gas was the only station between Mercury and Las Vegas.

"Fill 'er up, sir?" The attendant in the grease-covered overalls asked.

Georgiy nodded and fished some currency out of his wallet.

When the tank was full, the attendant replaced the nozzle and screwed the gas cap back on. "That will be three-ninety."

Half asleep, Georgiy pushed the five spot out his window. "Thank you, sir," the man said. Handing him back the change, he added, "Keep your head cool and your feet warm, and have a good day."

Georgiy's head snapped to attention at the sound of the words. *Keep your head cool and your feet warm.* It was a Russian saying, and the one he had been trained to listen for.

The attendant was slightly older than Georgiy but built more solidly, like a tree trunk. His hair was a yellow blond, just a hair lighter than his own and cut short and sharp like a military man, and his shirtsleeves were rolled up high on his arms to reveal large biceps. Georgiy looked into the man's blue eyes. "I'm sorry. What did you say?"

The man placed his hands on top of the car and lowered his voice. "My mom used to tell me all the time, keep your head cool and your feet warm. Good advice, huh?"

Georgiy stared at him for a few seconds, noting that he was clearly waiting for a response. "I ran from the wolf but ran into a bear."

The attendant nodded, reached into his back pocket, and handed Georgiy a folded road map. "Courtesy of the Thunderbird."

Georgiy nodded and drove out of the station, his heart pounding in his chest. He had just had his first contact with another illegal since he had arrived in Las Vegas almost a year and half ago.

Back at his apartment, Georgiy quickly unfolded the map and scanned it top to bottom and left to right. It was a map of Nevada, and at first glance nothing appeared to be marked, so he removed a magnifying glass from the drawer in his coffee table and looked again. He found several letters and numbers circled and knew instantly they were coordinates and a time to meet.

He shivered like a rabbit.

That night, Georgiy could not sleep. His encounter with the man at the gas station had his mind conjuring all kinds of worrisome situations. As soon as he saw the morning light, he completed his daily calisthenic routine and three-mile run, then took a luxurious twenty-minute hot shower, something which did not exist in the Soviet Union. As the powerful spray unwound his taut muscles, he wondered why the Americans had so much and his countrymen so little. It must be because they weren't ravaged by the war. Yes, they lost soldiers, but their cities had been untouched by the conflict, their population a hemisphere away from the slaughter. Simply put, they had not suffered.

At 10:30 he got into his Crestliner and drove north. Thirty minutes later, he pulled off the highway onto a dirt road and headed east through a sandstorm toward the map coordinates contained in his coded message. His instructions, provided by the gas station attendant, did not contain anything as simple as an X marking the spot of the meeting. Instead, the coordinates had to be deciphered from a series of letters and numbers subtly identified on the map. Twenty miles north of town in the middle of a barren desert was out of the way to say the least, and it meant the meeting required privacy and had to be of great import. A dozen possible scenarios ran through Georgiy's mind. Were they bringing him home? Had he somehow been detected? Were the Americans aware of him? Was he getting a new assignment? With every divot and rock in the road his tires collided with, he thought of another reason Moscow had deemed a face-to-face necessary. He had been in Nevada for a year and a half, so why now?

He drove slowly, stopping the car every few hundred meters to look around for the gas station man. But all he could see through the blowing sand were the heat waves shimmering off the desert floor, the hot wind sending the tumbleweeds tumbling, just like the song said. The dried-out diaspores, often the size of automobiles, would often blow right through the center of town in the strong winds, their sharp nettles drawing blood if you happened to be in their path. Georgiy rechecked the coordinates indicated on the map and continued driving.

After a couple of miles, he thought he saw an oasis in the distance and wondered for a moment if it was a mirage like he and Kitty had seen in that John Wayne picture, *The Searchers*. But as he got closer, he saw that it wasn't a mirage at all. Tall cottonwoods shot out of the ground along what must be a natural spring. And there were buildings too, more than a dozen of them from what Georgiy could see, a stable for horses, and strange, brilliantly colored animals that passed in front of his car and looked to be some kind of immense waterfowl with iridescent tails that spread out like a fan.

A small sign at the entrance said he had reached Tule Springs Divorce Ranch, and it had large tracts of green grass and two small lakes where ducks and geese sought refuge from the intense heat. Georgiy took off his shoes and walked slowly through the thick, cool grass, its green blades shooting up between his toes.

It was beautiful. Flowers of every color lined the gravel paths through the grass, and their combined smell was heavenly to a boy from Odessa, a boy who had come of age amid the acrid smell of gunpowder and the dead and dying of the Soviet and German armies.

He saw several people, men and women roaming the grounds, a few riding horses. But there was no sign of his contact. Finally, Georgiy sat down under the shade of a giant cottonwood. He checked his watch. The man was late. *Has he been caught?*

There was someone, across the lake. He appeared to be fishing, and under the large brown cowboy hat, Georgiy couldn't tell if it might be his contact. He watched him intently until the man finally looked up and in his direction. It was him. There was no feather protruding from his hat, which would have indicated danger, so Georgiy sprang to his feet and walked quickly around the water to the other side.

"Slow down, Freddie," the man said as Georgiy approached. "We are new friends, not lovers. Be cool, as the American beatniks like to say."

Slowing his pace, Georgiy then took a seat on the grass a short distance away.

"Do you know what this place is?" the man asked, wrestling a large catfish out of the lake.

Georgiy picked nervously at the grass around him. "It says divorce ranch on the sign."

"That's right," the man said, his voice as pleasant as a singer's in Georgiy's ears. The man extracted two beers from a green metal cooler and took a seat next to him in the grass. He opened both bottles by twisting the caps with his hands, a feat Georgiy had never seen before. Handing one to him, he said, "There are movie stars here right now who pay to live here for six weeks so they can get a divorce. Have you ever heard of such a thing?"

To see and hear another Russian in front of him, his first in almost two years, was almost more than he could bear.

His English was good, with only a trace of foreign accent, Georgiy noticed. He could pass for Polish or Slav, and he had the steely gaze of a killer in those blue eyes. Georgiy scanned his surroundings to see if there might be FBI agents hiding in the bushes, but everyone else was far away. As a precaution, he rose to one knee. "What do I call you?"

"You don't call me anything. I was never here."

Georgiy nodded. "Do you have news for me? Instructions?"

The man studied him for what seemed to Georgiy to be an interminable amount of time. "You are Ukrainian."

"So?"

"Not ethnically Russian."

"The majority of the world is not ethnically Russian. What is your point?"

"Where exactly?"

Georgiy was growing perturbed. "Where exactly what?"

His contact took another drink of his beer. "Where in Ukraine?"

"Odessa."

The man winked at him. "On the Black Sea. Very nice."

"It was," Georgiy replied. "Before June twenty-second. Before Hitler dropped his bombs."

The man nodded. "And of those who survived that invasion, millions starved."

Georgiy's mind flashed fifteen years back to 1941 when three million Germans streamed across the border. He was eleven years old. "My parents and sister never made it long enough to starve," Georgiy said.

They sat in silence for a minute. "You can call me William," the man said softly. "It's nice to meet you, Freddie." He extended his hand and Georgiy took it.

"Pleased to meet you as well, William."

"So, on to business. Your intelligence has been brilliant thus far, Freddie. The information on the U-2 plane has the Defense Ministry and our bosses back home fighting over every picture you send, I'm told. By the way, Comrade Khrushchev sends his regards."

"That is good to hear. I was afraid the photographs wouldn't be of much use." Georgiy doubted very much that the leader of the Soviet Union even knew of his existence, but it was nice to know the Lubyanka regarded his work so highly. It struck him that William probably did not know his real name, just like he didn't know William's. Their worlds were entirely fake. "I've been trying to get closer to the drivers to learn more about the cameras on the plane, but they keep their distance. They are all CIA, by the way, not Air Force."

William nodded, baiting his fish hook with a fresh worm. "Yes, you were very clear on that. It is this Project 57 that has our attention at present." Project 57. The file Georgiy had frantically photographed at Dr. Ellison's home. "What do you know about it?"

"I had no time to read it. I just photographed it. What do *you* know about it?"

William stood up and cast his line out into the lake. "We know it is going to be a very secret test."

Georgiy started to laugh. "They are all very secret tests."

William reeled in a bit of line and set the drag. He planted his pole in the cooler and closed the lid so that it kept the fishing line taut. Sitting back down next to Georgiy, he said, "This one even more so. The Americans are going to simulate the crash of one of their bombers to test the effects of an accidental release of pluto-nium. A very original idea."

And one that made no sense to Georgiy. "Why would they do

that? They explode things all the time here. They already know plutonium is deadly."

William turned to Georgiy. "Yes, they know it's deadly, but they don't fully understand the effects of exposure to it yet. Neither do we. Freddie, you have provided us with very important intelligence here."

Pride surged through Georgiy's veins. How proud his parents would have been to know he was helping his country. "When is the test?" he asked William.

"Sometime early next year, it appears. That is one thing we need to know for certain. You will have to find this out."

Georgiy nodded enthusiastically. "And then you want me to access the results, through Dr. Ellison?"

Seeing a slight bob on his line, William put his hand on the pole for a moment, feeling for a bite. "Not exactly, though your work with Ellison and his daughter has been extraordinary. We have something else in mind for this, something that could derail the American nuclear program entirely." William looked at him for a moment, waiting for Georgiy to guess. "We're going to create an accident."

Georgiy's head dropped suddenly, the air rushing audibly out of his chest.

"You don't approve?" William asked.

Georgiy looked at him. "It would be far easier for me to simply steal the results. The Americans are going to do the test. I can access Ellison's papers again after the test is done. Or perhaps I can get a transfer to the site of the test and see it for myself."

William nodded. "But then it would be just another test that the public knows little about. The antinuclear protests here are already a nuisance for the government. Imagine if there was a nuclear accident. We think this might be the opportunity to kill the American testing program entirely."

Georgiy's head was shaking before William even finished. "I don't think you appreciate how much security you're dealing with out there. The place is in the middle of nowhere, and within the middle of nowhere are testing areas that are even more remote. I can't just drive someone out there so he can create an accident with a bomb."

William swatted at a fly on his ear. "This is true, Freddie. We would never attempt something so stupid."

Georgiy silently chided himself, realizing that while he had successfully reported on things happening at the Nevada Test Site, he had failed to ensure Moscow had a full appreciation for how compartmentalized and secure the installation was. "What then? How are you going to do this?"

William just stared back at him until Georgiy figured it out.

"No, no, you don't understand. I don't have access to these areas. I'm stuck guarding airplanes."

"Then we have a few months to find out how to get you moved to Area 13."

"Where?"

"Area 13. This is where Project 57 will be conducted."

Georgiy's voice rose in irritation. "There is no Area 13, William."

"I imagine there will be soon."

"Even if I can get posted there, I don't have the technical knowledge to do this myself, and if you're thinking of stealing this thing and creating an accident somewhere else, I can't just slip a warhead in my pocket and walk out."

William stood and reeled in his line. "You've done outstanding work so far, Freddie. You are good at thinking on your feet. Start thinking about how you can help the Soviet people do this very important thing. Figure a way to get the device off the test site. I will worry about what we do with it afterward."

The last time he had heard such lunacy was during the war when a leader of Ukrainian partisans ordered Georgiy and his compatriots to charge more than two dozen German tanks. He recognized a suicide mission when he heard it. "Look, William . . . even if I could do this, an accident would kill innocent people. I've already seen firsthand what these tests and their radiation has done to people living downwind."

William reached down, grabbing him roughly by the upper arm. His squeeze was viselike. "Innocent? Comrade, this is the enemy we are talking about. Yes, some may suffer, but think of the thousands, maybe millions who might be saved by stopping the American program." He paused, releasing Georgiy's arm, his tone softening. He began packing up his things. "You will keep us advised of ongoing preparations for the test, especially the timing of the plane carrying the bomb from New Mexico to the test site. After this is done, we will both return home as heroes. Yes?"

The dream of going home, especially as a hero, tugged on Georgiy's heart, but his mind wandered quickly back to the beauty of the American West and the people that were growing on him. Give me a rifle, he thought, and I will fight any soldier. I will kill the enemy. But women and children, people simply going about their daily lives? That's what the Nazis had done. "Such an accident will not slow anything down, William. The Americans are like us, they will never abandon such an important program."

William shrugged. "Neither of us can see the future. Let us do what we can do."

# CHAPTER 9

The cell phone buzzes to life, and with each ensuing vibration creeps closer and closer to the night table's edge. I spot it with one eye because the other is still buried in my pillow. But I don't recognize the night stand, or beyond it, the rest of the room. I check my watch as the cell phone continues to buzz. It's just after 6:00, and only a single ray of sunlight has made its way over the horizon and through the window. The phone vibrates again and I want so much for the person on the other end to tell me we have found Michaela Edwards and that she is safe and sound.

"Beck," I say with a cough into the phone.

"Sheriff, it's Jimmy Green. We have what looks like a suicide out here in Panaca."

*Including our Russian out at Big Rocks, that's three deaths in three days. What are the odds?* "What do we know, Jimmy?"

"Old guy in his late eighties. Son is a long-haul trucker, came home about 4:30 this morning and found him."

*Old guy in his late eighties.* "Text me the address and get Tuffy up. Be there in thirty." I hang up and dial another number. "Swinging by in fifteen to get you," I say. "Be out front and bring your kit."

As soon as I click off, Sana's arm reaches over my side and down to my groin. "Ah, good morning," she murmurs into my ear, sucking the lobe into her mouth.

The night comes immediately to life in my brain. The Pioneer Hotel, a rush to her room, a removal of garments as lovely and choreographed as an Argentinian tango, followed by the most incredible two hours of my life in which she somehow summoned from me a sexual stamina I did not know I possessed. It was a master class in the *Kama Sutra,* and she was the master. Or mistress. Whatever. What came after was the sleep of the dead.

"We're still alive," I say, turning over to face her. "I thought for sure you had killed me."

"I tried my best," she answers, kissing me. "It was touch and go there for a while."

My grin is growing as quickly as something else. "Mostly touch, as I recall. We have another body, by the way."

"Can it wait?" she asks.

"Well," I say, "we can't save him now."


Thirty minutes later we're showered and Sana notices we seem to be headed back to Lost Meadows. "Are we going to your dad's for some reason?"

"Yep, gotta pick something up first."

"So," she says. "About last night."

"And this morning," I remind her.

"Yes, and this morning," she says with a chuckle. "It was all quite beautiful."

I go ahead and interrupt her since I know what's coming. "But it really shouldn't happen again. Yeah, I know."

She nods and lays a hand on my leg. "I was going to say that you are incredibly adept in the sack, sir. I consider myself a bit of an expert in that area, so I'm qualified in scoring these inter-actions. And I don't believe I've ever enjoyed myself as much as last night."

"That makes three of us," I say with a quick glance at my nethers.

Her laugh is as sultry as the rest of her. She looks out her window as we pass a few elk nibbling on some brush just off the right side of the road. "If things were different . . ."

Sana is the type of woman I could fall heavy for. Beautiful and fearless gets me every time. "No worries," I tell her. "Gather ye rosebuds while ye may. That's my motto."

"Exactly," she says, turning back to me. "Maybe we'll have a chance to gather some more later on."

When we pull up to the house, I tell her I'll be right back. "You want coffee?"

"Sure," she says.

Inside, I shoot up the stairs and see Brinley in the bathroom bent over at the sink in nothing but a skimpy T-shirt, spitting her tooth-paste out and rinsing.

"Jesus, Brin," I say, trying to look away. "I asked you to be ready."

She turns to face me, laughing at my obvious discomfort. "Do I not look ready to you?"

Brinley is promiscuous, especially when she's manic. I think it's one reason she leaves home as often as she does and hangs out in places like Hollywood and the south of France. She can pick up a man with a single, inviting glance, but her relationships are like a false spring, just warm enough to deceive the local vegetation. I know this is the product of what happened to her all those years ago as a little girl, and I also know she will never concede that fact. I think C. S. Lewis was right: denial is the shock absorber for the soul.

"Move it, munchkin," I say, slipping by her and into the bathroom to the toilet.

"Did you get some of that Fed stuff last night?"

"And this morning," I say proudly. "Got a dead body in Panaca. We gotta go." I stand over the toilet, waiting.

"What? I've seen you pee before."

We arrive half an hour later at the address, just off State Route 319 and east of the unincorporated town of Panaca at a remote lot with no other homes around it, not uncommon in the small community. Three of my patrol vehicles are parked in front. Through the windshield, I can see Wardell Spann talking to a heavily tattooed middle-aged tank of a man at the rear of an eighteen-wheeler, the son of the dead man, I'm guessing. The house is a 1960s ranch-style, the exterior not well maintained, decaying day by day, decade by decade. The paint is chipped and faded from the elements, and the yard a veritable junkyard with all manner of auto parts and other rusted scrap metal lying among the natural high-desert scrub that grows in the area.

"Very scenic," Sana says as we traipse up the gravel drive.

She's been a little put off since Brinley jumped in my truck, so I try to lighten the mood. "Did you know Panaca is only one of two cities in Nevada where gambling is illegal?"

"Thanks, that's helpful." Her tone feels like a paper cut.

Brinley grimaces as we approach the front door, her evidence collection kits in hand. "Someone's a little grouchy today." She opens one of the black cases and hands out crime scene gloves.

Sana looks at me as we pull them on. "I want to ask why I'm here, but I would really like to know why *she's* here. Didn't you say this was a suicide?"

Brinley puckers her lips and makes a kissing noise, stepping by Sana. I wait until she's out of earshot. "I said it looked like a suicide to my guy, and she's here because she knows forensics about as well as she knows guns, so if she happens to be in the county when something goes down, I use her. You're here because I'm going to be surprised if this is really a suicide."

"You think—"

"Let's go see," I say, as three cats scamper out the door at my feet.

The interior of the home is as run-down as the exterior, with beer cans on every tabletop, unemptied ashtrays, and torn fabric on most of the furniture. The place reeks of cat piss and foul litter boxes.

The dead man is lying on the linoleum floor at the base of one of two old leatherback bar stools across from a well-stocked bar in the living room, the blood from his head wound spattered on the adjacent wall and pooled on the floor. A large revolver rests loosely in his dead fingers.

Tuffy is in the middle of her photography duties and Jimmy is collecting blood. "Tuffy, what do we know?"

She takes a few more quick shots and clicks off the details just as rapidly. "Hey, Beck. The decedent is Guy Pollack, eighty-seven. Not married. One child, Lyman, that miserable tub of lard you saw on your way in. We've had some dealings with him in the past, nothing major. Large caliber round to the left temple. Dead as a doornail, obviously. I would say seven, eight hours, by the look of it, but that's purely my opinion."

I nod, watching Brinley slip some covers over her boots before carefully lowering herself to the floor to examine the body.

"Do you know him?" Sana asks me.

I should mention here that while the county only has about six thousand residents, the population of a very small town, it might be presumed that among an entire sheriff's department, we know everyone. The fact is that a lot of people come here to be left alone. They are not by nature neighborly. So, when I'm constantly asked if I know someone, my response might have a bite to it. This time, however, given Agent Locke's present mood, I say, "I've seen him around but don't know him. You guys?"

Tuffy and Jimmy shake their heads. "Wardell knows him," says Jimmy. "The son drives for a freight outfit out of Salt Lake. Arrived about 4:30 A.M. today. Stays here between runs."

Already, something doesn't look right to me. I'm just not sure what. "Brin?"

Brinley looks up at me and shakes her head. "I don't think this is a suicide."

Sana is stunned. "You've been here ten seconds. What on earth makes you say that?"

We get our share of suicides out here, and Brinley has seen quite a few. She points to the old man's hand and revolver. "Colt Python .357 Magnum, double-action revolver, six-inch barrel."

I glance over to Jimmy Green. "The gun is registered to Mr. Pollack," he says.

"I'm sure it is," Brinley adds. "But here's the thing. You shoot yourself in the head with this gun, your brain shuts down in a microsecond."

Sana drops into a crouch to get a better look. "So?"

"So, in that same moment it shuts down your nervous system. The gun has a considerable kick and the round a considerable amount of force. You fly out of your seat—and I mean *fly*—and you still have the gun in your hand?"

"Wait," Sana says. "A gunshot to the brain can also have the opposite effect. It can cause the fingers to tense around the grip and trigger."

Brinley nods. "For an instant, yes. But you're being launched out of this bar stool, right? By the time you hit the floor, that tension is gone because your nervous system is turned off." She gazes up at me. "What else is wrong with this picture?"

I cross my arms in contemplation. "He's lying at the bottom of the bar stool, not a few feet away, like he fell straight down."

Brinley nods again. "Or was lowered. What else?"

"The bar stool," Tuffy interjects. "It's still standing. That much force, the stool goes down with you."

I look at Jimmy again. "Checked with the son. He said he didn't touch anything."

Sana turns to Jimmy. "Did you?"

"He knows better," I say confidently.

Brinley points at the back legs of the bar stool, sitting in more of Pollack's blood. "Hasn't been moved. If it had, we would have disturbances on the floor." Tuffy snaps a couple of pictures of the bottom of the stool.

Sana climbs back to her feet. "All valid observations, but can I play devil's advocate for a minute?"

"Please," I say.

"Okay, the position of the body is a solid point, not so sure I agree on whether he would or wouldn't hang on to the gun, but you can see what looks like soot on his left hand. You can test it, but I can tell you right now that it's going to turn out to be gunshot residue. The dead guy fired the gun."

Brinley looks bewildered. "That's a quantum leap in logic. If the decedent's hand was in the vicinity of the gun when it was fired, whether he fired it or someone else did, it would have GSR on it." She looks over at me. "I'll collect whatever I can, but I agree that's probably what it is."

I step closer. "The question is, did he fire it or did he have help?" I pick up the other stool, the one not sitting in blood, and move it into the middle of the living room where there is some open space. "Jimmy, let's do a test. Take a seat."

Jimmy Green walks over and sits down on the stool. "How much force from the gunshot?" I ask Brinley.

Brinley approaches, considers the question for a moment. She looks back at the dead man on the floor. "Jimmy, what are you, Two hundred? Two hundred five?"

"About two hundred."

"Mr. Pollack here is about a buck-ninety." In her mind, Brinley visualizes the shot, placing her hand on Jimmy's left temple. "I'm going to give you a shove, Jimmy. Just let your body go." With that, she pushes hard on the deputy's head, sending him sprawling to the floor where he lands a few feet away, the bar stool on top of his legs.

I nod. "He had help."

Sana throws up her hands. "I'm sorry, guys, but this is hardly scientific."

"Jesus, woman," Brin says. "It's the definition of scientific. It's how you would re-create this man's death in a crime lab."

Wardell comes in through the front door just then and does a big knuckle cracking, like it's a symphony we all want to hear. "What's all this?"

I take a beat before saying, "We're trying to figure out how Mr. Pollack shoots himself in the left temple with a .357 and somehow falls straight to the floor without knocking the stool over."

"Doesn't make sense," Wardell says.

"Most of us seem to agree on that point," I reply, looking at Sana.

Wardell walks over to the body. "No, I mean it doesn't make sense because Pollack wasn't left-handed."

Sana's irritation grows. "What is it with you guys and hands? Yesterday, it was the Russian Pete killed. Today, it's this guy. So what if he wasn't left-handed?"

Brinley takes Sana's hand in hers, raising it up and pointing it at Sana's temple. "You take yourself out, you're going to do it with your dominant hand, your shooting hand."

Sana yanks her hand back and turns to me with pleading eyes. "Says who?"

I can take this one. "Says a bunch of forensic studies. Handedness is not, in and of itself, definitive in determining a self-inflicted injury, but it is one major indicator." I recite this information like I read it in a book because, well, I read it in a book.

"Okay," Sana says, looking at Wardell. "But how do you know he wasn't left-handed?"

Wardell scratches his chin. "Because, Miss Hot Shit FBI, I bowled with the man every Thursday night for ten years. He was a righty."

Okay, so Mr. Pollack did socially interact on occasion. His choice of bowling partners is a little suspect, but at least someone in the department knew him. I step between Wardell and Sana, shutting down the discussion. "Let's double-check our work here guys. Wardell, go outside and check with the son. Not doubting you, just want to be sure. Jimmy, look for photos, anything you can find that verifies Mr. Pollack here was right-handed."

Wardell and Jimmy go their separate ways, and I bend down and carefully remove the Colt Python from Pollack's hand, marking the cylinder position with my Sharpie. Then I open it and check all the chambers. They're full. I show them to Tuffy so she can document them. "Lot of bullets when you only need one." After I empty the remaining rounds, I place it in a plastic evidence bag that Brinley opens for me. Then I check his hand. My nostrils flare a bit.

"What?" Brinley asks.

I hold Pollack's fingers up to my nose. "What's that smell like to you?"

Brinley bends and takes a whiff. "Engine degreaser? It's got that citrusy smell."

I nod and study the fingers more closely with a penlight from my pocket. On the underside of the man's thumb, there is a small trace of something black. "What do have we here?"

Tuffy snaps a picture, the flash blinding everyone for a second. "Looks like ink of some kind?"

"Fingerprint ink?"

She exhales in agreement. "The guy used the degreaser to remove the ink. Missed a spot. I'll collect a sample, but that's what it looks like."

I look at Brinley. "Find me that degreaser. Garage maybe. Ask the son, if you need to."

"Maybe the son killed him," Sana says.

I stand up. She's still miffed about Brinley, and it's clouding her judgment. "Anything is possible, but it doesn't look like there's a big inheritance for Lyman here. Tuffy, get with the freight company and get the location of Lyman's truck all last night. Should be LoJacked." Turning to Sana, I say, "But why does the son fingerprint him?"

Sana runs a hand through her hair. She looks like she wants to kick something. "It's the Russian, isn't it?"

"Beginning to look that way."

"Assuming that's the case," she says, "and he believed Pollack might be the spy the Soviets sent here in the 1950s, he would have the guy's fingerprints. If he wanted to do a match, he could have lifted a latent print from anywhere in this house and used some portable biometric technology. Why actually print the man?"

Brinley returns, holding a bottle of Purple Power All-Purpose Citrus in an evidence bag. "Because those things are nowhere near as good as taking actual prints. Do they not teach that in the FBI?" I glare at Brin, a warning to her to retract her claws. "Found it under the kitchen sink," she says.

"They're good questions," I tell Sana. "Keep going."

"Okay, no forced entry into the house, just like at Atterbury's.

It's the middle of the night. No apparent struggle with the victim. How do you force him to shoot himself in the head—given the gunshot residue on the hand—with no struggle?"

I look at Brinley again, who shrugs.

"Drugs," says Tuffy, dropping to her knees by the body. With her hands, she carefully examines Pollack's neck. "Holy shit." She exposes the right side of the neck, the part not covered in blood. I shine my light on the skin.

"Puncture wound," I say. "Good spot, Tuff. Let's get a tox screen, and ask Vegas to rush it."

"Shit," Sana mumbles. "He's checking off a list."

This killer is pissing me off. "He printed poor Mr. Pollack here after he drugged him. When he determined the prints didn't match, he shot him, making it look self-inflicted, old guy, tired of living, sitting at his bar in the middle of the night. Couldn't leave him alive, obviously."

"Yes," Sana says. "But how did he know about Pollack? He can't just be driving around the county looking for men in their eighties. How is he staying one step ahead of us?"

My phone starts to vibrate. "That is the million-dollar question." I listen for a few moments. "Shit, okay, I'm on my way." I click off. "That was the other Jolly Green. He found Michaela Edwards's bike."

# CHAPTER 10

Johnny Green leads Brinley, Sana, and me over yesterday's light snow to the red-and-white bicycle Michaela Edwards had been riding when she left the Pony Springs Fire Station three days ago. The wind is whipping the bitter chill, yet it somehow feels warmer than the forty-five-minute ride up, the tension between Sana and Brinley palpably icy.

Michaela's bike is no more than fifty yards off the highway and partially sticking out beneath the unruly branches of a large creosote bush. No one touches it until Brinley snaps some photos.

"Well, stating the obvious, it does look like blood," she says, pointing to the white seat tube as her breath condenses in the open air like a heavy fog. She looks back at me, sliding her mouth to one side, which puffs up one cheek. "Doesn't look right, though."

I'm careful stepping closer to the bike. "Almost looks like someone took blood and wiped it across the tube," I say upon closer examination. "No drops."

Brinley nods. "Yep. Don't see blood like that typically."

"And no damage to the bike," Sana observes. "So, the blood wasn't caused by an accident on the road."

Johnny points to the rear wheel, where a piece of blue cloth is wrapped in the chain. "This could be part of Michaela's dress."

"Yeah, let's recover that and have the blood analyzed for DNA. Have the handlebars and grips checked for the same. Process the whole bike for prints." I look around the immediate area. "Any other tracks around?"

Johnny motions me to come around to where he's standing on one side of the bush. "We got about an inch or two of the white stuff yesterday, so any tracks leading in here or back to the road are ours. But I did find this. Okay to move the bike, Brinley?"

"You're good, Johnny."

Johnny Green puts his thick winter gloves back on his hands and carefully lifts the bicycle by the top tube out of the bush. He looks straight down. "See that?"

I step over and look down. There is a boot print in the dirt at the base of the bush, only partially covered by snow. In the moist ground, I can see the outline clearly. "Nice work, Mr. Green. Outsole is complex with a distinct pattern. Not a cowboy boot." I hover my boot just over and to the side the print. "About my size, so we're not looking for a giant here."

Brinley takes a couple of close-ups. "There's enough here. I can cast it."

"Do it," I say. "Johnny will take you back to the station. We'll head over to Mill Valley and have another conversation with Clem Edwards."

Brinley nods. "She didn't ride it out here, Beck."

"No, she didn't." I turn to Johnny. "See if you can get Bugsy out here to track this blood. Might be more under the snow."

"Hey," Brinley says as Sana and I start back to the highway. "I have a gig in L.A. tomorrow."

My head swivels back. "I'm really shorthanded. Can you reschedule it?"

"Can you pay me?"

I nod. "I'll tap our emergency fund. Not like your normal pay-check, though."

She looks at Sana and winks. "That's okay, might be nice to stick around for a while."

Clem Edwards isn't at the farm in Mill Valley, though. "He's off looking for her, Sheriff," Amon Jessup tells us. "Did you find her?"

"Not yet. I need you to find Clem and bring him to the station in Pioche. This can't wait."

Dread gives Amon a hitch in his throat. "Oh no, what is it?"

"Just get him to the station, Amon. That's all I can tell you now."

"Can we go hunt our Russian now?" Sana asks as we once again head south toward the county seat. "I'm anxious to see what your team has come up with. And by the way, I have to say I've been really impressed with the knowledge and investigative instincts your people have."

There is no sincerity like a woman telling a lie. "Pop trained most of them. He was a good cop for a long time."

"Well trust me, I know some FBI people who aren't that good around a crime scene."

Uh-huh. "Well, thanks. I was thinking about our Russian. You said he was checking off a list, that he couldn't just be driving around randomly selecting men in their eighties."

Sana nods. "Based on what we saw at Pollack's house, that's the obvious conclusion, I think."

"Right. List of old men at least eighty years old in the immediate area. Where would you get such a list? How would you know where to start?"

She thinks for a moment. "DMV?"

I consider that. "Okay, assuming you could access their records, people here have licenses from all over the West. Vegas, Utah, other states, not just this county. I'm the sheriff, and it would take me getting a warrant to get that information. So, if you're not a cop, where would you look to isolate demographic information on people in a specific area? I mean how would an SVR agent do it?"

"Voter rolls," she says. "But you would have to have access to the data."

That's a fair point, and I shift my eyes from the road to Sana. "For us, that's the county clerk's office." As soon as those words escape my lips, I slam on the brakes. "Shit."

Sana reaches out to grab the dash, steadying herself. "What? Did you hit something?"

We're at a dead stop on the highway. "Just a week ago, I got a call from the clerk's office. They thought their server had been hacked. I didn't think much of it. We took a report."

"You think it was the Russians."

I must look like a bobblehead doll right now. "I understand they have some experience at that kind of thing."

Sana nods. "Detour?"

"Detour."

The county clerk's office is located on Main Street just across the Great Basin Highway from my office. Martha Floyd is the county clerk and has been as far back as I can remember. She is well past retirement age but will not be budged or bullied into quitting. A short, round woman with stray whiskers on her chin, Martha manages a staff of three people who, in turn, manage a number of county functions, including voter registration and elections.

"Hell if I know," Martha says when I ask her what information had been accessed in their computer server. "I don't understand that stuff." She stands up from her desk. "Jerrold," she yells. "The sheriff and FBI want to talk to you about our thingamajig getting hacked last week."

Across the open office space in the opposite corner of the room, a reed-thin Gen-Z man with unkempt hair peeks sheepishly out from behind two large computer monitors. Sana and I walk over to his desk. He has the face of a twelve-year-old.

The clerk's IT man quickly reveals what he remembers of the incident. "They only accessed voter rolls, nothing else. We have a lot of data here on people in the county, but that's all that was downloaded."

"Were you able to tell if the hacker was looking for a specific group of people within the voter rolls," asks Sana.

The young man nods eagerly. "That was the weird thing. It was men between the ages of seventy-five and ninety-five. Who the heck would want that?"

"Can you print me that list?" I ask.

Jerrold looks over at his boss. This is the advantage of living in what used to be called a one-horse town. She gives him the okay, and we have our list two minutes later. It's a short list. I show Sana one of the names.

"Guy Pollack," she says.

Pulling into my parking space at the office a few minutes later, I say, "But what about neighboring counties? The guy could be living in Vegas for all our Russian knows. That county has more than two million people. Why is he focused on my county?"

"You're right," Sana replies. "But he's here. Pollack's death proves that. The real question is why the Russians are so sure of it."

As we head into the office, I touch her on the shoulder. "It's in the intel that was leaked to them. It has to be. You have to find out for us."

She hangs her head. "I can't risk it. We can't risk our asset in Moscow, and we can't risk tipping off the mole on our side."

"Find a way," I say. "Find someone in Washington you can trust."

She laughs. "You have no idea how big an ask that is. But I'll do my best."

As soon as we enter, Tuffy motions us to her desk. Arshal and Pete are seated nearby and roll over for a confab. Tuffy says, "We've been running the prints from Pollack's house. Still have a few sets to go, but the interesting thing is his prints don't belong to anyone named Guy Pollack."

This is great news, I think. "Please tell me his real name ends in *ov* or *ev,* and we can forget about the Russians until the next election."

"No such luck," says Tuffy. "Real name is Eldon Lee Mathers, wanted in Tennessee for armed robbery. Guess when?"

I am all out of guesses.

"In 1960."

Sana appears confused. "I don't get it. Why is that important?"

I turn to her. "Because it confirms our theory. Pollack was on the list, and there was something about him that made our SVR agent suspect he wasn't who he claimed to be. His name wasn't first on the list. He was almost near the bottom. So, our killer is running names through a filter. He's able to check these people out. How would he do that?"

"What list?" Arshal asks.

"Voter rolls."

Sana takes a chair that Pete offers. "Has your computer server been hacked?"

Beats me. I look at Tuffy. "Have IT do a complete analysis. Borrow the guy from Vegas who works on Metro's stuff if you have to. Let's find out." I folded my arms tightly. "Christ, this is one time I'd be inclined to help the Russians if I knew who they were looking for."

"Hell yeah," Tuffy says. "What do we care about some Russian spy who's been here for sixty years?"

Sana sits straight up. "Don't even joke about that."

"Relax," I say, turning to Pete and Arshal. "How are we coming on Atterbury's files?"

Pete points to his desk. "Still going through them. He had a big head start on us."

I pull the list from the county clerk out of my coat pocket, handing it to Pete. "This is what our Russian has. Start with this. Run them all. But keep working the files. We have to find who he's looking for before anyone else gets killed. I'll bring my dad out in the morning to see if he can help."

"Beck?" Mary Elizabeth Bauer, my office manager and second-grade teacher, calls from the office entryway. I turn to see Amon Jessup and Clem Edwards. "Keep at it," I tell the crew. "I'll be in my office." I lower my voice and say to Tuffy, "We found blood on Michaela Edwards's bike."

"Damn."

"In your spare time, have the Jolly Greens pick up every registered sex offender in the county and bring them in. You do the interviews. Do what you do, Tuffy."

"It's going to pull me off Atterbury's files," she says.

I look back at Clem in the foyer. "Yeah."

After asking Amon to wait, I bring Clem into my office and sit him down in a chair opposite my desk and then take the chair next to him. "We found some blood on her bicycle, a piece of cloth that might be from her dress." I let the words hang in the air, watching Clem's face closely.

Slowly, the big farmer's eyes get wet, and a single tear escapes. He bites his trembling lip. "Someone hurt her then?"

In that instant, I know that someone isn't Clem Edwards. "We can't be sure until we test it against her DNA. To do that, we need something like her toothbrush or a disposable razor that might have some of her skin cells on it. Can you get me something like that?"

As he wipes his eyes, I look down at the floor and Clem's boots. He's wearing black Ropers with a smooth outsole, not even close to the print we found in the desert near Pony Springs. His feet are inordinately big for a man of his height, probably at least size twelve. I don't bother to ask. This is not a crime he has perpetrated. We can dicker all day about how the man lives his life, but he didn't make one of his wives go missing.

I lean forward in my chair. "Clem, listen to me. At this point, we are operating under the assumption that Michaela is alive. We have her picture out to every local law enforcement agency in the state, as well as NHP and the state of Utah. We're going to find her."

Clem Edwards looks down into his lap where his tears drip onto his folded hands. "When you do, Sheriff, you bring the man who done this to me." He looks up into my eyes. "Will you do that?"

It is well into the night when Sana walks into my office and closes the door. I'm into a pile of paperwork, and she drops a slice of room-temperature pizza on top of it. "Eat," she commands. "I've spent more than two full days with you now, and you've only had two meals."

"Any luck?" I ask, taking a bite.

She takes a seat on the corner of my desk. "I know why our Russian is looking in Lincoln County."

I drop the pizza. "Tell me."

"My boss reached out to one of the agents who handled the illegal when he was still communicating with us, the agent before Atterbury. Much better than potentially tipping off the person who's been leaking to the Russians."

"And you trust your boss?"

"Have to," she answers with a nod. "He's the one who sent me here."

I rock back in my chair, its ancient wooden parts creaking and tired, like me right now. "That was good thinking."

"The guy is living in a retirement community in Arizona now but still has all his faculties. He and Atterbury had stayed in touch, and he said Atterbury told him the NSA logged a call to the Russian embassy in Washington five years ago from inside the U.S., about the same period Atterbury came out here." Sana begins to read from her notes. "The caller was male and only got to the switchboard in the embassy. He spoke in Russian but had trouble with a few words. He purported—"

I interrupt. "Like he hadn't spoken it in a very long time."

Sana nods. "Exactly. Anyway, he purported to have been an agent in place in America at one time and wanted to let Moscow know— his words—'I am sorry for what occurred in 1957. I was young, and I was a patriot, but you were asking me to do something horrible.'"

"Stop," I say. "What does that mean?"

"What?"

"Do something horrible?"

Sana shrugs. "Since nothing horrible happened at the test site in 1957, we're assuming he meant spying on our atomic testing program. Anyway, NSA tracked the call to a pay phone outside a gas station in Omaha, Nebraska, but the caller was long gone when we got there. There were no cameras, so there was no video of the caller."

I hold up a hand. "Wait. There is a Lincoln County in Nebraska. Are you saying the Russians are looking in the wrong state?" I ask this, of course, because I am something of a geography savant. Idiot savant, Brinley would say. She sometimes calls me Rain Man.

"We wondered that, too. But the cashier inside the store recalled that the man using the phone was older, probably in his seventies or early eighties, and was wearing a hat that said Meteor Mine. He remembered it because it had a picture of a meteor on it, and he thought that was pretty cool."

My body tenses. "The Meteor Mine is in *this* Lincoln County."

"It is. And he said he thought the guy's truck had Nevada plates. So, it proves the guy was here."

I rotate my tired shoulders and crack my neck. "At one time. That mine hasn't been in operation since the early '70s. It's one of our ghost towns now."

"Ever seen that baseball cap?" she asks. She's got me there. They're sold at any number of souvenir shops around here. Sana raises her foot and rests it in my lap. "Come on, Beck. Fifty-five years after 1957, the guy was wearing a Meteor Mine hat and driving around with Nevada plates. Just five years ago. If he was still here then, why wouldn't he be here now? That's why the Russians think he's here. That information must have been in the leaked files."

I cogitate on this latest information for a moment. "What does your boss want you to do?"

"Well, after pulling your Army jacket, he said it's convenient that you happen to be the sheriff here because you're probably one of the most qualified people to hunt down an SVR assassin.

He was confident we could get the job done without raising any alarms in D.C."

I don't respond.

"Someday you're going to have to tell me about your time in Russia."

"Someday," I say.

# THE PAST

It was September 1956 and a few weeks had passed since Georgiy's meeting with William. He spent it all at the test site, working overtime and extra days to find out as much as he could about Project 57 and determine a way to get a warhead into the hands of his people. At the same time, however, he was also actively avoiding another meeting with William. The thought of creating an "accident" with nuclear consequences occupied most of Georgiy's waking life, preventing him from getting more than a few hours' sleep every night. Reluctantly, he finally returned to Las Vegas, bypassing the gas station in Indian Springs, where he knew William would be waiting.

He killed the last hour before Kitty's shift ended in the casino, mindlessly dumping nickels into the slots, the sound of coins dropping into their metal trays drowning out the noise of uncertainty in his brain. The place was dark inside, the cigarette smoke thick and heavy under the dim lights and much like the fog in Georgiy's head. His training and dedication to duty were sewn into the fabric of his being, as permanent and essential as his organs. To abandon them now was not only traitorous, it was cowardice. From the day he had been plucked from university and sent to Coca-Cola City he had known his country might one day require him to kill the enemy, uniformed or not. Now, when called upon to do just that, Georgiy felt the shame of fear and weakness.

After winning ten dollars, he scooped his jackpot into a large paper cup and headed to the cashier, wondering if breaking one innocent girl's heart might somehow be worse than everything else he was about to do. He didn't see the man walking just as fast and approaching to his left. The collision sent Georgiy and his two hundred nickels sprawling to the hideous multicolored casino carpeting.

"Oh, crap, I'm so sorry, buddy," the man under the dark fedora said, reaching down to help Georgiy up. "Wasn't looking where I was going."

As he rolled to his back, Georgiy couldn't immediately see the man's face under the black hat. "No problem, Mack. I wasn't looking either." He grabbed the extended hand and started to rise to his feet.

That's when the man pushed him back down on the ground and knelt close to his ear. "You've been a bad boy, Freddie," the man said softly. "I suggest you check your mail and respond to the interested party right away." He tilted his hat up, so Georgiy could see his face.

Georgiy recoiled, pulling his hand away from William's, and then William was gone, like a cat in the night. He got to his knees, his face flushed as the other gamblers watched him pick his coins up off the floor.

From the top of the Groom mountain range, Georgiy could see all of Area 51 below him and to the south, the morning sun bathing the dry lake bed in a warm, yellow blanket against an azure sky. He tapped Dr. Ellison on the shoulder and motioned for the scientist to stay silent. The two men squatted low and Georgiy pointed south.

"That's Delta," he whispered. "Look, you can see the airstrip just across the dry lake bed."

Ellison eased the butt of his rifle to the ground and peered through his binoculars. "That's where you work."

"Yep."

Kitty's father seemed surprised. "It seems so close, and yet this area isn't restricted. You could be a Soviet spy sitting up here taking notes all day long about what you saw coming and going down there."

"I suppose that's true," Georgiy said with a laugh. "Come on, let's keep going."

After William had delivered his very stern warning to provide regular updates on his intelligence-gathering activities regarding Project 57, Georgiy had spent as much of the last few weeks as his work schedule permitted with Kitty. Kitty was the gateway to her father, and Georgiy urgently needed to discover the details of the simulated nuclear "accident." One night after dinner, over pipe smoking and brandy, when Georgiy was letting the physicist pin his king in a game of chess, Dr. Ellison mentioned that he needed to learn how to hunt deer, as his boss was coming in from Washington in a few weeks and had heard the hunting was good in the Nevada mountains.

"I don't know the first thing about hunting deer," he confided to Georgiy.

The words were music to Georgiy's trained ears. "I can teach you how to hunt deer. I mean, if you like."

"You hunt?" Kitty asked from her chair in the corner of the study where she was reading the latest *Sky and Telescope* edition. "Is there anything you don't do?"

"Sure, I hunt." Georgiy said. "All my life. Grew up hunting deer." It was a true statement. He had learned to shoot the sika and roe deer in his native Ukraine for the same reason he had learned to shoot men—out of necessity.

Ellison was ecstatic. "Freddie, that would be fantastic. When can we go? What do I need?"

Georgiy took the following Friday off and spent the morning packing his trunk with supplies. The FSI office in town loaned out camping gear to its employees, so he picked up a tent and sleeping bags and loaded up with groceries, and then headed to Woolworth's on Fifth and Fremont where he purchased two rifles, a Marlin Model 336 lever action, and a Winchester Model 70. He added a scope for the Winchester. After the ammunition, he had spent almost $200 of the KGB's money, and Georgiy knew his bosses would be expecting a significant return on that investment.

He picked Kitty and Dr. Ellison up just after 2:00 P.M. Ellison was decked out in the strangest hunting garb Georgiy had ever seen. His red and black flannel suit and cap made him look like a walking checkerboard. Around his neck hung binoculars so large Georgiy was certain they could be used to view storms on the sun. "Don't laugh at him, Freddie," Kitty whispered as she climbed in the seat next to him. "He went shopping."

Georgiy stifled a laugh. "The deer will appreciate the heads-up."

They camped that night in Groom Range, at a spot Georgiy had been told by a few guys in his dormitory was the perfect place to use as a base. Always good with his hands, he had the four-man tent up in no time. Then he taught Dr. Ellison how to hold the Winchester securely to his shoulder and how to load and fire it. That night in the chilly autumn air, with Kitty's telescope they observed Saturn's rings.

"Thank you, Galileo!" she yelled.

"I'm the guy who bought you the telescope," Ellison said, smoking his pipe. "Thank me."

That made Georgiy laugh. "We'll go there some day," Kitty announced. "You'll see."

He loved her unbridled exuberance and love of science. Putting his arm around her, he wished upon the four stars that form the body of Pegasus that he could somehow leave behind the world in which he was an intelligence agent planning on poisoning an American city and live in a new one with Kitty.

Having no love for killing animals, Kitty stayed in camp the next morning when Georgiy and her father set out while it was still dark. After pointing out the facilities at Area 51 to him from a clearing in the trees, Georgiy led him up a moderately steep game trail.

As they trudged up through the thick forest, Ellison asked Georgiy how he liked his work at the test site. It was the perfect opening. "I like having the responsibility for protecting the things that are important to our future, but honestly I'm a little bored. And I would like to make more money. Don't get me wrong, Dr. Ellison, the money is much better than I was making at the Dunes, but I would like to get married someday, so I need to have some real long-term plans." He turned around to find Kitty's dad smiling at him.

"And did you have someone in mind to share your life with, Freddie?"

Georgiy looked into the man's eyes. "I think you know who I'm talking about, sir."

Ellison took a seat on a nearby rock. He had little physical stamina and needed frequent breaks, the result of long hours behind a desk. "Does Kitty know your feelings?"

*I don't even know my feelings.* He had been with women before but had never been emotionally close to one, never been . . . Georgiy couldn't even say the word in his head. "I wanted to speak to you first. I know I haven't finished college yet, but I will. I would love to work on the physics side of things at the site."

Before Ellison could respond, Georgiy spotted a small buck with a basket rack through the trees about fifty yards ahead of them. It could not have come at a better time. He held a finger to his lips and motioned to Ellison to stay low and follow him. They circled to the left for a minute until Georgiy found a line of sight through the brush that gave them a broadside view of the grazing mule deer. He pulled Ellison up next to him and pointed with his finger.

Ellison started to raise his binoculars but Georgiy pushed them down. "Just look," he whispered. "See him?"

Ellison nodded. "Now find him through your scope." Ellison raised the rifle to his shoulder and tucked it in tight, just as Freddie had shown him. He peered through the scope. "I have him."

"Now," Georgiy whispered. "You're aiming for that spot just behind his forelegs in the center of the body. Heart, lungs, liver, all there. Take a deep breath in and slowly let it out." When he heard his breath release, Georgiy told him to slowly squeeze the trigger.

He saw the animal lifted from the ground as the round caught it high on its back, shattering its spine.

Ellison was exuberant. "I got him!"

Georgiy clamped a hand on the man's shoulder. "Yes, you did. Great shot for a first-timer."

They pushed through the brush and found the young male on the ground, still alive and shaking. "Good Lord," Ellison said, "he's still alive."

Georgiy released the safety on his Marlin and shot the deer in the heart, ending its life instantly. He stood over the animal, silently apologizing for using it in a war that, with each passing day, seemed to make less and less sense. "Great shot, sir," he said, uttering the lie with as much conviction as he could muster.

Laughing like a child, Ellison started walking down the mountain. "Kitty is not going to believe this."

Georgiy couldn't believe the man was leaving. "Where are you going?"

Ellison turned. "Isn't this the way to our camp?"

Georgiy nodded. "It is, but we need to field dress the deer first."

Ellison's face said it all. It was blank. "Why?"

Georgiy looked into the man's eyes and saw clearly his utter detachment from the life he had just taken and for the death and disease he and his government were spreading in the wind every day. "Because you killed him. You're a hunter. You owe it to the animal to feed on it. You don't kill something for no reason." He pulled a long knife from the scabbard on his belt and held it out for Ellison to take. "I'll walk you through it, Doctor."

Thirty minutes later, Ellison was jubilant as they packed his trophy down the mountain toward Kitty and their camp. "Freddie, that was amazing. You've made me a hunter. I can't believe I killed a deer."

Georgiy couldn't believe it either but said nothing. Ellison put his hand on his back. "You know, Freddie, I've got something big coming up in the next few months. I might be able to get you on that project in some capacity. How does that sound?"

Before Georgiy knew it, it was Christmas already and Project 57, like the year for which it was named, was knocking on the door. Dr. Ellison had been true to his word, moving the levers of his power and influence to get him reassigned. In the six weeks since his promotion to sergeant and his move to CP-1, the test site's primary control point located just south of the parched expanse of Yucca Dry Lake, Georgiy had learned much. His new clearance and badge provided him access to just about everything at the rapidly expanding nerve center for all nuclear test activities, and already he had photographed the interior of the most important structures like the main building and the Radiological Safety Building.

He photographed at night typically when the majority of the engineers and Dr. Ellison had gone home, leaving only a handful of military clerks and FSI guards on the grounds of CP-1. More than his photographs of instrument panels, which Moscow would soon determine were how the Americans monitored radio signals and recorded voltage, wind velocity, and wind direction, all key measurements for nuclear detonations, Georgiy was now within earshot of the conversations taking place in preparation for the project. And one of the first things he heard was that, unlike the other tests, the public would not be made aware that its government would be conducting a simulation involving an XW-25 warhead and the subsequent release of deadly plutonium particles. That intelligence would be crucial to Moscow's plan because if the test could be "accidentally" relocated by Georgiy and his handler to another place, the public outrage would be too much to overcome. The corrupt American government would have to shut down its program or find a new location to conduct nuclear tests. Both prospects were hugely problematic.

It hadn't taken him long to figure out how the planners in the Lubyanka intended to do this. Las Vegas was the only logical target, especially once he had photographed the huge balloons the site technicians were experimenting with. The Americans hoped the balloons could be used as detonation platforms instead of the metal towers normally constructed to suspend warheads. In his head, Georgiy saw how it could be done. A balloon, untethered from the earth, floated in the air and drifted on a current of air. A stiff wind out of the northwest could easily carry such a balloon in the direction of the glitzy city in the desert whose population now exceeded 55,000. It was a puzzle that was starting to come together for Georgiy, and he enjoyed the mental challenge, all the while trying hard to believe that none of it would ever come to pass and that he could somehow just continue gathering information and living his fantasy life with Kitty. Still, a sense of duty is a habit hard to break, especially one forged in the fires of war, so Georgiy felt he had no choice but to pass his intelligence along.

"Freddie, I'm proud of you," William told him in early January as they sipped beers in the near-empty bowling alley inside the Boulder Bowl in the little town next to the Hoover Dam about forty miles from Las Vegas. "You've positioned yourself perfectly, and your information is of the highest quality." He grabbed his upper arms. "Congratulations, Captain."

Georgiy was stunned. "Captain?"

"Your promotion is official. The ceremony will have to wait until your triumphant return to Moscow, but know that you are doing heroic work that is not going unnoticed."

*Captain Georgiy Dudko.* It had a nice ring to it, but even upon his eventual return home, there would be no one to enjoy it with. His parents and sister were gone, and he was living in a world where fools contemplated chess moves with nuclear pieces.

"Now, these balloons," William said quietly, "where are they made?"

"Texas. A company there has been contracted to produce them for the Atomic Energy Commission."

"And what is the projected date for the test?"

"Early April."

William frowned. "When in early April?"

"The date is dependent on the wind."

"Of course."

"And the warhead? Do you know when it is being flown from New Mexico?"

"Not yet, but I will as the date gets closer. I know it will be housed in Building 11 until the day of the shot when it is moved to Area 13. But I have no idea how we can possibly get it or a balloon off the site."

William nodded. "Let me worry about the balloon. What do you know of the warhead itself?"

"I have photographed the specifications," Georgiy responded, pushing William the tiny film cannister under his palm. "The XW-25 is relatively small, approximately forty-four centimeters high and sixty-eight centimeters long." He paused for a moment, knowing these last words would make all the difference. "It weighs just under ninety-nine kilograms."

William's face lit up. "So small?"

"Well, they only need the warhead for this particular test. It won't be in a bomb casing. But it is heavy."

William nodded. "Just slightly heavier than me, then. And as you said the first time we met, not something you can put in your pocket, but you could carry it."

Georgiy looked into his beer. "If I could get to it, if I could manage to remove all the security around it. If I could access it after the physics package had been assembled. And then if I could somehow manage to get it all the way back to the main gate and off the site before they knew it was gone. All of which seems quite impossible."

William grabbed Georgiy's head with both hands. "Impossible is what we do, Freddie. It's what we do."

Georgiy nodded uneasily. "Have you determined the best location for the accident to occur?"

"Not yet, but it is not your concern."

Georgiy knew he was lying. He could see it in his eyes. Moscow had certainly reached the same conclusion he had. It was to be Las Vegas. And by the sound of it, a balloon would be used—perhaps not to get the warhead off the site but to deliver it and its plutonium payload to the city, making it appear every bit an accident that would be undeniable by the American government. That is why William wanted to know who manufactured the balloons. As to how they would ensure one would be guided to its intended target or the warhead would be triggered to release the deadly radiation, Georgiy had no idea. But he was certain there were a lot of very smart people sitting around a room in Lubyanka Square formulating answers to those questions. And Georgiy knew one more thing. Regardless of what happened, he was not going back to Russia. He could see that in William's eyes, too.

# CHAPTER 11

Sana's update on the illegal's call to the Russian embassy and his apology for something that happened in 1957 has my Spidey-sense tingling. I spend the night in my office researching everything available about the era of aboveground atomic testing. I'm aware of a lot of it from my time growing up here when many of the long-term effects of living downwind from the Nevada Test Site were still being felt by my friends and neighbors, like the cancer that took my mother. I've waded through reams of information on the tests from 1955–1957, the time period the FBI believes the illegal gathered his intelligence. Oddly, the first part of 1957, the year the illegal referenced in his call, was a relatively quiet time at the site. There were only four small safety tests conducted. Still, having spent the majority of my military career working in and around intelligence operations, I know things are not always what they seem. Or what the public is told.

While I'm doing all this, I'm growing more and more nervous about Michaela Edwards. Statistically, the odds of finding her alive are not good now. It's already Tuesday. Three full days have passed since she vanished. The blood on the bike will turn out to be hers, and it's likely to take a day or two for the Vegas crime lab to come back with the type, manufacturer, and size of the boot print, so I have no evidence to help me find her.

With my deputies almost evenly split working her disappearance and our hunt for two Russians, I'm getting nowhere fast on either case. I need a lucky break and I need it now. I also need bodies on the street.

Sana walks into my office in a fresh change of clothes and a couple hours sleep under her belt. She's literally dressed to kill, I see, with the Walther tucked in her shoulder strap.

"Good morning," she says, handing me a hot coffee. "You here all night?"

"Let's go," I tell her. We walk into the larger office and I get everyone's attention. "Okay, listen up, folks. We're going to do some active policing today. Wardell, I need you to take the Twin Peaks and Pete here and fan out across the county. I want you to run every license plate you see on any vehicle you don't immediately recognize. If it comes back to someone you don't know, you radio it in, and the closest two of you make a stop. Identify the driver and look for anything suspicious."

Tuffy holds up her hand. "Boss, Pete is still on administrative leave because of the shooting."

I nod. "I know, but we have someone out there who has already killed two people and is looking to kill at least one more." I look at Pete. "Pete, this is my call. The shooting board isn't in yet, but I need you on the street now. My responsibility. My call. The county can fire me later if it wants." I see Wardell smirk. He knows I've just put another bullet in his gun.

Pete nods. "No problem, Sheriff."

"Listen," I say. "I can't emphasize this enough. We have every reason to believe the man doing this is a trained killer. You only do the vehicle stop if you have backup. If this guy is driving around our county looking for his next victim, don't let it be you. He will do what's necessary to keep going. Use your backup. Do not approach someone alone. Are we clear?"

Everyone nods. Wardell and the three deputies gather their gear. As they are heading out, Brinley walks in.

"Where's Pop?" I ask. "I thought we were going to have him look at some of these old pictures."

She shakes her head and speaks into my ear. "He's not with it today, Porter."

I fucking hate dementia, especially the incremental decline it inflicts on people. I walk over to Tuffy. "No Pop today, sorry. How are you coming on the list we got from the clerk's office?"

"We've found a few who are already deceased. Checking the others and seeing if there any matches with Atterbury's photos, any other assumed names."

"Look for anyone who resembles Guy Pollack," Sana says. "Our guy is probably working from an old photo. Maybe he thought Pollack resembled his agent."

"Good point," I say. "And focus on anyone who wasn't in the county until 1957 or later."

"Why 1957?" Sana asks.

I rest my backside on a corner of Tuffy's desk. "I was thinking about this all night. If you were an illegal who had access to intelligence at the test site back then, you would have had to have been employed out there or had access to someone who was, right?"

Sana nods. "I think we have established that, yes."

"And if you later began informing to the FBI, you would have already disappeared. And because you're on the run from your own security services now, you're no longer using your original cover identity. You know the FBI and the Kremlin are out looking for you. So, you're someone else now. Under this assumed identity, you would have been a resident of Lincoln County no earlier than 1957, the year the illegal said he stopped working for the Soviets."

"That makes sense," Sana adds. "This new identity would be carefully built, just like the first one, with documents and a history proving he is who he says he is."

"Carefully built," I say. I swivel around to Tuffy. "How are you coming on the sex offender list?"

"Two down, four to go," Tuffy replies, holding up some manila folders. "Arshal is bringing them in, and I should have those knocked out by noon. Wish we had better news, boss, but two manhunts at once is giving us fits."

She's right. The last time we had two major cases running concurrently in Lincoln County was never. We have effectively exceeded our capacity. The problem has been tumbling around in my brain all night, but now the answer hits me like a lightning bolt.

"Oh no," I say softly.

Sana gets up from her chair. "What?"

"How did I not see this? If you were this Russian and you needed to move about in a county where a stranger, any stranger, would stick out like a sore thumb after a few days, how would you do it?"

She shrugs. "I don't know. How would I do it?"

"Remember what you said when we were up in Mill Valley? You said this is a distraction we don't need right now. Michaela Edwards's disappearance is a distraction, isn't it?"

The shock registers on Sana's face. "You think he's doing this, that he's taken the girl to keep us busy until he finds his agent."

"The Russian?" asks Tuffy.

"Yes," I say. "The Russian. He hides her bike just off the highway. Leaves a small amount of her blood so we know she didn't just hitch a ride out of there. No body, just a little blood. He knows we're looking for him, so he gives us someone else to look for."

Sana crosses her arms reflexively. "That's not very . . . definitive. There's some logic to it, but—"

"It's definitive," Brinley says. "The blood wasn't taken from any struggle with her on the road. Whoever grabbed her took some of her blood and smeared it on the seat tube of the bike. He wanted us to find it."

"How do you know that?" Sana asks.

Brinley sets her equipment down on a desk. "Because I was at the crime lab in Vegas all night, and that's what they said."

I give her a brotherly hug. "Thanks for doing that, Brin. This guy is very smart. The good news for us is that it may mean that Michaela is still alive. Tuffy, radio Wardell and the guys and let them know what we're thinking."

She looks at Sana and me. "What about you two?"

"We're going to see X-Files. Maybe he knows something about the history of this the rest of us don't."

"Better you than me," Tuffy says with a grin.

The sun is out again today, warming the interior of the truck, and the snow on the ground outside is making a hasty retreat. Normally, that would be enough to put me at ease, but the idea that Atterbury's killer has also taken Michaela Edwards has me jittery. On the one hand, the Russian having her might be better than the alternative. The thought of an abduction by a sexual predator terrifies me. On the other hand, if he took Michaela simply to distract us and split our resources, he has no practical reason to keep her. He may have killed her immediately and hidden her body, knowing we would continue to look for her. The more we look for her, the less we look for him.

"Who is X-Files?" Sana asks as we speed south, my flashers

and occasional siren causing anyone ahead of me to pull off the road. "And why are we going to see him?"

"He used to be an investigative journalist in Los Angeles. Was pretty well respected for most of his career. And then he started doing stories on aliens in Area 51 and hanging out with a lot of the UFO crazies. Largely fell out of favor with his bosses at that point, developed a bit of a drinking problem, and got the boot. Used to be married, but even his wife finally gave up on him. Outside of the people who actually work there, he knows more about the test site and its history than anyone. I met him a few years ago when I got a call from the Feds saying that he was flying one of those hobby drones into Area 51 and taking pictures."

Sana takes a sip of coffee, searing her lip as I round one of the many sharp curves. "Sounds like a crackpot. Why are we wasting our time with somebody who's looking for little green men?"

I look over at her. "I was thinking about what you told me last night. There's nothing online about any event at the test site in 1957 that was not planned."

"Right," Sana replies.

"But the illegal's handler said he used the words, 'you were asking me to do something horrible.' What if something did happen, or came close to happening, something so serious it still wouldn't be declassified?"

It takes her too long to answer. "But nothing happened."

Greg Knutson, the man they call X-Files, lives in the town of Alamo, not far from the Nevada Test Site. He resides in a double-wide in a run-down trailer park with laundry hung on the line out front that is flapping in the wind and looks like it has been out there for months. He answers the door in his boxers and no shirt covering his enormous potbelly, squinting into the southern sunlight and smelling of booze.

"What do you want?" he asks, fixing his glasses over his blood-shot eyes. "Who are you?"

"Great," Sana says to me.

"Greg, it's Sheriff Beck. Remember me?"

The man is haggard, his unkempt brownish-gray hair partially stuck to the stubble on his face. "I remember you arrested me without cause. Who's this?" he asks, looking at Sana.

"This is Special Agent Sana Locke with the FBI, Greg. Could we come in for a minute?"

"Do we have to?" Sana implores.

X-Files crosses his arms over his chest, and they sit like a shelf on top of his stomach. "You people will never shut me up," he tells Sana. "I know what you're doing out there, and I know my rights."

Sana turns to me. "You can't be serious with this guy."

"Please, Greg," I say. "I need some information."

X-Files steps closer, his veined, bulbous red nose against the outer screen door. "What's in it for me?"

"Depends on your information."

The inside of the trailer isn't any better than the outside. It is pure chaos, and when the former reporter goes into the bedroom to put on some clothes, I take a seat on a cheap folding chair while Sana tries to find a clean place to sit on the dingy sofa, finally giving up. She notes the hundreds of books and magazines stacked on bookshelves or piled on the floor. The titles alarm her, I guess, because she holds up a number of them so I can see. They are all about aliens and secret government conspiracies. The posters of UFOs on the walls are equally discomfiting to Sana. She turns to me and makes the "cuckoo" noise.

"I heard that," X-Files yells from the bedroom. He walks out in sweats, a yellow T-shirt, and some ancient slippers. "I'm not crazy, young lady. The government tells everyone I am, but that doesn't make it true." He plops down in his recliner. "I'm listening, Sheriff."

I lean forward in the chair. "I need your help with an investigation."

At the sound of the word, the recluse's eyes bug out. "Investigation? My specialty." He reaches down to the coffee table and pours himself a bourbon, gesturing to us with his glass.

"Little early for me," Sana says disapprovingly.

I wave off the drink. "I need to know what happened at the test site in 1957." It's a wide-open question. If something occurred that's not on the official record, he'll know about it.

X-Files's eyebrows shoot up, and he slurps excitedly at his drink. "What happened? Operation Plumbob is what happened. Boom, boom, boom, all the livelong day. Twenty-nine detonations from late May to early October. Some really big suckers, too. And don't forget the thousands of servicemen we put in trenches or dropped in parachutes next to ground zero to see how they would stand up to radiation on the nuclear battlefield." He takes another sip, gripping the glass tightly. "That's thousands of guinea pigs, all long dead now, I'm sure."

He's right, of course. I found the same in my reading last night, amazed by the things I didn't know went on a few miles to the west of my home back then. Men in trenches or dropped from parachutes, and even pilots forced to fly through the radioactive cloud itself, all to learn how we could survive a nuclear war. "I'm aware of those," I say. "What I'm curious about is whether something might have happened out there that wasn't scheduled, wasn't planned."

The ex-reporter swallows loudly and looks nervously at the FBI agent sitting in his home. "I'm not sure what you mean."

Sana and I have a quick visual exchange in which she's telling me she has better things to do. "We're not looking to put you in a bind, Greg. I just figured if anyone might know about something peculiar out there, it would be you."

X-Files rises from his chair and moves behind it, as if it somehow provides him a useful barrier between himself and the law. "Are you recording this?"

Sana rolls her eyes. "Here we go."

"You don't think I know what they call me? X-Files, Greg Knutjob with a *K*? You all think I'm paranoid about the government watching me. The F-B-I. I tell people the NSA is tapping my phones. They say I'm looney tunes."

"We're not recording this, Greg," I say. "I'm trying to solve two murders and prevent another, and I need a break pretty quick."

X-Files is suddenly intrigued. He sits back down. "Murders, you say." He looks at Sana again. "One of them your man up at Big Rocks?"

"How did you hear about that?" Sana asks.

He laughs. "Young lady, please. I have tentacles into many places here, some very secret places."

I turn to Sana and say, "It's not important, Agent Locke." And then to X-Files, "Yes, Greg, he was one of the victims."

"And the other?"

"Again, not important."

The man who believes aliens from outer space are being kept just thirty miles from here sits back in his chair and mulls over what he is hearing. "I don't trust law enforcement, Sheriff. But I hear you're a fair man, and when you tell me you're trying to solve a murder, I will take you at your word."

Sana sighs sarcastically. "You can't imagine how much we appreciate that."

"You're asking about Project 57," he says. "You want to know what really happened."

I had read about Project 57 in the middle of the night as well. There wasn't much information, really, just a blurb or two. "I know it was a safety test that simulated the crash of a plane carrying a warhead. Plutonium was involved. *Did* something else happen? Something that hasn't been declassified?"

X-Files laughs. "How crazy do you think I am now?"

"We probably shouldn't go there," Sana says, staring at the floor.

I shoot her the stink eye. "Tell us what you know, Greg."

X-Files pours himself another. "Well, you are correct, Sheriff. Project 57 was a safety test simulating a plane crash. Its intention was to measure the dispersal of plutonium over a large area that might occur in such an accident. You have to remember bombers were a huge part of our nuclear strategy then. Land-based ICBMs were still in their infancy, and submarines carrying nukes were still a few years off. Bombers in the air 24–7. Sooner or later, one was bound to crash. In fact, one did over Spain some years later, but that's another story."

It is clear the man's mind is better ordered than his living space. "So, what happened?"

X-Files rubs his hands vigorously together. "They did the test. They collected their data and went home. Kept it secret for many years. It's only recently been declassified."

"I don't understand. You're saying nothing went wrong, nothing happened that wasn't supposed to happen?"

The journalist stares at me for a long moment. "I never said that. I told you the official version."

I glance at Sana. "I take it there is another version."

His pupils flare. "As I said before, what's in it for me?"

"I told you, Greg. I'm trying to solve some murders. You would be helping me."

"Uh-huh, and what is that worth to you?"

I throw up my hands. "You tell me, Greg. What is it worth?"

He motions for me to lean close to him and then whispers in my ear. "I want a Get Out of Jail Free card. I want a heads-up from you about any federal warrants the Feds may decide to serve on me, and I want you to hide me from them if necessary."

"Done." I have absolutely no idea if this is something I could pull off. I'll have to worry about that when I have the luxury of extra time on my hands.

We both sit back. "All right then," X-Files says. "My source for this information is reliable. He has since passed away, but he was solid gold. Trust me on this. Shortly before Project 57 occurred, the Russians stole the warhead being used in order to create the same accident, but in Las Vegas."

Sana starts for the door. "Okay, next we're going to hear the moon landing was staged. I'm out of here."

My eyes never leave those of the man seated across from me. "Go on."

Sana stops in her tracks and drops her head in defeat while X-Files continues. "Obviously, Vegas was never bombed, but a few people were killed."

I can sense I'm getting closer to some answers I can use now. "Killed how?"

"Three shot, one burned up. Russians, all of them."

The pieces are sliding together now. I can see them in my head. "How did your source come by this information, Greg?"

"That's the beauty of it, Sheriff. They stole the bomb from him. He was the scientist in charge of Project 57. Very embarrassing. Ended his career and his security clearance."

I think about it all for a moment. "The men who were killed. You said three of them were shot. Who shot them?"

X-Files grins insanely like Jack Nicholson in *The Shining*. "Who do you think?"

"We executed them," I say, nodding.

Sana spins around. "Oh, come on. You're not buying this, are you?"

"And the fourth man, the one who was burned?"

"Burned beyond recognition," X-Files replies. "But, Sheriff? When I asked you who you thought killed them, it would be a logical deduction that agents of the federal government did. No witnesses, secrecy maintained, keep a lid on everything, right?"

I stand. "But?"

X-Files looks up at me. "My source said they were dead when our people got there."

# THE PAST

On an unseasonably warm February evening, Georgiy Dudko kissed Kitty good night on the doorstep to her father's house in Las Vegas. He waved to her one last time as he climbed in behind the wheel of his Crestliner. Loose from a couple glasses of wine, he did not immediately see the man dressed in black and holding a satchel who appeared in front of his car as he reached the end of the block. Slamming on the brake, Georgiy's heart practically flew out of his chest. *"Yebat!" Fuck!*

"Can you believe how warm it is?" William asked with a grin, climbing in to the back seat. "And this is February! Keep driving, please."

Instead, Georgiy shifted into park and turned around. "Go to hell, William. We have predetermined methods for contact. This isn't one of them."

William took his time lighting a cigarette and then leaned forward so that his face was only inches from Georgiy's, his blue irises glowing in the dim light of the streetlamps. He blew the smoke in Georgiy's face. "Mind your tone with me, Captain. I decide how and when we meet. Now drive."

Georgiy turned slowly in his seat and moved the gear shift. He drove for a full minute before William spoke again. "She's not very pretty, your girlfriend. Not like our women back home."

It was a jab, sharp and intended to bruise. Georgiy wanted very much to punch back, to actually use his fists on William. He had encountered many Williams already in his young life, men who delighted in antagonizing others, unfortunate products of a

Soviet existence. But now was not the time. "What is that to me? She is Ellison's daughter, a tool."

William laughed. "Come now, Freddie. You like her. That much is obvious."

"I do my job. The girl means nothing to me personally."

"Turn right here," said William, "into the alley."

Georgiy did as he was instructed. The alley bisected the two halves of the neighborhood. "Now what?"

"Stop here." When the car stopped, William leaned forward and handed Georgiy some photographs. They were taken from a distance, but even in the dim light inside the car, he could see they were pictures of him and Kitty. Holding hands, kissing. Georgiy could see they went back many months, some of them before William had come out of the shadows. Whoever the photographer was, he was good because Georgiy had never noticed him. "You never detected the surveillance," William said. "Not once. Moscow would not be pleased to know you have forgotten so much of your training."

Georgiy was incensed and afraid all at once but laughed, throwing the pictures back in William's face. "This is how you spend your time? Is Moscow aware of this foolishness? Perhaps we should telephone the Lubyanka and ask them."

William grabbed Georgiy painfully by the ear and slapped him. "Developing feelings for your asset is not uncommon," he said, wrenching the delicate skin. "We discourage it, of course, but if you are any good at your job, it's natural, I guess. I am sorry you have to have sex with her, though. I can't imagine how horrible that must be." He released Georgiy, sat back and smoked for a moment.

Georgiy knew he had to control himself or risk everything, so he turned around and placed both hands on the steering wheel. "Is there a point to this conversation?"

"Just that we are getting close to the finish line, Freddie. Let's make sure that all goes well so that nothing bad has to happen to Miss Ellison."

The threat was clear. Deliver the warhead or Kitty would be harmed. Georgiy felt his skin getting hotter. "The warhead is scheduled to be flown in during the last week of March."

"And when were you going to get around to telling me that?"

Georgiy didn't answer. Anything he said would be a lie. They both knew that.

"And the security around Building 11?"

"Six guards, rotating in groups of three over twelve hours. Half the guards will be FSI, under my control. Half will be Army from Camp Desert Rock."

William was immediately concerned. "Why Army guards?"

"Technically, it's a military project. They're simulating a bomber crash, remember? They want their guards outside the storage building at all times."

William nodded. "So, we have six weeks to determine how to steal the warhead."

Georgiy turned back around to face William and slowly shook his head. "There is no way to steal the warhead, William. You have to trust me on this. Building 11 is reinforced concrete. There is an electronic lock on the outside, and only the project engineers and Ellison have the code. There will be roving patrols around the clock once the warhead is flown in. We should let the Americans conduct their test, and I can steal the documentation of the results. I'm sure of it."

William cocked his head to one side. "That is not the plan, Captain. You know this."

Georgiy was exasperated. William was a fool. He simply did not appreciate the logistics involved in such an undertaking. "Look, even if I could somehow get the warhead out of the building, I would have to load it in my work truck and drive it thirty minutes and get it off the site without the gate guards seeing it."

William nodded. "Let me think on that. What time is the test scheduled for?"

Georgiy expelled the air in his chest. "0630. But that is highly dependent on the wind."

"So, we have to steal it with enough time to get it off the facility before they know it's gone. And we need a couple of hours to get it where it needs to go."

"And where is that?" Georgiy asked.

William shook his head. "Not your concern."

Georgiy got out of the car and slammed the door.

"What are you doing?" William demanded, rolling down his window. "Get back in here immediately."

Georgiy leaned in through the back window. "Listen, if you are going to risk everything I have done so far, and my life, you are going to have to read me into the rest of the operation. I know this place, and I know these people. Do not shut me out."

William bared his teeth, his two upper canines distinct and pointy like a wolf's. "I am ordering you to get back in this car."

Georgiy's voice rose. "Or what? You'll report me? Who is going to get you what you need then, William?"

"Lower your voice . . . please."

Georgiy did not. He leaned farther into the car. "Let me tell you something, William, or whatever your name is. I'm doing exactly what you sent me here to do. I got close to the girl. I got close to Ellison himself. I work at the most secret facility in the American nuclear program. I'm doing my duty." He picked up one of the photographs from the car seat and looked at it again. It was when he and Kitty had been in Zion National Park more than a year ago. "And what are you doing? You're following me around taking pictures you think you can threaten me with? That doesn't make me feel very good, William."

William moved slowly to the opposite side of the car and got out. Without saying a word, he walked around the back of the Crestliner and faced Georgiy. He produced a small envelope. "From this point on, I will be at the gas station in Indian Springs around the clock. Every time you leave the site from now on, you pull in and fill up on gas. This is how we will exchange information regarding the operation." He handed Georgiy the envelope.

He peeked inside and saw a small gray capsule, knowing immediately what it was.

"Just in case," William said. With that, he turned and walked back toward the street.

Georgiy threw his hands into the air. "How are you going to be at the station around the clock?"

William turned his head back. "We bought the place." He turned the corner and was gone.

Area 13 wasn't on anyone's map, and almost no one knew of its existence. It had been created specifically for Project 57 and occupied a ten-by-sixteen-square-mile block of land northwest of Area 51 that technically wasn't even part of the official test site. It was open, barren land. In the days and weeks leading up to the shot, Georgiy watched as the engineers set up thousands of fallout collectors and tethered huge air-sampling balloons to the desert floor, some of which rose to more than a thousand feet off the ground. As he drove his daily patrol around the site, he saw construction workers laying strips of asphalt as long as city blocks, and then other city features like sidewalks, curbs, buildings, and automobiles were added.

On one such day, Georgiy drove Dr. Ellison on a tour of the site to check that everything was being put in place as required. The wind was howling out of the north and kicking up sand everywhere. Ellison seemed particularly anxious, and Georgiy noted on more than one occasion the scientist stealing sips from his flask.

"See those?" Dr. Ellison asked him, pointing at the galvanized steel pans several men were laying out in various locations. "Those are sticky pans. They're designed to capture plutonium particles released into the air, and that way we can measure how plutonium behaves when dispersed."

"Hmm . . . and what are those cages over there for?" Georgiy pointed to a group of metal cages that were being unloaded from several trucks.

"For the animals," the project director responded, puffing on his pipe.

"Animals?"

"Sheep, burros, goats, dogs, lots of dogs." Georgiy bit his lip, and Ellison noticed his discomfort. "Well, we can't test it on humans."

"Science never sleeps," Georgiy responded, slowing the jeep to a stop.

Ellison said, "Exciting, isn't it, Freddie?" He took another drink.

Georgiy nodded. This was Ellison's baby, and every day the scientist was revealing more about the nature of the project, a measure of his trust in the man who was dating his daughter. "A lot more exciting than when I was sitting at Delta all day guarding airplanes."

"Oh, that reminds me, those CIA idiots are trying to throw a monkey wrench into my project. They are convinced that the Soviets know all about their precious U-2 spy plane, even what it looks like. Those paranoid fools think there might be a Soviet agent working here."

Georgiy felt the blood rush to his head. "Why would they think that?"

Ellison threw his hands in the air and reiterated he thought the entire intelligence apparatus was a waste of money. "They see Soviet agents everywhere. When they told me their investigation could delay the project, I told them to check out the Groom mountain range where we went deer hunting. They need to seal that place off. A spy doesn't need to be working here to see secret airplanes in Area 51. How did they miss that, I wonder?"

Georgiy started the jeep forward again. "When will you know if the project is delayed?"

"I told them they have two days to wrap up whatever it is they need to do," Ellison replied. "Because that's when the warhead is being flown in. So, this might be your last free night for a while, depending on the wind. If I were you, I would go home and take Kitty out for a nice dinner."

Georgiy left the test site late that afternoon, driving in a near panic and checking his rearview mirror obsessively, certain that every vehicle behind him might be the FBI or CIA. There were no city streets to take that could help identify a tail, there was just that lonely stretch of two-lane road that ran seventy-five miles from the test site back to Las Vegas. Thirty minutes later, he pulled his Crestliner into Thunderbird Gas. William met him at the pumps and pointed to an adjacent side building.

"Pull it into the garage," he said.

Georgiy waved him off. "I have news. We have to abort."

"We'll talk about it inside," William said sternly. "Now pull it into the garage."

Once inside, two men lowered the garage door behind Georgiy. They were both substantially larger than William and built like weight lifters chipped from marble. Moscow had sent muscle, Spetsnaz most likely, the most highly trained and dangerous Soviet soldiers. In seconds, they had the trunk open. Georgiy asked what they were doing and William told him they were preparing a space for the warhead.

Georgiy threw up his hands. "I told you, I cannot bring my vehicle beyond my dormitory."

William spoke calmly as his men pulled the spare tire out and removed some of Georgiy's tools. "Yes, I heard you."

"You have to stop. The Americans are hunting me."

The two men stopped working, and William turned to Georgiy. "What do you mean?"

"Ellison told me. The CIA has received intelligence that the Soviet Union knows about the U-2. They are checking everyone who has worked at Delta. They could pull me in tomorrow, or even tonight. They could be watching me now. We have to abort. I cannot go back."

The KGB major said nothing for several seconds, carefully choosing his words. "I don't know how they could know that."

Georgiy's eyes clamped shut. "Well, maybe the Americans have their own Directorate S inside our country. Or maybe someone is selling our intelligence secrets. They've seen the pictures I took."

"Is that what Ellison said? Did he use those words?"

Georgiy thought back to his conversation with Kitty's father earlier in the day. "He said they believed we knew what the plane looked like."

William shrugged. "That could mean anything. Do you know yet when the warhead is arriving?" He motioned to his men to continue.

Georgiy seized his superior by the arms. "Are you insane? If they catch me, all will be lost."

"What will be lost?" William asked. "They may interview you.

They may put you on their lie detector. You've been trained for this. If they put you in chains or start to torture you, bite down on that capsule I gave you."

Georgiy stared at him in disbelief.

"Now, what about the warhead?"

Georgiy took a seat in a folding chair next to his car. "It will be flown in the day after tomorrow. Barring unfavorable winds, the shot will happen in three days. Beginning tomorrow, I and the rest of the project staff will be locked down until the shot is completed."

"Excellent," said William. "We will be ready."

Georgiy suddenly felt dizzy. "Ready? Ready how? I told you I cannot get into the storage facility. To steal the warhead, I have to get into that building. I do not have the combination to the electronic lock."

"You will," William replied. "Once the warhead arrives and is in the building, I will give you the combination."

Georgiy appeared stunned. "You have it? Give it to me now if you have it."

William shook his head. "I do not have it yet."

The truth suddenly dawned on him. "You have another source."

William ignored him, producing a small slip of paper from the pocket in his coveralls. "Memorize this number. Use it only on the night you are ready to move the warhead. Ask for Susan. You will receive the lock combination and further instructions then. Ideally, this should happen late at night but no later than midnight."

Another source, Georgiy thought. An asset. Someone on the test site with access and clearance. Someone like him, or perhaps an American who had been compromised. *Who the hell could it be?*

Whoever it was, his identity was being protected. Ironically, it was the same kind of security employed at the test site. So, this madness was moving forward. Moscow would not be dissuaded. Georgiy had his orders. They were suicidal, but apparently that mattered only to Georgiy.

It took forty minutes for William's men to assemble the hidden compartment in the trunk of the Crestliner. After hollowing out a portion of the lower chassis, they inserted a rubber mold in the exact shape of the XW-25 under and to the left of the spare tire well, securing it with bolts to the outer edges of the trunk. Above it, they laid a perfectly cut piece of sheet metal and covered it with the original matting. The end result was a slightly elevated trunk bottom, and even Georgiy had to admit it would pass a cursory security inspection by the gate guards. Of course, that would only be the case if he could somehow get into Building 11, steal the warhead, conceal it in his work vehicle, drive to the parking lot outside his dormitory at Mercury, and transfer it to his car without being seen. Madness, he told himself.

As he was getting back into the Crestliner, William approached him. "One more thing, Comrade." He handed him a small vial of liquid. "You may find this useful." He then went on to explain why.

Georgiy pocketed the vial. There was no use arguing with William, so better to just shut up and leave. He drove to the Ellison's and was waiting on the porch swing when Kitty arrived home from work just before 7:00. The sun had dipped behind the mountains, and the air was cooler now. Seeing her, Georgiy felt a chill run down his spine. Kitty jumped into his arms and kissed him deeply. "Oh, a man in uniform, how nice! Wasn't expecting you."

He closed his eyes and inhaled her into his lungs, her devotion to him strangling his breath. He wanted to tell her everything at that moment, to implore her to run away with him. They could make a life together somewhere. She could forgive him his deceit, his sense of duty and patriotism for the only country he knew. They could go to the American authorities, and he could confess it all. But she wouldn't forgive him. His betrayal of her trust would crush her, the embarrassment and humiliation too much for her and, ultimately, for her father. His career would be over. If Dr. Ellison had been a Soviet scientist and had allowed an American intelligence operative access to classified information, even unwittingly, he would be sent to a camp or shot. Maybe both.

*And I will spend the rest of my life in prison.*

Kitty saw the sadness in his eyes. "What's wrong, honey?"

His words were barely audible. "I'm sorry, Kitty." As soon as he said the words, he saw the fear clamp onto her heart.

"Sorry? What's . . . happened?"

"I can't stay," he said. "I'm so sorry."

She shook her head slightly. "Can't stay? You mean right now? You have to go?"

He stared at her for a long moment, knowing it would be the last time he would look at her. Finally, he nodded. "Yes, I have to . . ." *To do my duty, to do something too horrible to imagine.* "I have to get back to the site."

Her eyes were wet now. "Oh, you scared me. I thought you were going to say something else."

"I love you, Kitty."

She nodded, unable to pull her eyes from his. "Is everything all right, Freddie?"

Georgiy stroked her face. He ran his fingers gently through her hair, committing to memory the sensation of touching her. "Everything is fine. I'll see you soon."

# CHAPTER 12

Leaving Alamo, I realize I've spent more time with Sana driving around my county than in any actual productive activity, unless you count the other night at the Pioneer Hotel. I'm also wondering how much of what X-Files told me she already knows.

"Problem?" she asks.

I glance over but say nothing.

"What is it, Beck? That guy was three sheets to the wind before lunch. He's pickled. You think the Russians almost nuked Las Vegas?"

"It would make some sense."

"How on earth would it make sense?"

I take my foot off the gas pedal and pull off the road, slowing to a stop and shutting down the engine. As a matter of fact, I'm about to shut this whole thing down. "You've been holding out on me, Sana." Before she can speak, I place a finger over her lips. "Please choose your next words carefully because I don't have time for any more lies. I have people dying here. I have a young woman who is missing, and I don't have time."

Sana turns away and looks out her window, clearly exasperated.

"You're not cleared for this. It's need-to-know, and I know you know what that means."

I grab the collar of her jacket and drag her onto the console between the two seats. "Please hold while I transfer you to someone who gives a fuck about need-to-know."

We sit for a moment in silence, me holding her face close to mine. She just stares into my eyes and doesn't say anything. Obstinate. Finally, I release her and reach for the ignition button. "There were four of them," she says. "One we identified as one of their scientists from Kazakhstan. He was probably there to make sure the plutonium would leak out of the warhead when they exploded it, just like the test was meant to."

I lower my window, and the cold air braces me. "Jesus."

"Two guys were muscle, we think," Sana continues. "Low-level thugs, probably Spetsnaz."

I nod. "And bachelor number four?"

Sana turns to me. "Some guy employed as a security guard at the test site. Probably also Russian, although he was the one that was burned. No positive ID, but there were a few pieces of his uniform and badge. His legend was well crafted. Frederick Meyer. He had been working there for eighteen months and was dating the daughter of the scientist who was in charge of the project."

"Jesus, it really happened."

Sana nods. "I didn't know until this morning, I swear. It's all still highly classified, and we never had this conversation. Do you understand?"

"What happened? Why did they fail?"

"We don't know," she answers, and she can see I don't believe her. "Hey, I'm telling you what I have been told, okay? So, don't give me that look. We don't know. They came this close to dropping plutonium all over the city of Las Vegas."

I hit the steering wheel. "There was a fifth man, another illegal."

"It would seem so."

"And the reason Moscow is hunting him is that it was his fault they didn't succeed." I run through it all in my mind again. "But why? Missions fail. The world kept spinning. The Russians weren't hurt. Why do they want this guy so badly now?"

"I don't know," Sana says. "That part does not make any sense."

I stare at her in frustration. "Why didn't you just tell me all that this morning?"

"Because it doesn't help you," she replies. "And if it ever got out that this happened, it could be the Cold War all over again."

I start the truck and pull back onto the highway. Before I can respond, my cell rings. "You're on speaker," I tell Tuffy.

"I have two possibles for you, boss, and only two," she says. "We've cross-indexed everything Atterbury had with the list from the county clerk. Hank Tyler is the first."

That surprises me. "Hang 'em Hank Tyler? The judge?" Tyler had been a county judge for many years after being the district attorney for many before that, all of which occurred well before I joined the military. I don't know the man well but heard many stories from my dad about him when I was a boy. Tyler was known for putting the screws to anyone he found guilty in his courtroom, and everyone was guilty.

"Roger that," Tuffy says. "Eighty-eight years old. Been here since the early '60s. Appears he knew quite a few people who worked at the test site during the '50s, so he would have had access. But he's out of the county now."

Interesting. He would have known plenty of people who worked out there. Construction guys probably since a lot of them lived out here, but maybe even some of the men from the large defense contractors at the time. But I find it hard to believe Judge

Tyler could possibly have been a Soviet spy. He would have a documented history of college and law school before coming to Lincoln County. And, I remind myself, the man being hunted would have had a different identity back then, otherwise the Russians would have killed him long before now. It makes no sense for Tyler to have been a Russian asset. "Who's the other guy?"

"Chuck Wolverton. Age ninety. Lives alone. Been here since '65."

I search my memory. "Is he the guy that ran that auto shop in Caliente back in the day?"

"Same guy," answers Tuffy. "Business license says it opened in 1979. Retired about twenty years back. One of his boys ran it for a time, but it closed in 2005. The old man lives on Social Security now. He and Tyler are the best candidates when we look at age and when they first resided in Lincoln County."

I think for a moment. "Tuffy, I know about Hank Tyler. What did Wolverton do before he ran the garage?"

"Checking." Sana looks over at me, and we can hear Tuffy leafing through some papers. "He was a miner," she says.

My face lights up. "Which mine?"

"Uh . . . Meteor Mine."

"Go, go, go," Sana says. I mash the gas pedal and flick on my light bar.

It's brightly lit inside the house despite it being well past Chuck Wolverton's bedtime. The ancient former miner and mechanic normally retires by 8:30 P.M., and I have no doubt he is already fast asleep in the place I have secluded him. It took more than an hour to convince him that his life was not only in imminent danger but that he should somehow give a crap about it. I never mentioned Russians. He's frail, emphysemic, and attached to the oxygen concentrator in his small dining room by a sixty-foot plastic tube that uncoils to either end of his home like a giant snake. More than once, I had to disentangle the tubing from his walker as he paced the floor. Eventually, the old man relented and agreed to vacate his premises for the next few days, but only if I promised he could watch all the pay-per-view movies he wanted.

Now, alone in the house, I speak softly but loud enough for the Bluetooth device in my ear to pick up. "It's nice and warm in here. How's everything outside?"

"Up yours," Sana responds. "Freezing my ass off."

From behind the drawn shades, I peer out through a corner of the living-room window into the two acres of high desert scrub that constitutes Wolverton's front yard. It is almost pitch-black, with a third-quarter moon casting just a bit of light over the grounds. "What's your location?"

"Your ten o'clock."

Now you might think that this would be the time for me to admit to Sana that, even with my binoculars, I cannot see in the dark, that I have this horrific eye condition, and that she is truly out there on her own. But for some reason, I fail to do this simple thing. Somewhere in my brain, I've rationalized that if the Russian takes the bait, he will come inside the house, and that Sana is in no real danger, so there is no need to admit my disability.

So, I lie. "Thank you. I register one FBI agent in the dirt next to the '78 Trans Am. Solid choice." Having been a mechanic, Wolverton has apparently collected cars over the years like some people do garden gnomes. The empty hulks of at least a dozen rusted-out autos pepper the front of the property, acting like pots for the natural vegetation to grow through.

I can hear Sana, prone in the dirt, shifting her body to get warm, and I picture her slowly pulling the collar of her jacket higher on her neck. "Yeah," she whispers, "I know you're just punishing me for not telling you everything before, but that's okay. Although it's not like you've been completely honest with me either."

"How's that?"

"You have night blindness," she says.

I swallow hard. "How do you figure?"

"My first clue was when you tried to stop me from running out of Atterbury's house after the first Russian, not the most instinctive reaction for a cop. But then I thought maybe you were just being extra careful. Then you didn't want to drive me back to the hotel after we had dinner with your dad the other night."

I don't speak for a moment. "That hardly seems conclusive. I hadn't slept in almost two days."

"Then my boss told me it was in your records jacket. It's why you retired."

I withdraw from the window and sit down on the crummy sofa next to it. "What else did he tell you?"

There is a long pause on the other end of the connection. "He said you had an operation in Moscow that went bad."

"Yeah, well we all have our days."

The memory of that night floods into my brain. I'm not sure how much time passes before Sana's voice floats back into my ears, and the image of an old friend dissipates.

"Earth to Beck. You still there?"

"I'm here. Sorry."

"Do you think this is actually going to work? I mean, it seems like a shot in the dark, no pun intended, for our friendly neighborhood SVR assassin to know what we know about Chuck Wolverton and show up here tonight."

"Why? He seems to have access to the same information we've

been looking at, with the exception of Atterbury's files. He got to Guy Pollack before we did, so I think we have to assume he'll identify Wolverton as a possible target."

"Then why is it just us out here? Why not pull in some of your officers?"

"Because I'm assuming our SVR man is listening to the police band. If he is, then he'll just hear normal radio traffic and know my guys are out running license plates and stopping random vehicles. We want him to think we're just stupid small-town cops."

"I'm not sure . . . wait one—"

I wait few seconds. "What is it?"

"Thought I heard something," Sana whispers. "I was going to say I doubt he thinks that. He knows you've already taken out his partner. He might be expecting a trap."

"It's our best play. I'm going to head out to the deck for a while, so keep an eye on me. My vision will be limited to what's about six feet in front of me."

"Oh wonderful," Sana whispers. "Thanks for the heads-up." A few seconds later, she adds, "Sorry about outing you like that. Who else knows, by the way?"

I can hear the concern in her voice. I'm a liability to her now. "Until a minute ago, I would have said no one. Now I'm not so sure."

As I head outside, I try not to let the thought of my secret being out clog my mind, transformed as I am now into Chuck Wolverton, wearing the old man's baggy clothes and fur hat and using his walker, the oxygen tube trailing from the nasal cannula looped around my ears and the ratty slippers exposing my otherwise bare feet. It is not my first time in a disguise—I actually went to school for this. When I emerge from the front door onto the long deck that runs the width of the house, backlit by the interior lights, I'm hoping my impersonation is sufficient to make a Russian hit man believe he is looking at a man with one foot in the grave.

I take a seat on one of the wicker rocking chairs. With my mouth under Wolverton's old hunting jacket, I whisper, "Goodness, it's a tad chilly out here."

"Again, up yours," comes the reply.

I sip hot coffee from Wolverton's mug and peer out into a black void. The night sky, away from city lights and so abundant with the stars and colors of the Milky Way, are just foggy dots in my eyes. The massive 15,000 units of vitamin A my doctor prescribes are slowing the progression of the disease but not enough to help me on a dark night.

I whisper again, hoping the microphone under the nice, fleece-lined earflap of my cap can pick up my voice. "Which direction would you approach from if you were him?"

"West side of the property," Sana answers after a moment. "It's more protected."

"Agreed. We need to let him in, so if he comes, let him come."

"The hell with that. I'm going to put him down."

"When we were out at Big Rocks, you were insistent on taking the guy alive. But you want to ice this one?"

There's a pause. "Yeah, that was before I knew what happened in 1957. I say we shoot first."

"No, Sana. He's not going to kill me right away. He needs to make sure I'm the right guy so he can torture me and make me pay for screwing up their operation and whatever else I might have done. And we need to know he's the right guy."

"Hey, he's out here in the middle of the night, he's the right guy. I will blast that asshole into oblivion."

I try not to laugh. "Okay, fair point, but it would be nice to find out why this is so damned important to Ivan."

"Ivan?"

"It's how we always referred to the Russians when I was there."

"Oh, the collective Ivan."

"Right."

We wait. Another half hour rolls by, and I'm freezing my nuts off. Just as I'm about to go back inside for more coffee, there is a sharp pop and the lights in the house go out. Now, everything is black. I'm assuming Sana has already toggled on her night vision goggles. I, however, have no such advantage.

"Heads-up. Power in the house is out," she whispers.

"Thanks for that," I say back. I attempt to look surprised, like Chuck Wolverton would be if his power had suddenly gone out, and rise from the rocker unsteadily. The breaker panel, I know, is located at the back of the house.

"That has to be our guy," Sana whispers. "Be careful."

I nod, knowing she can see me in the surrounding infrared light. Stooped over the walker, I shuffle to the front door and enter the house into complete darkness, my breath coming in short gulps, knowing that if the SVR man is inside, he will have the advantage over me. Bumping into everything, I silently swear for not having familiarized myself with the layout of the furniture.

I do my best to sound like a man rapidly approaching the century mark. "Goddamn fuses. Where the hell is that flashlight?" I stop and listen intently for a moment. A breath, a footfall, anything. But there is nothing.

Sana's voice explodes in my ear. "Beck!"

I throw off the oxygen hose and slippers and try to bolt for the front door, tripping twice.

"Fucker!" I hear Sana yell, followed by some gurgling sounds.

"I'm coming!" By the time I find the front door, I've managed to pull the small flashlight out of my pants and click it on. I leap over the deck railing, running barefoot over the hard ground toward the

Trans Am where Sana had been, barely able to make out anything in front of me. I catch something hard, full into my forehead, and go down like a bag of cement. The small amount of light coming from the flashlight a few feet away begins to ebb, and I can just see the shape of a man. Something sharp enters my neck, and then the man becomes an inkblot. My last thought is of Anatoly Rudenko.

It's late August and the Moscow Zoo is just a quick three-minute car ride from the U.S. embassy, where I am the acting foreign area officer. I'm not driving, though. I'm running. Over the past months, I have established more than twenty circuitous routes ranging from six to eight miles through the streets of the capital city, so that whenever I leave the embassy on foot the Federal Security Service watchers assigned to me will have trouble anticipating where I am going or how long I might be gone. I have made it practically impossible for the FSB to track me in the city's heavy rush-hour traffic, even with several teams in vehicles. Whenever they try putting other runners on me, I happily confound them with bursts of speed and dashes across busy intersections that result, on more than one occasion, in my pursuers getting clipped by traffic. I have created this predictable pattern of behavior for one reason. Not to improve my health, for I hate the monotony of running, but to allow me to occasionally meet with my contact from the Russian Army. As long as I am back within ninety minutes of leaving the embassy, the FSB has no reason to suspect I am up to no good.

My main job is to supply Russian political and military knowledge to my senior commanders and embassy officials, build relationships with my counterparts in the Red Army, and develop reports on military, diplomatic, and economic activities in the host nation that might impact the U.S. Army's strategic direction in the region.

Despite my fluency in German, I have a deeper love for the Russian language, especially its literature, and due mainly to a college professor who took me under his wing, I speak the consonant-heavy Slavic tongue as if I were born into it.

It is at a reception at the Spanish embassy that I first approach Colonel Anatoly Rudenko with a proposition. Rudenko, twice passed over for promotion to general and stuck in the Strategic Missile Forces, is a man on his way out. He is forty-nine at the time, stately, and the very picture of a Russian military commander in his uniform, and he reminds me of those old photos of Soviet May Day parades with Brezhnev surrounded by sycophant generals, where you pick out who is next in line for a top job by how close he is standing to the old man. Rudenko, much to his glee, has not been in any such photographs with Russia's current strongman president, Maxim Zhilin, and never will be. His problem is he isn't political, and he doesn't drink, a cardinal sin in the new (or old) Russia. For this heresy, he has been relegated to the Missile Command where he works for a man who believes he is still fighting the Cold War and who relishes testing the operational readiness of his charge, the land-based ICBMs that can destroy the planet.

When the party at the embassy begins winding down, I cozy up to Rudenko. "Anatoly, have you heard the one about the guy standing in line at the liquor store for so long, he finally says to his friend, 'Save my place, I'm going to shoot Zhilin.' He comes back two hours later and the friend asks, 'Did you get him?' 'No,' the guy says. 'The line there was even longer than the line here.'" The joke about the Russian president is an old one but still makes Rudenko laugh.

Since that night, the Russian colonel and I have met on thirteen separate occasions.

At this last meeting, Rudenko tells me that he might be blown. He tells me he thinks he is being followed after he leaves his office on some days and wants to know if anyone on my side could have done anything with the information he provided on Russian ICBM controls that can be traced back to him. I have provided him some rudimentary training in surveillance detection, but he has no real tradecraft. He is strictly military. But I'm inclined to trust the man's senses. We agree to lie low for a while to see if that will shake any formal curiosity.

Now, two months later, I receive a distress signal from Rudenko, his Russian Federation flag pin worn upside down on his lapel. The message means two things: Rudenko feels he is in imminent danger, and he will be at three different locations around the city on successive evenings. The first two potential meets aren't meets at all. They are simply designed to see if Rudenko is being followed. The third night is the actual meeting and it is scheduled to take place at the Siberian tiger exhibit at the Moscow Zoo. Rudenko will be on the bench to the east of the exhibit and holding a zoo map in his left hand if he believes he is clear of surveillance. If the map is in his right hand, Rudenko is signaling he has been interviewed regarding his activities of late. That will also mean his apartment is almost certainly bugged and that the FSB is watching his every move. If this is the case, the meet is off and I will know to activate a secondary protocol, one in which Rudenko will elude his watchers on the following Sunday and take one of three early morning trains to St. Petersburg, where we will smuggle him out of the country via Finland, an enormous feat that has only been accomplished once by the British during the Cold War.

I'm tense when I leave the embassy at 6:40 sharp and quickly realize my pace is too fast. I am running a seven-minute mile instead of my normal eight, and everything depends on perfect timing. After turning north onto Konyushkovskaya Street, I make a left on Krasnaya Presnya, which takes me just south of the zoo. I wonder if Rudenko is already there waiting, but knowing there are surely FSB agents doing their best to stay with me, I continue west for about a mile before turning left again on a side street where I dive into a grove of trees. Thirty seconds later my minders turn the corner, and as soon as they pass, I dart into the shadows of the strip mall across the street and then into the Adidas store, where I proceed quickly past the athletic gear and the shoppers into the back room, where I find a satchel waiting for me.

Inside the bag is my disguise for the evening. I kick off my running shoes, and two minutes later emerge from the store in the coveralls of a zoo custodian, along with a fake stomach suspended from my shoulders under the coveralls, a blond toupee and blond beard and mustache over my clean-shaven face. Underneath my work hat and eyeglasses, I look like a fat Muscovite in his fifties. I walk with a limp to the car that had been parked for me because I have placed just enough gravel in my shoe to make it painful every time my right foot hits the pavement. Once in the car, a battered tan Lada one of my CIA colleagues has lifted just an hour ago from the airport, I drive down the street and turn in to the zoo. I check my watch. It's 7:01 which means I have about twenty-five minutes until sundown and an hour until closing. The first deadline is of more immediate concern, as over the last few months I have started to realize I can't see too well in low light. I've also been getting headaches, a condition completely foreign to me, and some occasional eye pain as well.

To make matters worse, I am completely on my own tonight. In an effort to convince the FSB that no one is interested in Rudenko, all CIA personnel have been ordered to stay inside the embassy for the evening. My disguise is my only defense against Russian surveillance. With that caution firmly in my head, I get out of the car.

Once inside the zoo, I hobble to the employee entrance gate and put the key card in the lock. It opens immediately. Minutes later, I'm pushing a trash cart in the direction of the Siberian tiger exhibit, stopping occasionally to empty a waste bin, checking each time for the typically easy-to-spot FSB grunts. The only people I see are real visitors, and when I reach the large mammal island, there are still lots of people gawking over the railing to get a look at all the animals. But Rudenko is not on the bench where he is supposed to be. Nor is he in the crowd.

My window is closing. If Rudenko doesn't show by 7:30 it means either he couldn't shake surveillance or he has already been arrested. If he's been arrested, there is a chance the FSB already knows about me, but knowing Rudenko, that possibility is remote. I keep walking and emptying the trash, and then I hear it. A low hum, a buzz really. I glance upward in the direction of the noise. *Drone!*

It's a few hundred feet above the ground making a circular sweep of the area. Only about the size of a computer bag, the flying black spider has four arms, each with a propeller. I've seen them before. Both the military and intelligence organizations in the U.S. are using them extensively now, and I only heard this one because here in the center of the zoo, away from the noise of street traffic, it's relatively quiet. While there is a chance this one is simply the toy of a rich Russian kid, I doubt it.

Two FSB thugs suddenly brush past me, one on each side. Both have small earphones with a trailing cord behind their neck that I know are attached to radios. These boys are in a hurry, following in the general direction the drone is flying, and they are looking for Rudenko and whoever he is meeting with. I hear one of them say *"poka nichevo,"* essentially "nothing yet." They haven't spotted Rudenko.

The smart move is to abort. In fact, those are my orders. If I am caught, it will be an international incident. Worse, if Rudenko is caught there will be repercussions at the embassy as well as the death of an asset I have developed, fought to keep from CIA control, a man who has entrusted me to keep him safe.

With every tick of the clock, my field of vision begins narrowing by degree, objects and people in the distance becoming less clear. I have to find Rudenko now and get him out. In thirty minutes, if not earlier, the entire FSB will be out looking for me, and the noose around the city's neck will quickly tighten.

As I round the far end of the island, I see a blur in some bushes just over the fence in the camel pen. *Rudenko!* I limp quickly toward the fence and position my trash cart alongside it. "Anatoly," I whisper.

"Yes," comes the reply. "They are on me. You must go, Beck. Get out."

I bend down to tie my shoe and speak quickly in Russian. "No, my friend. We are going together." A quick glance of the darkening sky shows no drone, but I can hear it about a hundred yards to my left on the other side of the island, above the Siberian tigers. "When I tell you, fall over the fence into the cart and cover yourself with the trash."

I scan the people around the exhibits, many of them beginning to head to the exits. I see no one who looks to be FSB. "Now," I say.

Rudenko launches himself to the top of the fence, his waist bending over the six-foot metal railing, and somersaults into the trash bin, landing with a thud that echoes off the surrounding buildings. I am wheeling him away as Rudenko scrambles to get under the trash. For good measure, I stop at the next waste receptacle and empty it directly on top of Rudenko.

Just as we are rounding the corner, two other FSB men running the other way almost run into us. As they pass, one of the men speaks into his radio. "Where?"

I keep moving but only get another few feet before the man yells at me to stop. I don't. The man yells at me again. In Russian society, when an adult male voice yells *"Stoi,"* people freeze, and everyone in the vicinity does. I have no choice. Without even looking up, I hear the drone draw nearer. The two FSB agents come up behind me.

"You," one of them says. "Stop, please."

I stop and turn, sizing them up immediately. One is tall, maybe forty, in good shape. The other is closer to fifty and overweight, out of breath. "Me? Did you need something, sir?"

"Your cart," the taller man answers, holding up his official identification. "Step away, please. FSB."

I do as I am directed, limping two steps away from the cart. "Of course. Is there a problem?"

As soon as the taller agent bends down and begins to comb through the trash with his hand, I sweep my right leg high into the air and bring it crashing down onto the man's neck. The shorter, fatter agent's instinct is to go for the gun strapped to his shoulder, and that gives me all the time I need. I take one step forward and swing a straight arm in an arc, my rigid fingers catching the man in the throat. I can feel the tough cartilage of the windpipe buckle, the agent reaching instinctively for his throat with both hands, his knees buckling. I grab the Grach semiautomatic from his shoulder holster as he falls. Several people scream. Pivoting to my right, I see the taller man still bent over, half in the cart, Rudenko's arms around his neck. I kick him hard in the side of one knee and can hear the crack of his ligaments giving way. The man shrieks in agony, and as he pulls free of Rudenko's hands, he falls perfectly into my waiting arms, where his neck is snapped an instant later.

The drone practically falls out of the sky on top of me and Rudenko, hovering ten feet above, a mistake. I point the Grach at it and fire three rounds. It spins out of control and crashes into the restrooms next to us. Everyone in the area is running now, many of them screaming, "Police!"

I reach down into the cart and pull Rudenko out. "We have to run."

We do, moving in the opposite direction from the zoo entrance and into the trees on the north end. The perimeter wall is like a prison fence, about fifteen feet high, and the trees are too far from the fence to be of use; at least I am counting on our pursuers believing that. Earlier in the day, one of the zoo groundskeepers lowered a rope from a tree limb that extends down the wall.

"Up and over," I say to Rudenko. "There is a cab waiting across the street with its hood up. Wait at the top of the wall until you can drop undetected. When you hit the sidewalk, walk slowly to the cab. Don't run, and don't wait for me. I'll get back to the embassy another way."

We can hear the voices of men running through the grounds, frantically communicating via radio. I peer through the trees, but my eyes cannot focus in the distance and my peripheral vision is cloudy at the edges. Rudenko reaches into his pocket and extracts the tiny camera I had long ago given him. "It's all there," he says. "Everything you need. But I'm blown now. This is it for us. You have a leak somewhere, Beck."

I nod. "They will question you, Anatoly."

"I know. I will be okay."

I reach out and take his arm. "I can get you out. It will take time, but I can get you out."

Rudenko shakes his head. "No, my friend. But thank you."

Rudenko climbs the rope like a monkey. When he reaches the top of the wall, he pauses to check the darkening street below.

In my narrowing field of vision, I don't see the Russian creeping through the trees from the north. The crack of the bullet is loud, and it strikes Rudenko in the neck. He falls like a sack of cement at my feet, the rope with him.

The next round smacks into the tree next to my face. Dropping to my knees, I can barely make out a figure moving along the wall, fifty-plus yards away. I raise the Grach and fire seven times. When the man leaps back into the trees for cover, I take one last look at my brave friend and scramble up the rope.

Fifteen minutes later, I jog back up to the front gate of the American embassy. Since the Russians can't be sure who Rudenko had met with, my status in the country will not be affected, but at my own request, I fly to Stuttgart the next day for an eye exam. My military career is over.

# CHAPTER 13

I wake much like I had gone to sleep, my vision blurred and dark. Slowly, my brain begins analyzing the visual data, and the popcorn ceiling in Wolverton's living room takes shape. I'm lying on the couch, and my temples feel like abused bass drums in a marching band. My left eye and forehead are wet. Blood.

She must have gotten me back in the house. "Sana?" No answer. I swivel my legs over the edge of the couch. The sole dim light in the room emanates from an electronic screen in the kitchen. I stagger to my feet, holding a hand over the wound on my head, and move toward the glow.

"There he is. Welcome back, Sheriff." The voice that comes through the speaker has been electronically altered and sounds like one of those confidential sources on *Dateline*. These days you can download an app for that, so I'm not overly impressed or surprised. I set my hands on the kitchen island and peer into the iPad. What I see horrifies me. Sana is hanging upside down from a hook attached to what looks like a floor truss somewhere, maybe a basement, her bare arms tightly bound, a gag in her mouth, her clothes torn away with only her underwear covering her. She appears otherwise unharmed and is squirming against her restraints.

"Hey there, sleepyhead. How are you feeling?" the voice asks. I say nothing. "That's a nasty cut you have there, Sheriff. I think you're going to need stitches."

A man backs into the camera shot. He looks to be of average height, maybe a bit taller, it's hard to tell. He wears a black mask covering everything but his eyes and a long black leather jacket. "Let her go, Ivan," I say.

The masked man takes a seat in a folding chair next to Sana and laughs. He pushes on her torso, and her body swings freely back and forth. "*Ivan,* that's good, Sheriff. How very Cold War of you."

I unspool some paper towels from the stand nearby and plaster them to my forehead, wondering why he's using a voice disguiser when he's wearing a mask. "Nothing personal, Slick. If I don't know your name, I have to make one up. What should I call you?"

He laughs. "Ivan is fine."

"What do you want?"

"I think you know. We're both looking for the same man, if that helps."

"You assaulted and kidnapped an FBI agent. Now you're going to have a couple hundred feds out looking for you. Where you gonna hide?"

"I suppose the same place I am now, if it comes to that. Seems to be working okay so far. And if I sniff the foul odor of another federal agent in this county, bad things are going to happen." He pauses a moment. "Or I could release your precious colleague. All you have to do is deliver mine."

I think about his offer for a moment. Well, that's not actually true. I'm berating myself for screwing this thing up so badly. "I have to tell you, man, I think your agent is long gone, if he was ever here to begin with. Just release her, along with Michaela Edwards and we'll call it a day. You can leave my county and go back to Moscow or whatever hellhole you were hatched in. Just walk away."

The electronic voice chuckles again. He seems to think I'm very funny. "Very good, Sheriff. Yes, I have the other girl, too. Although you should give me a reward for taking her from that place. It's barbaric what they do to their women. The indoctrination, the servitude. All in the name of a God that doesn't exist."

I feel my knees giving way and scoot a bar stool under my butt. "Yeah, well, we call that religious freedom here. It's not perfect, but we find it preferable to living under a murderous tyrant."

The masked man gets up and moves out of the view of the camera. I pick up the sound of metal clanging in the background, and then I see terror in Sana's bulging eyes. "You still there, Ivan? Did I hurt your feelings?"

The Russian comes back into view, although it suddenly strikes me that the man could be American. There are people with a very particular set of skills, people like Liam Neeson, the Russians could have hired for this job. He is holding something in his hands I can't quite make out. Some kind of tool, and the sight of it makes Sana scream through her gag.

"I have to say, Sheriff, I've become very impressed with you. Especially how quickly you put the pieces together. And finding the FBI man's files, that was genius. We missed that."

I try to smile, but it hurts too much. "Well, don't beat yourself up, Ivan. You're just trained to kill people. Nobody expects you to do the heavy mental lifting."

Ivan sits down in the chair again and begins twirling the tool in his hand. It is shaped like a razor but bigger and with a thicker handle. Now I recognize it. It's a dermatome, the medical tool for peeling human skin the Vegas coroner showed us. My stomach turns. It's the same thing he used on Atterbury. "You also seem to be pretty good at killing, Sheriff. Or should I say *Lieutenant Colonel?*"

That's a surprise, although I should have anticipated that they would have researched me.

"Oh, yes, I know who you are, Lieutenant Colonel Porter Beck. My bad luck to get someone with your background and skills running the police out here."

I chuckle. "Ivan, your bad luck hasn't even started. You lay another hand on her and I'll never stop hunting you. You'll never get a good night's sleep again. So why don't you just let the women go?"

"Like you hunted me last night? When you stumbled out of that house and nearly killed yourself on that tree branch? You know, I stood over you after you went down, Sheriff, and I gave serious thought to putting a bullet in your head."

My jaw tightens. "Why didn't you?"

"Because you have my illegal, obviously. Everything is just a lot easier if you hand him over to me."

"A lot easier for you maybe. I'm pretty sure I would have a hard time living with that decision."

Ivan rises from his chair and holds the dermatome next to Sana's exposed thigh. Her body jerks, but she's strung up like a piece of raw meat. "Why? What is he to you? A spy in your country. A traitor in mine. He's not American, not one of you. Why would you lose any sleep over that?"

"Well, there's the whole problem with you already having killed a couple of people here."

"Old men, both of them," says Ivan. "What is it you say here,

Sheriff? You have to break a few eggs to make an omelet?" He presses the skinning tool hard into Sana's thigh and she shrieks.

I know I have to buy her time. "I didn't say no, Ivan. Let's keep talking." When the masked man sits down again, I add, "You place a pretty low value on human life."

"Don't sound so somber, Sheriff. You're going to come through this okay if you just do as I ask. No one else needs to die."

Maybe he's right. I've worked with spooks before, and most of the time they can be counted on to stick to a deal. Most of the time. "So, how do we do this? I mean, if I can identify your illegal, how do we handle this?"

"That's the spirit." Even electronically altered, the voice sounds jovial. "I'll call you in twelve hours. That's all the time I can give you, I'm afraid. If you can't give him to me by then, I'll kill the women. Of course, I will peel every inch of skin from them first."

I pound the kitchen counter. "How do I know Michaela is still alive? Let me see her."

"No. Call you in twelve hours, Sheriff." Ivan rises and moves toward the camera.

"Wait," I yell, before he can disconnect us. "Why is he so important to you after all this time?"

There is no response, and all I can do is wait. "He's a traitor," the Russian finally replies.

"It's more personal than that, though, isn't it?"

Ivan backs up a few feet, so I can see his masked face. "Isn't it always, Sheriff? By the way, speaking of personal things, I believe I went out for a run with you one night in Moscow several years ago."

My brow furrows. "Don't tell me you were one of those fat FSB guys in the hideous track suits that used to follow me around."

"No, Colonel," he replies, the voice deadly serious now. "This was a night in late August. I was the one who shot that other traitor, Rudenko, as he was climbing the wall at the zoo. That was a great shot, don't you think?"

I feel rage rising in my chest. "Doesn't ring any bells for me, Ivan. Talk to you in twelve."

# CHAPTER 14

"You need stitches," Tuffy tells me, applying a butterfly bandage to top of my forehead. "And you probably have a concussion. You shouldn't have driven here." She dabs carefully at the blood in my hair with some gauze.

After my encounter with the Russian and seeing Sana being stretched from a rope with a human potato peeler against her bare skin, I somehow managed to get to my truck in the dim early morning light and drive to the station.

Tuffy places some pills in my hand, and I swallow them, leaning back in my desk chair. "Should help with your headache," she says.

"Nice gash, Columbo," Brinley says from the doorway.

Tuffy leaves with her first aid supplies, and Brinley sits down on the desk. She carefully reaches toward my face as if she wants to adjust the bandage and then ruthlessly thumps the laceration hard with her finger. I rock back and howl.

"Are you a moron?" she yells.

I nod slowly and painfully. "I believe the jury has returned with a guilty verdict on that count."

"I could have been there with you. I could have been in a tree two hundred yards away and killed the bastard."

I look at her, the woman who has grown from a frightened feral child into the Annie Oakley of the modern West. "Or, he could have killed you, Brin. I didn't want to take that risk."

Brinley's expression softens, the corners of her mouth lifting. She gets up and shuts the door to the office, then returns to her seat on the corner of the desk. "I really appreciate your concern for my safety," she whispers, "but you can't see in the dark, dumb fuck. I can."

*Jesus, who else knows?* I get to my feet and she has to steady me. "What did you find?"

"He blew the breaker box on the back of the house with a remote charge. After that, who knows. How he sneaks up on her is a mystery. Even to get close enough to dart her like he did you, it's like he's invisible. The ground out there is covered with patches of snow and hard, thorny vegetation. You can hear every footfall. The two of you would make a cute couple—you're blind and she's deaf, apparently."

My eyes close. "Any tracks?"

"Same one we found near Michaela's bike. So, we know it's the same guy. And he didn't make any attempt to hide them this time."

"He's very good, Brin. Better than me, obviously. I don't want you caught in the cross fire. You should go take that gig in L.A."

She gazes up at me, wounded. "I can help, Porter. You know that."

I straighten. "I mean it. Go. You don't work here."

"I'm not leaving you," she says with a shake of her head.

"Fine. I'll put in you in protective custody in one of my cells. You can help Tuffy go through those files. But you will be locked up." I know that last part will do the trick. Brinley has been locked up before, by her asshole father, and the thought of confinement of any kind is the only thing I know that terrifies her.

She backs slowly toward the door, her hands squeezed into fists. "He's going to fucking kill you!" she yells. "You know that, don't you?"

"Get out of here!" I yell back, the words banging off the walls of my brain. I don't like talking to her this way, but I know she won't go unless I get her good and pissed. Following her into the outer office, I see everyone's eyes on us.

Brinley marches toward the station's entrance. "I'll send you my bill," she announces, flipping me the bird on the way out. She doesn't look back.

So, let's look at the scoreboard. Two men are dead on my watch, two women taken. I have a concussion, my third, and I have less than twelve hours to produce the illegal for Ivan. And the day is just getting started. I walk to the center of the office, my face flushed with heat. No one wants to speak first, so I have to do it. "Where are we, people?"

Tuffy, Wardell, and Pete all look at each other nervously. From his desk, Pete slowly raises his hand, a pen dangling from his fingers. "Umm . . . I think Chuck Wolverton is the illegal, Sheriff."

I stare at him for a long moment. "Tell me."

Pete swivels in his chair, nodding toward his computer screen. "He first shows up here in '61. We knew that. Goes to work at the Meteor Mine. But I can't find diddly on him before that. I mean the guy does not exist. I've checked NCIC, military, and every other database I could think of. Social Security says they didn't issue him a number until 1962."

"That wasn't uncommon back then," Tuffy adds. "A lot of employers didn't require a social back then."

Pete nods. "That's true, but it is interesting that there is no record of him anywhere before '61. I mean the guy does not exist. No birth record. Nothing."

Wardell stands. "We should bring him in. Question him. Interrogate the son of a bitch."

"Maybe," I say.

Wardell scowls, his legendary lack of patience already at an end. "Where do you have him stashed? Pete and I will go get him."

In my brain fog, I consider the options for a minute. "He's safe. Let's leave him be for now. He's not going anywhere. The way this guy has been ahead of us, I don't want to risk more people getting killed right now."

Wardell's cracked lips draw back in a snarl. "You should have brought us in on this thing you were running last night with that FBI lady friend of yours. Now this Russian has another hostage. You're not even going to tell us where you have Wolverton? What if something happens to you?"

My arms cross my chest. "If something happens to me, Wardell, I guess you'll be in charge and you can do any damn thing you want. For now, I need you guys back out on the roads. Tuffy, you stay here and man the fort. I'll go talk to Wolverton and see what I can find out."

Pete rises from his chair. "I'm happy to come along, Sheriff. I did a lot of interviews in my time as an MP."

"I'll manage, Pete, but thanks. You guys get back out there and start knocking on doors. This guy has Michaela and Agent Locke both. He's keeping them somewhere close. Any house you don't know. Check the abandoned ones first. God knows there are plenty of those up here. Start poking around. Look for places with basements. You guys take Caliente and Panaca. I'll have Arshal and the Twin Peaks do Pioche. Anything that looks hinky, call it in. Nobody else is dying in our county, got it?"

———

Forty minutes later, I pull up at the home of Amon Jessup on the FLDS compound in Mill Valley. Arshal is waiting for me.

"How's he doing?" I ask, getting out of the truck.

"Which one, in particular?" the old deputy answers. "Wolverton, or my brother the mighty prophet?"

"Wolverton."

Arshal laughs. "He tried escaping a couple times during the night. Practically had to tie him down at one point." He points at my head. "Lost a fight with a tree branch, did ya?"

I fill him in on what happened during the night. Then one of Amon's four wives leads us into the massive living area where Amon and Clem Edwards are waiting, along with Chuck Wolverton. I wonder what I'm going to do if Pete is right and Wolverton turns out to be the illegal from the 1950s.

"Damn it, Sheriff," Wolverton groans loudly. "You can't keep me here. I know my rights, and while these people have been good about feeding me, they don't have any TV, let alone pay-per-view."

"I'm sorry for the inconvenience, Mr. Wolverton," I say, taking a seat in a high-backed leather chair. "It won't be long now."

"You haven't found Michaela then?" Clem asks.

I bring my hands together. "Not yet, Clem. We're starting house-to-house searches right now. If she's in the county, we will find her." There is no point in telling them that Michaela's disappearance is tied to the hunt for a Russian spy.

Amon puts a hand on the younger man's shoulder, and I ask them both to give me and Arshal a few minutes with Wolverton. After they leave the room, I walk over and sit down by the old man, the sound of his oxygen concentrator humming in the background.

"Chuck, I need to ask you some questions about your past."

Wolverton is bone-thin, a thick gray stubble covering his weathered cheeks. "The hell do you mean, Sheriff? What's so danged important about my past? I'm . . . nobody."

It was how he said it. Nobody. With a little crack in his voice.

"Chuck, someone came out to your place to kill you last night. That someone has already kidnapped Clem's wife and is holding an FBI agent, and it all seems to be tied to you. So, I'm thinking you're . . . *somebody*. Why don't you tell me who?"

The grizzled miner turns away. "I got no idea why someone would do those things. I got no enemies."

"What did you do before coming to Lincoln County, Chuck?"

Wolverton doesn't meet my gaze. His tired eyes dart around the room as if trying to find a way out. "Nothin', I was a kid."

"From where?" Arshal asks. "Where did you spring from, Chuck?"

Wolverton cackles. "Nowhere special, I can tell you that." The old man nervously adjusts the tubing that keeps slipping out his nose.

I reach over and steady the cannula in his shaking hands. "We can't find a birth record on you, Chuck. As a matter of fact, we can't find any record of a Chuck Wolverton anywhere. I really need to know the truth here, and I need to know now."

Wolverton's head twitches back and forth until Arshal nudges him in the leg with his big boot. "Answer the man's question."

Arshal is an imposing figure in any room, and I know from experience that sometimes a little intimidation can go a long way. Eventually, Wolverton's head cranes in my direction.

"Illinois. I'm from Illinois originally."

I nod. "And?"

"I worked on cars through high school. Only thing I was ever good at, really. Only thing I wanted to do. Then in '51 I got drafted to go to Korea."

The corners of my mouth turn downward in dejection. I know what is coming. Wolverton is not the illegal.

"Was getting ready to go to basic and realized I just couldn't do it. Didn't want to kill no one. Had seen all those boys that was killed over in Europe and the Pacific a few years earlier, or worse, coming home all mangled and without their limbs." The old man fights back the tears now and lowers his head, his already scattered breaths quickening. "I just didn't see no reason to go halfway across the world to fight for some idea some people thought was important that I didn't."

Arshal and I exchange glances. "Where did you go, Chuck?"

Wolverton looks up toward the ceiling, searching his memory. "Oh, thought about running to Canada. Some guys were doing that. Vietnam wasn't the first time that happened. But it's too cold up there, so I wandered around, picking up odd jobs under different names at farms and garages. Did a lot of field labor in the South for a few years. Warm down there." A tiny smile tugs at his lips. "Did that for, oh, nine or ten years before I saw an ad for miners out in Nevada. That's how I got here. Just made up the name, like I did all the others."

Arshal looks down at him. "Chuck, what is your real name?"

Wolverton looks up through one eye at the towering deputy. "Arnold Fletcher, sir, though it sounds funny when I hear it now. Haven't said those words out loud in almost seventy years. You going to turn me over to the Army?"

I place a gentle hand on Wolverton's arm. "Chuck, do you have anything that can substantiate what you're telling us? Anything that can prove you are actually Arnold Fletcher from Illinois who was drafted in 1951?"

Wolverton's head bobs slowly, his eyes narrowing. "Think I do. I believe I have my actual birth certificate down at the house." He looks over at me. "I'm sure the Army has my draft notice. They don't forget deserters, Sheriff."

I nod. "Okay, Chuck. I don't think we need to involve the government. Could I ask you just to sit tight here awhile longer?" I stand and turn to Arshal. "Deputy Jessup is going to hang around if that's okay."

Arshal rolls his eyes. After we leave the house, Arshal remarks on what happened at Wolverton's. "So, your Russian probably has good reason to think that cranky old miner is his spy."

"Yep, and we're going to keep him thinking that for now. Might keep him from going after anyone else."

Arshal snickers. "Who's left?"

I get back in the truck. "No one except us knows Wolverton is out here, Arshal. Let's keep it that way. Have Amon keep men at the front gate. Anybody trying to get onto this compound that you don't know . . ."

My deputy nods. "Yeah, no shortage of guns out here. What are you going to do?"

I drape my arms over the steering wheel and stare out through the windshield. "Ivan has a couple of bargaining chips right now. I'm going to see if I can find one."

He points a gnarled finger at me. "Keep your head down, young buck."

I close the driver's door and start to back up, but then something occurs to me. "Hey, Arshal, when you called me a few days ago about those graves down in Rachel, didn't you say that was the second time they had been disturbed?"

The big deputy twirls his gray mustache to trigger his memory. "Ayup. Someone dug them up about three years ago. That's why there was nothing in there this time. Probably some stupid kids."

I look at my watch and pray that isn't the case.

# THE PAST

The air was unusually calm over Yucca Dry Lake, a perfect day to land an airplane carrying an XW-25 warhead. As Georgiy watched the C-124 Globemaster circle the airstrip, his stomach rumbled like a volcano. On the seat next to him, Dr. Ellison grinned like a silly schoolboy. "Here she comes, Freddie. If we're lucky with the wind, this time tomorrow we'll be measuring plutonium dispersal."

Georgiy had the sudden urge to slam the scientist's head through the passenger window. He was as much a devil as William, wanting nothing more than to see a large area of land poisoned. In William's case, and his masters in Moscow as well, that desire included people, but even Ellison seemed to be fine with unleashing the deadly radioactive element in the open air, not knowing or caring how far it might travel and who it might ultimately kill.

Once the warhead was loaded onto the truck, Georgiy turned his vehicle onto the road and followed.

"Let's pray the weather holds," Ellison said. "Let's pray for that."

Part of Georgiy was doing just that. He could ignore his duty and let the test proceed as planned. But if the wind came up and the test was delayed, he would have to act. Or he would have to run.

Ellison noted Georgiy's hands gripped around the steering wheel. "Easy, son, it's just a nuclear warhead. Don't go getting all white-knuckled on me."

When they returned to CP-1, the control point for all nuclear tests at the site, Ellison set about the final preparations with the engineers from the Sandia National Laboratories in New Mexico.

The waiting wore on the man, and Georgiy could smell the alcohol on his breath. Around midday, Georgiy headed over to Area 13 as part of his scheduled patrol and check-in with the guards under his command. The animal cages were now occupied, and many of them were in the process of receiving their last supper, a thought that sickened Georgiy. He got out and walked over to them. The rats he didn't care about. He had seen enough rats during the war to wish them all dead. The nine burros appeared sad but oblivious to their coming fate. Then came the dogs, a hundred or more of them, beagles for some reason, all black, brown, and white. Why beagles had drawn the short straw in the dog lottery, he could not fathom. They yelped at him, some climbing the walls of their cages in a plea for a last-minute pardon. Last, Georgiy walked over to the where the sheep were being kept, ten of them resting under the shade of their pens, unwitting participants in a deadly experiment. He imagined their deaths, cooking from the inside and bleeding from every orifice. Madness.

When he finally arrived back at CP-1, it was 6:00 P.M. Just over twelve hours to detonation. The air wasn't exactly calm, and neither was Ellison, who was pacing back and forth from panel to panel and dial to dial watching the wind readings from north of the test site.

"Damn it!" Ellison's voice boomed from his large chest, pipe smoke puffing from between his lips like steam from a train. "It's picking up, and it's out of the north now."

"Thirteen knots," another man said from his chair as he watched the needle move on the dial. "Not good for us."

From the papers he had accessed and photographed over the weeks, Georgiy knew anything more than a ten-knot wind would effectively kill the shot, even if it was blowing east toward Utah. But a wind blowing south from the test site was an automatic kiss of death to any planned detonation. By 9:00 P.M. the decision would be made.

Arms folded across his chest and leaning against the entry door, Georgiy watched as Ellison sat down at his desk in a huff. The scientist badly wanted this monkey off his back. A phone rang. One of the technicians held up the receiver and nodded to his boss. Ellison got up and grabbed it. "Dr. Ellison," he said gruffly. He listened for a moment, and Georgiy could see the man's face contort. He looked at Georgiy and rolled his eyes. "That's outrageous," he said, his voice rising. "We're twelve hours away, and Sergeant Meyer is running the security for this operation. I cannot spare him for some silly inquiry right now."

The alarms sounded in Georgiy's head as Ellison continued to argue. It was the CIA on the other end of the line, he was certain. They wanted to interview him—interrogate him—about the U-2. A cold current of terror ran through his veins. He would be found out, imprisoned for espionage.

"Look, I'm telling you, sir. This man has passed every security review required of him. He has been here for almost two years. You can speak to him after the test has been conducted, and if you have a problem with that, you can call Dr. Teller." Ellison slammed the phone down. "Idiot," he said to Georgiy with a wink. "You're the only guy from Delta they haven't spoken to yet, so as soon as this is over, you'll have to go down to Mercury and strap on their stupid lie detector. Sorry, Freddie. The witch hunt continues."

Georgiy waved a hand. "Not a problem, Doctor." But it was. He was fucked three ways from Sunday now. If the shot went as scheduled, there would be no opportunity to steal the warhead. There simply wouldn't be enough time, and he still didn't have the combination that would get him inside Building 11. If it was delayed, he would have to get the combination and try getting it out of the building and off the test site, which was bound to get him killed. If he somehow avoided that, he would end up being grilled by the CIA about how the Russians found out about the U-2 and dragged to the gallows. He was going to live a very short life, of that much he was certain.

From the small control room, they waited, watching the minutes tick by and checking their gauges and dials. At 9:00 P.M., the shot was officially postponed. Georgiy saw Ellison's shoulders slump. He would have to wait at least another day. Until his God changed the wind.

An hour later, after releasing the engineers and technicians at CP-1 for the evening, he turned to Georgiy. "I need to eat. Walk me over to the cafeteria?"

Georgiy swallowed the knot that had been forming in his throat. "Sure thing." And just like that, everything had been decided for him. He would steal the warhead tonight. Or die trying.

The cafeteria at the NTS Control Point was nothing like the one at Camp Mercury. Smaller, and without the turnstiles that required a silver dollar, its primary use was to fill the bellies of the arming and firing parties who resided at CP-1 in the days leading up to a shot. The food, however, was just as good, and the weary scientist grabbed up a double order of pot roast and some mashed potatoes. Georgiy, too nervous to eat, got two cups of coffee, one for him and one for Ellison.

"You're not hungry?" Ellison asked, as the man he knew as Freddie sat down at the table.

Hungry? Georgiy couldn't remember when he last felt like eating. "I had something earlier." He placed a cup of coffee on Ellison's tray and watched the man pull it down under the table where he added some whisky to it from his flask. He quickly took a few sips.

"You look tense, Freddie. I hope it's not that silly interview the spy guys want to do."

Georgiy paused a moment, feigning a look of uncertainty. "Actually, sir, it's something else. I was hoping I could . . . well, I would like it very much if . . ."

Ellison's stuffed his mouth with a forkful of meat. "Just spit it out, son. Whatever it is won't be as disappointing as this shot delay, I can assure you."

Georgiy looked down at the table. "I want to ask Kitty to marry me, and I was hoping you would give me your blessing." He loved the sound of those words and wished more than anything they could be true. But he needed Ellison's help right now, and he was certain this was the way to get it.

The older man extended his hand. "Freddie, this is very great news." They shook hands. "When are you planning on proposing?"

"As soon as the test is over, I think." He produced a small box from his jacket pocket and opened it on the table. "Think she'll like it, sir? It's all I could afford."

Ellison stared down at the ring with the small diamond setting. "I think she's going to be over the moon." He reached out and grabbed Georgiy's upper arm. "This is the best news, Freddie. You certainly have my blessing."

As Ellison finished off his meal, he became pensive. "We're going to have to get you a better job out here, Freddie. If you're going to be taking care of Kitty, you'll need something with a better salary."

If only that was my universe, he thought, his hands trembling beneath the table. "That would be fascinating, Dr. Ellison."

Project 57's director leaned forward on his elbows, cradling his bearded chin in his hands. "Let me tell you just how fascinating."

Georgiy listened intently as Ellison, his tongue already loosened by the whiskey, related what his team projected would happen once his device was detonated. Now he knew why William and Moscow were so intent on going forward with their plan.

"Incredible," Georgiy said. "You know, I would really love to see the warhead up close. Do you think since we're delayed anyway, we could take a quick look at it?"

Ellison grinned, and Georgiy could tell the whisky was already working its magic. "What the hell, why not? I have clearance. You have clearance. Let's go."

"Now?"

The big man winked and held up his flask. "Maybe another coffee first."

Georgiy rose from his chair. "I'll get it." At the coffee counter, before adding cream and sugar, he looked around the mostly empty dining room to be sure no one was watching and then placed six drops of the liquid William had provided in Ellison's cup. He checked his watch. Thirty to forty minutes, William had said. No more.

As the scientist finished his second cup, Georgiy said, "I just need to make a call before we go. Check in with my guys."

Ellison grinned. "Well, make it quick, young man. Your future awaits."

A few seconds later, Georgiy entered the phone booth by the cafeteria front door and picked up the receiver. A moment later, a switchboard operator at the test site answered. "Number please?" Georgiy gave her the exchange and number. He knew full well that his call was probably being monitored. In fact, the small sign in the phone booth indicated as much. Half a minute later, he heard a ring and a woman answered. "Hello?"

"Hi, Susan? It's Freddie. I'm sorry to call so late."

"Oh, hey Freddie. Don't apologize. I'm still up. I know you needed those measurements for the deck. Are you ready?"

She sounded like she was older, middle-aged perhaps. "Yes, please. Go ahead."

"It's 95 by 88 by 38. Do you have that?"

He memorized the numbers instantly, subtracting one from each digit as he had been trained. That meant the combination was 847727. "Yep, got it. Thanks very much. Anything else?" William had indicated there would be further instructions.

"Just that Tom and I really liked meeting Kitty the other night. She's a wonderful girl. We know you're busy out there, so we'll keep tabs on her for you."

Georgiy felt his chest tighten and his jaw go rigid. The message was clear. We have the girl. "Oh," he said. "I'm so glad you like her. I'll see you soon." He hung up.

Georgiy drove faster than he would have liked, but with Ellison already dozing in the other seat, he was worried the man would change his mind about showing him the warhead. Even with the combination to the electronic lock, he needed a legitimate reason to be inside the storage facility, and Ellison was the best possible reason.

Building 11 was surrounded, mostly by fence, two separate rows of chain-link and razor wire, but a full complement of guards was there as well. Outside of a very small group of people, no one at the site even knew there was going to be a test. There were Army guards at the front gate and the two posted in a jeep next to the building. Georgiy's pulse quickened at the sight of the .30 caliber machine gun mounted just behind the front seat of the jeep.

The Army corporal checking Ellison's credentials seemed surprised. "Sir, we were notified the project has been delayed. Can I ask what you're doing here?"

Ellison yawned. "It's my experiment, Corporal. My warhead. There are some final checklist items I need to run through. Shouldn't take long." He turned and winked at Georgiy. A minute later, they were waved through the gate. Georgiy heard the guard radio that Dr. Ellison was coming in.

Parking, Georgiy took a quick look at his wristwatch—11:25 P.M. Twenty-six minutes since he had administered the drug. He and Ellison got out of the truck and Georgiy addressed the lanky FSI guard at the entrance door. "Hey, Finn. Dr. Ellison has some final checks he needs to do."

Finn stepped away from the door. "This man is going to be my son-in-law," Ellison told him.

"No kidding? Well congrats to both of you," Finn replied.

Georgiy watched as Ellison entered six digits into the lock. 8–4–7–7–2–7. William's source was good. The lock made an audible click, and Ellison opened the door and went in. Georgiy followed but held the door for a moment. "He's pretty hammered," he murmured to Finn. "It's amazing the guy can still operate."

Finn nodded. "Smells like a still."

As the door closed behind him, Georgiy realized for the first time that it was really going to happen. He was inside the storage facility not twenty feet from a nuclear warhead. Under the intense fluorescent lighting that lined the ceiling, the XW-25 lay at a forty-five-degree angle off the concrete floor, strapped to a large four-wheeled yellow hand truck that easily supported its cargo. It was Georgiy's first time in the secret building, and he was disappointed that there wasn't more to it. It wasn't like CP-1 with its instruments and monitors. It was essentially a huge tool shed, with rows of cabinets along the walls and work tables with drills and pneumatic devices and hoses. Normally, he knew, this is where the device would be assembled and armed prior to a scheduled shot. For Project 57, that was unnecessary. The engineers in

New Mexico had simply removed the warhead from its existing bomb casing. It was ready to go.

"Look at it, Freddie. Come closer. It's spectacular, isn't it."

Georgiy approached the warhead slowly. When he had agreed to become an illegal and work in the American nuclear program, he believed he would be accessing intelligence that would help stabilize the world and reduce the chances of war. But staring down at this instrument of destruction, his heart sank. *How stupid to believe such things.* He was trapped in a game played by madmen, and his only possible way out was to do his duty.

Ellison looked over at his young charge, sensing his sadness. "I was hoping for a little more enthusiasm, Freddie. This is the future of physics."

Georgiy looked up at him. Ellison's face was damp with sweat and flushed. "Are you all right, Doctor?"

Ellison's eyes clamped shut, his brow suddenly knitted together. "Yes, touch of heartburn from the pot roast, I think."

Moving quickly around the warhead, Georgiy caught the man just as he grabbed his chest and collapsed. Ellison's face contorted and his mouth opened. "Oh no," he groaned. Georgiy laid him gently on the floor and checked for a pulse. It felt like machine gun fire.

"Easy, Doctor."

"My chest," Ellison croaked.

Georgiy raced to the door. "Finn!" he yelled, loud enough for the Army guards in the jeep to hear. "I think Dr. Ellison is having a heart attack. We need to get him to the hospital."

Everyone came running. One of the soldiers said they needed an ambulance. "Too far away!" Georgiy yelled. "You need to transport him. Now."

The guards, both privates, both younger than Georgiy, gazed at each other in complete confusion. "Can we do that?" one asked. "Are we allowed to do that?"

"Back your vehicle up to the door," Georgiy commanded him.

"You should take him," the other private said. "In your truck. We're posted here. We can't leave."

Georgiy seized the man by the collar of his coat. "Listen to me, Private. You can call another unit to take your place. I will wait here for them. Right now, you are transporting Dr. Ellison to the hospital in your jeep, which has a back seat. Finn here will go with you. Call the gate guards and let them know."

"Me?" Finn said apprehensively.

"You. Building 11 security is our team's responsibility now. I'm the head of the team. Go with them, Finn. I'll meet you at the hospital as soon as I get somebody to cover me here."

"We'll take his arms," Georgiy said to the men. "You guys get his legs." He looked down at Ellison. "Hang on, Doctor, you'll be at the hospital in no time."

They lifted him, and it took all four to carry the big man. "Kitty," Ellison said, grabbing Georgiy's hand as they laid him in the back of the jeep.

"I'll let her know," Georgiy said. "You'll be okay. I'll see you at the hospital."

As the jeep shot forward, Georgiy knew its headlights were blinding the two guards at the front gate a hundred yards away. He moved to the door, his index finger frozen above the numerical buttons on the lock. If he reentered the storage facility, he was committed to taking the warhead. If he didn't, someone else might. William had a plan B, a backup. Of course he did. Someone else had the combination in case Georgiy lost his nerve. He entered the code. *Click.*

"Sixty seconds, Georgiy," he said out loud. "You have sixty seconds." He ran to the bomb.

In less than thirty, he was out of Building 11 with the warhead at the side of his vehicle. Georgiy cursed himself for not backing the truck in, for now he would be in plain sight of the gate guards if they turned his way. But if he was going to be caught, it really didn't matter how. He would not let them take him. The capsule William had given him was in his pocket. All he had to do was place it between his teeth and bite down.

Bending down and pressing upward with his knees, Georgiy hoisted the warhead into his arms, all 218 pounds. His hands were slippery, though, and the bottom of the device slammed into the truck's side panel. The noise seemed deafening to Georgiy, but he didn't dare stop to look toward the gate. He found a better handhold and rolled it up to his chest. If he dropped it now, the game was up, so he braced his legs against the side of the truck and allowed the weight of the warhead to roll his upper body up over the side and into the bed, his back screaming the entire way.

Georgiy released the package and collapsed into the dirt. There were no lights streaming his way from the front gate, but he could hear the radio chatter, so he stumbled to his feet and pushed the hand truck to the side of the building and into the shadows where it could not be seen. Racing back to the truck, he removed a blanket from the bed and covered the warhead, sliding it lengthwise along the tailgate.

"Hey! You there." Georgiy's blood ran cold. Hearing the soldier's boots slapping the pavement at a run, he turned, expecting to see a rifle in his face. Instead, it was the sergeant who had checked Ellison's badge at the gate, but there was no rifle.

"What the hell happened?" he yelled.

"Hell if I know," Georgiy replied, gasping. "He was doing some final checks, and then he just grabbed his chest."

"Holy Christ," said the sergeant. "He's the guy in charge, right?"

Georgiy nodded. "He is."

"We got another jeep on the way. You're staying, right?"

"No," Georgiy said. "I have to rotate to Area 13 and relieve one of the guys up there. One of my men should be down here in the next hour."

"Shit," the guard said. "This is not procedure."

From his own experience in the Army, Georgiy knew that soldiers just want direction. They are not comfortable with and don't expect to be making decisions. "Just lock the gate, Sergeant. My guy should be here shortly. Nobody comes in until then. Are we clear?"

Absent any other authority and the will to wake his commander up in the middle of the night, the man nodded. "Clear." A minute later, Georgiy passed the front gate, a live nuclear warhead six feet behind him.

# CHAPTER 15

I believe in hunches. I think they're just the dots in your brain that aren't fully connected yet. As I drive out of the Mill Valley compound, my hunch tells me the only way to satisfy the man holding Michaela Edwards and Sana might be with something of equal value, and since I don't have the illegal or have a clue who he might be, I call my new buddy, X-Files. The conversation lasts the full thirty-minute ride back to the office.

When I arrive, Tuffy is manning the station solo. I pull a chair up next to her and check my watch again. I have eight hours to deliver somebody to Ivan. "Whatcha got, Tuff?"

She stares at me blankly.

"Okay," I say, "let's go back through it again."

"It? There isn't anyone else to look at, Beck. We've checked everyone in this county."

I nod. "Right. Maybe we should look at the people who were there at the time."

Tuffy seems baffled. "Where?"

"The NTS. The test site. We now know that in the early morning hours of April third, 1957, four Russians were found dead in the desert outside of Las Vegas, one of them a test site employee."

My senior investigator grabs at her curly temples. "Excuse me? How do we know that?"

"Agent Locke. It's all still classified, so you don't know any of this. I didn't know until yesterday. So, who was the employee they found in the desert?"

"Why do we care, if he's dead?"

I lift a shoulder in a half shrug. "Sometimes dead people can tell you things."

Tuffy pulls a thick sheaf of paper off her inbox and begins scrolling through it. "From Atterbury's files," she says. "Everyone who worked there from 1955 to 1958. Do we have a name?"

I think back to the conversation I had with Sana, my verbal memory coming fully online. "Meyer. Frederick Meyer."

Tuffy scrolls through the alphabetical listing. "Yep, there's a Frederick Meyer here. Employed by Federal Services Incorporated as a security guard, October 1955 through April third"—she looks up at me—"1957."

"Anything else?"

Tuffy pops up from her desk. "Follow me. Maybe Atterbury had a file on him." We walk into the adjacent detention facility where Atterbury's boxes and filing cabinets are still taking up a cell. Tuffy goes to one of the cabinets. "He had test site employees in here. None of these are actual personnel files. Mostly just summaries of work histories and the occasional photo. Like he had compiled them himself." She fingers through the third drawer. "Nope, no Meyer here. That's strange."

"No," I say. "That makes sense. He was Russian. The Feds would have erased any record of him." A memory, vague and unformed, floats behind my eyes, and I can't grab it just yet.

We walk back into the main station and my office. "What's this?" I ask, picking a file off my desk.

"Shooting board. It's all there. I took the liberty of running it by our two civilian members. They signed off. Pete's good for active duty again, officially. Just needs your signature."

This is good news. I've been using Pete for more than the normal desk duty required when an officer is out on administrative leave until being cleared by the shooting review board, which consists of me and two of our five county commissioners. I take a cursory look at the photos taken at Big Rocks where Pete shot the other Russian.

"Pretty good shot," Tuffy says. "He should be our main sniper, unless you can convince Brinley to come on full time."

I nod, my eyes now glued to one photo, taken from where Pete was standing at the time of the shot and looking down to where the Russian lay in a dirt clearing two hundred or so yards downhill.

"What?" Tuffy asks.

"This is the exact line of sight?"

She nods. "Yeah, from Pete's position up above. Had the .308 set on a nice flat piece of rock. Why?"

I look up at her. "I thought he said the only thing he could see was the Russian's head."

Tuffy takes the photo from my hands. "Yeah." She looks at me. "There was nothing blocking his field of view. He would have seen the whole man."

I tuck the photos back in the file and hand it to her. "Guess I'll have to ask him about that."

"You want me to—"

"No, it can wait." That vague memory again is trying to come into focus. "See if you can get Pop on the phone for me, will you?"

When she's gone, I get up and close the door. Sitting back down at my desk again, I unlock my bottom right drawer and open it, removing Peter Alexander's personnel file. I know the acid sloshing around in my stomach is not from coffee. I leaf through the pages. Two tours in Afghanistan. Military police. Germany before that. Typical military CV, listing postings and responsibilities, medals and commendations. References listed. Peter Alexander.

I say the name out loud. And repeat it. Again. "Shit." I open my cell phone and speed-dial a number. "What's up?" Wardell Spann asks.

"Wardell, where are you right now?" He doesn't answer. "Wardell?"

"Meg's," the crusty cop says under his breath. "Just getting coffee."

My eyebrows snap together. In the two hours since I directed my lieutenant to start checking every house and building in Caliente, a town twenty-five miles from here, the man has managed to make it three blocks from the sheriff's department. "Are you alone, Wardell?"

"How do you mean?"

I want to reach through the ether connecting us and choke the man. "I mean, is anyone with you. Can you speak confidentially?"

"Give me a sec," Wardell replies. Ten seconds later, I can hear the wind blowing into Wardell's phone. "Good now. What's up?"

I pause a moment, gathering my thoughts. "Wardell, I need to ask you some questions, and I need you to keep this conversation between you and me because people's lives may depend on it. Do you understand?"

"I'm not a moron, Beck," comes the gruff reply. "Ask away."

I lean back in my chair. "Before you hired Pete, did you check his CV?"

"His CV? What the hell is that?"

"His military record, Wardell. Did you check it?" There is no answer. "What about his references?"

"What the hell are you into, Beck? Are you still hung up on me hiring him instead of letting you do it?"

"So that's a no, then?"

"That's a go fuck yourself," Wardell growls. "Sorry, go fuck yourself, *sir*."

I hold my breath a moment and then release it slowly, as if I'm about to put one in his brain from a few hundred yards out. "Wardell, I need you to come into the office. Don't speak to anyone. Tuffy will tell you what to do when you get here. Above all, say nothing to Pete. Do you read me?"

"I don't report to Tuffy, Beck. Tuffy doesn't *tell* me shit."

I get up on my feet. "Wardell, if you want to spend another day on this job, get your ass to this office now." I click off and quickly look up another contact in my phone.

"Colonel Berryman," the voice answers seconds later.

"Mike, it's Beck."

"Beck! You miserable shit, how are you?"

"I'm good, Mike. You still at the Pentagon?"

"Counting the days, brother. In forty-seven, no, forty-six days, I'm out of here. Maybe I'll come out to the wild west and work for you."

"Nah," I say. "You would have to qualify with a pistol."

"Fuck you." Except for Brinley, Mike Berryman is the best shot I have ever met. "What's up?"

"I need you to pull a jacket for me."

"Beck, I have forty-six days—"

"Mike, I need it, brother. It's important."

There is some dead air for a few seconds. "Name?"

I give him what I have in the file, including postings and date of separation. "I have no one with that name and date of separation," he says a minute later. "I could check those postings for you, but I doubt very much you're looking at valid information. As you know, we don't do a whole lot well in the Army, but nobody is better at record-keeping."

"I owe you, Mike." I hang up.

Peter Alexander. Something about that name. At the other end of my brain, another name starts pinging. Freddie Meyer. Freddie Meyer.

I walk out and give Tuffy instructions for Wardell. "When he drags his ass in here, make sure he stays put. Sit on him if you have to. I don't want him going anywhere. Have him go back through every file in those boxes and find whatever we can on Frederick Meyer. Do not let him out of this office, Tuff. And keep him off the radio."

Tuffy knows my expressions well but hasn't seen fear in them before. "What is it?"

I think about telling her, but all we have is a man with a phony record at this point. "I'm not sure. Were you able to raise the old man?"

She shakes her head. "No answer."

I tell her I have to run out to the house for a few minutes. "Won't take long."

On the drive out to Lost Meadows, I run through the facts. One: the man who took Sana complimented me on "finding the FBI man's files." How did he know I had the files unless he was in the vicinity of Atterbury's house when we removed them? Two: there was no forced entry at Atterbury's or the home of Guy Pollack. How did the killer gain entry? Someone in uniform, a fellow law enforcement officer would have tipped the scales for Atterbury certainly. Three: Pete knew where I was with every step of the investigation, including Chuck Wolverton, since he was in the office when Tuffy related the old miner's name to me over the phone. But he didn't know Sana and I were baiting a trap for him. Four: Pete Alexander's existence is artificial, yet carefully constructed. He has been on the county's payroll for two months, well after the Russians received the intelligence from their source in the FBI. Five: Pete shoots and kills the other Russian at Big Rocks behind Atterbury's place, saying he only had a head shot, when clearly, he could have seen the entire man. This one is odd, one assassin taking out a partner, but the guy was wounded and bleeding out, and shooting him solidified Pete's position. Six: and this one gives me a headache—Pete's name. In Russian, it is essentially Peter the Great. *How did I miss that?*

"Screw you, Pete," I say as I speed through the gate at Lost Meadows. Two minutes later, I pull up at the house. Now, I tell myself, now comes the part that makes no sense.

I note Brinley's Subaru Crosstrek is gone, and I instantly regret sending her away. "Pop!" I yell, coming into the house. "Pop, we need to talk."

The old man is nowhere to be seen. His truck is still in the drive, so that means he is probably out on the property somewhere. That's good, I think. I'm probably losing my mind anyway.

I walk down the long hallway to my father's bedroom. The bed is made, covers tucked in crisply at the corners just like every time I've ever seen it. The blanket is so tight you can bounce a quarter off it. Like we did it in the Army. But Pop was never in the military. I sit down on it and stare at the picture of him on the wall at his swearing-in ceremony as sheriff in 1974. So young then, just thirty-nine, the camera angled to avoid catching the scar on the right side of his face. *This is crazy.*

I rise from the bed and open his closet. Unlike a lot of people born during the Great Depression who grew up with next to nothing, Joe Beck is not someone who clings to the material things acquired over a lifetime. He has no keepsakes that I have ever seen and doesn't save anything that does not provide some immediate, tangible value. In short, he is not someone you would find reminiscing about "the good old days." I find a stack of photographs in a box on a shelf and return to the bed, where I dump them out. They are mostly of my mother through the years and me as a child, but there is nothing that shows my dad before coming to Nevada. He came from coal country in Pennsylvania. His father, my grandfather, had died on some island in the Pacific when Pop was very young. He had no brothers or sisters. I do find a picture of a man and a woman I remember as being my paternal grandparents. It's very old and they were very young when it was taken, and now that I think about it, it's the only photo I have ever seen of my father's family.

I pick up another ancient black-and-white, the edges yellowed and worn as if the picture has been visited a thousand times. It's my pop, in his early twenties probably, with his arm around a woman of similar age who is not my mother. Funny, I've never even considered the fact that he might have had a girl or two before meeting my mom. They seem happy, posing under a sandstone rock formation I recognize instantly as the Kolob Arch in Zion. Yet what really catches my eye is my father's unblemished face, slightly shadowed but clear enough. His scar is gone. I wonder if it is a trick of the light.

Thumbing through the rest of the photos, I suddenly stop at a shot of me and my dad at the county fairgrounds one August at what must have been the annual rodeo. I look at my younger self, on leave from the Army and early in my career. Before I stopped coming home. The scene replays in my head. A woman, someone I do not know, approaches us on Main Street. She has two ice-cream cones in her hands, and I remember wondering if she is planning on eating both of them herself. She is about the same age as my dad, mid-sixties at the time.

"Freddie?" she says. "Freddie Meyer, is that you?"

It's so vivid in my memory now, and I can see Pop's face turning away quickly.

"Pop, I think that woman is talking to you."

"Fred Meyer," the woman says loudly. "Can it be?"

Joe Beck is not someone who looks like other people, especially in a sheriff's uniform and with a large Stetson on his head. His features are distinct. He turns then. "I'm sorry?"

The woman stares up at him. "Are you . . . I'm sorry, you're just the spitting image of . . . I'm Dottie Ward. I was a friend of Kitty Ellison at the Dunes back in the day."

I remember looking over at my father then, thinking how very peculiar it is that this woman thinks he is someone else, especially with that big crease in his right cheek.

"I think you've got me mixed up with someone else," Pop says. "Sorry."

The woman stares up at him for a long moment, the ice cream beginning to melt on her hands. "Oh, you just look so much like him. But that was forty years ago."

Pop doesn't respond, I remember. He just tips his hat and turns away. I watch for a moment as the woman continues to stare.

*This is not possible.*

I have known my father all my life. And Freddie Meyer had been killed by fire in April, 1957. I think back to what Sana told me about the Russians found in the desert outside Las Vegas. There had been no positive ID of Freddie Meyer. His body had been burned, and he had been identified by pieces of his uniform and badge from the test site.

*But my father is not Russian.*

The arguments we had had, how upset Pop was over me studying Russian in college. And even more upset when I told him I was joining the military. "Armies are run by politicians, son," Pop said. "They will send you anywhere that suits their purpose, and you are always expendable."

I had chocked up his resentment to my mother's passing and a government that was still denying its role in the cancer that took her life. That was real, I tell myself, that was all real. And the woman on the street, did she really say Freddie Meyer? Maybe it was Phil Meyer or Frankie Meyer. I close my eyes and click through the View-Master in my brain. *No, it was Freddie Meyer.*

It's all circumstantial at this point, I remind myself. Freddie Meyer is, in all probability, dead. Long dead. I get up from the bed and return to the closet. I part the hanging clothes with a hand, looking for something, anything to prove my father is the man he claims to be. Angry, I sweep the collection of baseball caps off a shelf and onto the floor and then begin rifling the dresser drawers. Then some unseen force draws my eyes toward the twenty or so hats now lying on the carpet. None of them reflect the names of baseball teams. Pop is not a huge sports fan. The caps are all from establishments in the area, local bars, a meat processor called the Road Kill Grill in Vegas, three or four from the sheriff's department. And then I see the black-and-white one and hold it in my hand. Meteor Mine, with a meteor streaming through the sky.

*No, Pop. Please no.*

Dizzy, I return to the front of the house, the house I grew up in, the place my father taught me to saddle and ride a horse and drive a tractor and a truck. I walk out onto the porch and see him and Little Joe walking out of the east pasture toward the house. He waves to me, and Little Joe lumbers quickly ahead to greet me. After what seems like an eternity, Pop reaches the porch, stopping a few feet from me. He removes his cap and wipes the sweat from his brow with the sleeve of his jacket. He knows me well enough to know when something is wrong.

"What's got you all worked up?"

I lean against the porch railing for support. In perfect Russian, I say, "Tell me, Pop, what was it like when you were a kid?"

The words shake him, and he staggers to his favorite chair.

"You'll have to forgive me, I haven't spoken or heard words like that in sixty years, but if I heard you correctly, I guess I would say that the one thing I remember more than anything else is that we were always hungry. Always."

My eyes began to flood. "You bastard. You're a spy. How could you?"

Pop climbs slowly to his feet and faces me. "The same way you did. You served your country. They sent you to Russia. I served mine. They sent me here. No big mystery. We don't control where we're born."

Tears roll down my face. "Did Mom know?"

Pop shakes his head. "No. No one knows. Except you. Funny, I was just coming to tell you."

I turn away. "Bullshit."

He steps up and put his big hands on the railing. "If I had known what was going on, I would have turned myself in to you earlier. But Brinley just told me a few hours ago what you've been doing the last few days. Figured I would take one more walk around the place."

I spin around to face him. "What's your name? Your Russian name?"

Pop looks out over Lost Meadows. It's a nice day, and the grasses are doing their best to poke through the remaining snow to reach for the sun. "I was born Georgiy Dudko in Odessa, in the Ukraine."

I spit my disgust. "I know where Odessa is."

He puts a hand on my shoulder. "I've been Joe Beck a lot longer than I was ever Georgiy Dudko. And I really was coming to tell you."

I can't manage to look him in the eyes. "I don't know what's going to happen, Pop, but I have two women who might lose their lives because of you, and two men who already have. And now I have to go kill a man. If I can't do that, I may have to trade you."

Pop nods. "That's why I was coming to see you. You know who's after me then?"

"I do now," I reply, finally turning to face the man I thought I knew. "I need you to stay here. Don't go anywhere. I might be able to fix this. If I can't, we'll have to think of something else."

"Let me come, son. I might be losing my mind, but I can still shoot."

I can feel the heat on my skin, my face screwing into rage. I seize him by the collar and push him back into the chair with force, the spittle flying out of my mouth. "You will stay right here, do you understand? You will stay right here and wait for my call."

The old man's eyes seem to liquify. I launch myself over the railing and climb into my truck.

# CHAPTER 16

I leave a complete stranger at my house, a man I thought was someone else, a man I now know to have been a Soviet spy. I pull up the Find My app on my cell and see Brinley is about forty miles away, heading for Los Angeles.

"Turn around. I need you to sit on Pop until I call, do not let him out of your sight."

"A few hours ago you were ready to lock me up, you fuck."

"Just do this for me, Brin. Please. I can't explain right now."

"Shit. Fine. On my way."

My next call is to Tuffy. "What do you have Wardell doing?"

"He hasn't come in yet. You want me to call him?"

I pound the steering wheel. "No, do not call him on the radio or his cell. Check the LoJack on his vehicle, and tell me where he is."

I hear Tuffy clicking away on her keyboard. "Okay, that's a bit . . . irregular," she says. "Sure you don't want me to just call him?"

"Humor me, Tuff."

"Beck, what's going on? What aren't you telling me?"

"You by yourself?"

"Still," she says.

"Pete is the Russian we've been chasing."

I hear the keyboard go silent. "I'm sorry. What did you say?"

"It's Pete, Tuffy. He's been hunting the illegal from inside our department."

"I never liked him," she replies.

A few more keyboard strokes, and I know she is staring at a computerized map with the locations of every vehicle in the department. "I thought you said you liked looking at him."

"There's a difference, and now I'd like to shoot him. How sure are you?"

"Very."

"LoJack says Wardell is in Caliente."

"Is he moving?"

"Uh . . . nope."

"Location?" I don't wait, toggling on my light bar and siren just as I am passing the office.

"Uh, he's . . . wait one . . . shit."

"What?"

"He's at Pete's address. Just off of Holt and Second."

"How do you know Pete's address?"

"Umm, I may have driven by once or twice. But that's where Wardell is."

"Where is Pete's vehicle? Is it there?"

Tuffy taps the keyboard a few more times. "Stand by . . . weird, he's not coming up."

My truck goes airborne over a dip in the road. "He's disabled it."

"Meet you there?"

I think for a moment. "Yeah, I'm two minutes ahead of you. Get moving and come heavy, Tuff."

She doesn't hesitate. "Always do."

Twenty minutes later, I pull off the 93, turning right on Second

Street. I coast to a stop in the dirt a quarter mile in just before coming to the intersection at Holt. I'm a block away from the house Pete is renting, but I can see it clearly through the trees from my position. I can also see Wardell's Caliente Police truck in the driveway, but it appears he's not in it.

Returning to my truck, I yank the 12-gauge from the gun lock between the seats just as Tuffy pulls up behind me. "Vest?" I ask as she gets out.

"Got it," she says, opening the trunk. She pulls it over her head, tightening the shoulder and side straps.

"Okay, Wardell's vehicle is in the driveway. I'm guessing he's in the house. Let's hope Pete is, too. Can you give me a layout of the inside?"

She stares at me blankly. "What?"

"You've said you've been here a couple of times. What's the inside look like?"

"I said I've driven by a couple of times," she says, looking away. "I've never been inside the house."

"Just stalking him, then?"

"Fuck you, Beck," she says.

Despite the fact we're about to confront a Russian intelligence agent who has already killed at least two people, her retort makes me laugh. She laughs, too. "Okay, we go between these two houses and come in from the side. Stay low and out of sight. Let's see if we can peek in a window or hear something before we make a move. Looks like the house has a basement. Chances are that's where Michaela and Agent Locke are."

Tuffy nods and checks the slide and magazine on her Glock. "Copy."

I place a hand on her arm. "Remember, this guy is a trained killer, an assassin. Do not give him the chance to shoot first. Forget everything you ever learned about police procedure right now.

This is a bug hunt. You see him, you put him down. We'll worry about any shooting boards later."

Tuffy gazes up me and shrugs. "You think we should wait and get Arshal and the Twin Peaks?"

I shake my head apologetically. "Take too long to get them here. It's you and me, Tuff."

"Then let's go," she says.

We take off at a jog between the two houses just east of the single-story home with the decaying shake roof and a 1960s coat of brown paint. Lots here are big, not like ones you find in most cities where you can practically reach out and touch your neighbor's house from your kitchen, and Pete's is no different. It's at least an acre, with no landscaping and only native vegetation around the property. Peeking around the front of the house, I note there is no garage, just a dilapidated carport on one side. I whisper, "I don't see Pete's unit, but assume he's here."

"He's got foil over all the windows," Tuffy says. "Smart."

We creep along the side of the house to the back, and I nod toward a large metal shipping container at the far end of the lot, large enough to hold people but not very soundproof. It's a rusty red color and looks to have been there for years. Probably not where he's holding Sana and Michaela. "Single door in the back of the house."

Tuffy and I stay slow and low until we are on each side of the door. Kids from the house due west are playing and yelling, making it impossible for us to hear inside the house. I try the knob. When it doesn't move, Tuffy pulls out her lockpicking tools. It's a nice twenty-four-piece set that comes in a leather holder about the size of an eyeglass case, last year's Christmas present from me. Silently, she goes to work. In just a few seconds, she nods to me. I motion her back. Slowly, I turn the knob, withdrawing the strike into the door and nudging it open about the width of a safety pin until I can just barely see light coming from within. When I move it another millimeter, I feel the tiniest bit of resistance. Though I can't see much at night, my daytime vision is still sharp. I gaze up and down the crack between the door and the jamb. And I see it. A piece of red twine stretched tightly across the top of the door. Opening the door any farther will cause the twine to be stretched, activating whatever it is connected to.

"It's wired," I tell her. "Either alarm or explosive, I'm not sure." I gently pull the door closed and release the strike. "Let's keep going."

We move to the west side of the house where the basement is more above the grade of the property and one rectangular window sits just above the ground. Tuffy and I squat in the dirt on one side of it. The noise from the kids next door is decidedly less on this side, but even with my head pressed to the house, I can't hear anything coming from inside. No conversation, nothing. That doesn't bode well for Wardell.

"Okay," I say quietly. "This is our entry point. If he's using explosives, chances are it's just on the doors. If I'm wrong and this blows, fall back and seal the neighborhood off. Call the Vegas bomb guys."

"Boss," she says.

"If it doesn't blow, I go first and you cover. We clear the basement first and work our way up. Okay?"

Tuffy confirms with a head bob.

I grab the barrel of my shotgun and swing the stock into the window, shattering the glass. There's a scream from inside, female and desperate, and before it subsides, I go headfirst through the window, barrel-rolling off the cement floor six feet below and coming up in a crouch.

The basement is dark. I pop on my flashlight. "Move, Tuffy. Now." Another scream echoes off the concrete walls.

Tuffy drops straight in, landing on her feet. Her light comes on as well. We move quickly through the room to the basement steps, our flashlights sweeping back and forth. I spot a light switch and flip it. Even in the small glow of a single bulb suspended above the stairs, I know it's the same room I saw in the iPad from Wolverton's house.

"Here, I'm here," the woman cries from the other end of the basement. We move in tandem, looking for any movement. In a far corner of the room are two crates, the kind that are used for very large dogs. In one of them, Michaela Edwards lies fully dressed and shaking, curled into a ball, her wrists and ankles bound with electrical ties. The other is empty. "Please help me," she sobs.

I cover Tuffy as she slides to the ground next to Michaela's cage. "It's okay, Michaela," I say quietly. "It's Sheriff Beck. We've got you. Do you know if the man who took you is in the house?"

"I don't . . . think so," she stammers, as Tuffy frees her. "I . . . I heard . . . gunshots and then a car driving away. He took the other woman, I think."

I tell Tuffy, "Get her up, get her moving. I'm going topside." At the top of the stairs, I check for another booby trap but there isn't one. Slowly, I push the door open and can see into the kitchen. The long shotgun is a bit unwieldly for close quarters, so I set it down gently and remove the Glock from its holster. Stepping into the kitchen, I quietly close the basement door behind me. Something in the air catches my nasal passages, and I sniff. It's the pungent odor of nitroglycerin. The smell of spent ammunition. Every primal instinct I have comes alive.

Even without taking another step, I know Wardell is dead and that Pete is already gone and has taken Sana with him. He still needs her for the exchange.

Also, from where I'm standing, I can see the inside of the exterior door Tuffy and I tried a few minutes ago. My eyes trace the red twine near the top of the door to the pin of an M-84 flashbang just on the other side of the jamb. If I had pushed any harder, it would have gone off in our faces.

Three short steps to the left allowed me to peek into the living room, where I see Wardell's body on the ground, blood still dripping from his forehead onto the brown carpet beneath him.

"God damn it, Wardell." I hit the ground and place two fingers on his carotid artery. In addition to a double-tap to the head, he took one in the chest and was certainly dead before he hit the floor. "All because you didn't want to think I could be right about Pete, and that you could be wrong." A minute later, I've cleared the rest of the house and meet Tuffy and Michaela at the top of the stairs, Michaela wrapped in a blanket, still shivering and clinging to Tuffy.

With her arms around Michaela, Tuffy looks up at me. "I'm going to kill that bastard. Where is he?"

"Gone," I tell her. "Wardell's dead."

She hugs Michaela tighter. "She needs a hospital."

I nod. "I'll go and get your unit. We need to do this quietly. Pete may not know we've been here. The front door, just like the back, was wired to blow, but I've cleared them both. You take Michaela to the hospital. I'll call Arshal and have him tell Michaela's husband she's okay and to meet you there."

"What are you going to do?"

"I'm going to see if we can trick this asshole. It's worth a try."

Tuffy grabs me by the jacket. "We could just put out a BOLO on his vehicle."

"Can't risk it," I say, glancing at my watch. Four hours left. "I'm not losing any more deputies, and he might kill Sana. The question is, where does he go now? It's not like he can just drive around with her in the back. He's got to stash her somewhere. He's playing with the short stack now and he knows it."

A few minutes later, I'm on my way back to Pioche, feeling

horrible about leaving poor Wardell dead on the floor, but as I explain to Arshal over the phone, this is no time to throw up another crime scene.

"How do you want to handle it?" Arshal asks.

I explain the harebrained scheme in my head. As soon as I get back to the station, I walk to the dispatch desk and key the radio, sending a call out to all deputies. "Guys, it's Beck. We found our Russian spy, and his name is Chuck Wolverton. Nice job, Pete. You were right. Guy cracked like an egg. Arshal is bringing him down from Mill Valley. Sorry I didn't tell you where we had him before now. Just didn't want to risk anyone else getting hurt. Over."

The voice of Jimmy or Johnny, I'm not sure which, comes next. "Copy, Beck. So, we're still looking for the shooter, though, correct?"

"Copy. We are still looking for the shooter. I would like all of you to continue your patrols of the area. But at least we have Wolverton and might be able to trade him, if we have to, for Agent Locke and Michaela Edwards." I pause for a few seconds. This is the tricky part. "And does anyone know where Wardell is? He's off comms for some reason."

Arshal comes over the radio. "Old buzzard is probably at home taking his afternoon nap, boss."

"Copy," I say with a laugh. "Pete, you're the guy who picked Wolverton out. You know his background better than any of us. I could use you back here to take his statement and make sure we don't leave anything out."

Seconds pass with no reply, and I can almost see Pete wondering what to do next. Finally, his voice streams over the station's speakers. "Copy, Sheriff. I'm on my way. Be there in fifteen."

Good. If he thinks Wolverton will be here, he'll plan on taking me out first. Case closed. He takes his traitor back to Moscow or kills him here. "Copy, Pete." I breathe a sigh of relief and pump my fist. Then I head into to the adjacent detention center and have Mary Elizabeth lock everything down. If things go badly, I will not allow Pete to retreat into the jail where there are more people to hurt. Returning to the office, I see the Jolly Greens coming in the front door.

"Good timing, guys. Arshal bring you up to speed?"

They nod in unison, men of few words the Greens are. "This is some kind of crazy, boss," one of them says.

We head to the armory. "It really is. Where did you guys park?"

"Around back, like Arshal said to. Can't see them from the highway."

I yank some ammunition boxes out of the cabinet and lay them on the table. "He's already killed Wardell, boys. When he walks in that door, you shoot him, understand. No 'freeze' or any other command. You shoot the man."

My young deputies exchange concerned glances. "What about the FBI lady?" Arshal asks, entering the room.

I slam a magazine in one of the .45s. His question makes me realize now that I may have just ended Sana's life by telling Pete that Wolverton is the illegal. But I'm guessing he'll hedge his bet and hold on to her until he's sure of the hand he's holding. "He's either killed her, or she's alive and we'll find her. Trust me, we won't sweat the information out of him. So, find a spot behind a wall or desk and get ready. Arshal, you take the roof. If you can take him in the parking lot, do it."

As the men began dispersing, my cell phone rings. Everybody stops. I look at the caller ID. "Shit. It's Pete." The phone rings three times before I click the speaker button. "Pete, you close?"

"Well played, Beck," the Russian says, his breathing labored. I can hear the wind, so Pete is outdoors somewhere. "When did you figure it out?" he asks.

I grasp at my final straw. "Wolverton? That was you, buddy. I just confirmed it."

"I'm talking about me, Sheriff. You had me. I almost walked back into that station, but then I thought 'What would I do if I were Sheriff Beck?' So I drove up to the top of the hill here and watched Arshal and the Greens come in and park around back."

My heart sinks.

"Your skills are really quite remarkable," Pete says. "I take it you've already been to my place and found that useless shit Wardell. I wouldn't have killed him, but he just kind of barged in on me. So, I shot the lazy fuck. I guess you didn't get blown up on the way in. Did you find Michaela?"

I wave the guys back in. "Yes, we did. Thanks for keeping her alive, Pete."

"No problem. Nice girl. Terrible religion. So, you have Wolverton and I have Agent Locke. Shall we make a trade?"

"Sure. Where are you?"

He laughs. "Very good. Very good. No, I'm going to need a way out of here, Sheriff. With my prisoner."

I look at my deputies. "You mean you're not just going to kill him? You can't possibly be thinking you can get him back to Russia."

"Honestly, I haven't decided yet. I will call you in three hours and tell you what to do. I'm perfectly happy trading Agent Locke for him, but I will kill her if you do not follow those instructions to the letter."

The line goes dead.

# THE PAST

He had just completed the biggest theft in the history of the world, and with every bend in the road, Georgiy expected to see the bright blue and red flashing lights of the U.S. Army coming his way. The warhead was missing! The alarms would have sounded, and they would be in the process of sealing off the test site. The terror rose in his throat, choking him.

Twenty minutes into the drive back to Mercury, as he passed through the area known as Frenchman Flat, he had seen no other vehicle. If he could just get to the motor pool and transfer the XW-25 to the hidden compartment in the trunk of his car, he had a chance. It was just after midnight.

A minute later, he heard a *thwack*. It wasn't terribly loud. Then he heard it again. And again. The sound grew louder and more frequent. Looking into the rearview mirror, he caught sight of the problem. The heavy blanket he had covered the warhead with had come loose and was in danger of flying away. He had no choice but to stop. He took a roll of duct tape from his toolbox and sealed the device in the blanket like he was planning on shipping it through the post office. Of course, he had to climb in the bed to do that. It was a huge effort and required lifting the warhead several times, and midway through it, he saw headlights. He wrapped as fast as he could.

It was a car, that much he could tell. Not a jeep, not Army. More like internal security. Hopefully they wouldn't stop. He was just climbing back over the side of the truck when the black Ford Fairlane slowed to a stop alongside him. Georgiy's blood froze.

The CIA guys drove Ford Fairlanes. There were two in this one, both tall and skinny and wearing the same black suit and tie.

"Trouble?" asked the driver, rolling down his window.

"Just had some tools flying around the back," Georgiy responded, turning slightly to his left to keep the man from seeing the name on his badge. "Thought I was going to lose them." He was losing precious time, every second a greater chance he would never make it off the test site. "I'm FSI," he said. "May I see your badges, please?"

Miffed, the agent on the passenger side opened his door and got out. "What the hell, pal? We stopped to see if you needed help." He had an eastern accent that sounded like Boston or Philadelphia, impatient and guttural.

Georgiy put his hand on his sidearm. "I appreciate that, but it's late, and we keep things tight around here, so I need to see your badges."

The driver produced his badge and handed it to Georgiy. "You fucking security cops. You got nothing better to do?"

Georgiy scanned the man's ID. His name was Abbott, and he was, in fact, Central Intelligence, though his credentials indicated no such thing. Agent Abbott was the man Dr. Ellison told him to report to after the shot. *Damn.* He handed the credentials back. "Where are you guys headed?"

"None of your business, shithead," the other man shouted, as he started to make his way around the front of the car.

Georgiy drew his revolver and leveled it at the man, freezing him. "Did I tell you to get out of the car, sir?"

"Hey," Abbott said. "It's not a problem. What are you doing?"

"Get back in the car, asshole," Georgiy said to the other agent. The man spat at him but climbed back in the Ford.

"What's your name, asshole?" the agent screamed. "And who is your supervisor?"

Realizing he might have to kill these men, he decided he had nothing to lose. He bent down and peered through the driver's window. "My name is Sergeant Meyer, but I'm actually a Russian agent here to gather intelligence on the American nuclear program." He winked at them.

"You're Meyer?" asked Abbott. "We're supposed to talk to you."

"So I heard," Georgiy huffed. "I'll be at the admin office at zero nine hundred. For right now, I suggest you two secret agent clowns get back to your quarters."

It was a psychological trick that Georgiy had picked up in training. People searching for secrets seldom believe the truth when they hear it, often discounting it as absurd. After staring at each other for several seconds, the CIA men sped off.

Georgiy got back in the truck, his body shaking violently. *Breathe, Georgiy. Just breathe.* Finally, the truck was moving again. Five minutes later, he approached Gate 200, the main entrance gate just north of Mercury. Fortunately, like most of the test site, it was designed to keep people out, not in, and Georgiy just had to slow long enough for the guard to recognize his vehicle and wave him through. The lights of Camp Mercury and the main gate were below him now, where he would somehow have to transfer the warhead to his personal vehicle and exit the most secure facility in the United States.

He passed the hospital where Ellison was now being examined. The drug provided by Moscow was designed to work violently but only for a brief time. By now, Georgiy hoped, the physicist was beginning to feel better. Entering his row of dormitories, things appeared relatively quiet. There were eight long buildings on his right and three on his left, and tall overhead lights glowed at each end of the parking lot. If anyone happened to be looking out a window or walking by, they would see him instantly. He needed them all to be fast asleep right now.

Both parking spots next to his Crestliner were taken, which meant he had to park two cars over. It was 12:35 A.M. He had lost too much time with the CIA men and would have to move fast now. Quickly, he walked to his car and popped the trunk. Georgiy lifted the false bottom and removed it from the car, careful not to make any noise as he set it on the ground. The space William and his apes had created was a perfect mold of the warhead.

*For a warhead not taped up in a blanket, you fool!*

Opening the tailgate of the truck, Georgiy examined his handiwork. "Screw this," he muttered, pulling the XW-25 toward him. This time, however, it didn't lift so easily. The blanket was bulky, and Georgiy was tired, his muscles already strained. And he had no hand truck to move it. He set it back down with a thud.

*Leave it here. Just get in the car and get out. Run.* But he couldn't. With all his remaining might, Georgiy walked the nuclear payload to his car. Since he could not see through the blanket and couldn't remember which side was which, he simply set it in the mold as it lay in his arms. It did not fit. He would have to cut the tape away and remove the blanket. Except he had no knife. He checked his watch. No time. Reaching down, he pulled the new cover back into the trunk and tried mashing it down over the warhead. It rode so high, he would barely be able to close the trunk hatch, let alone screw the cover down as it had been intended.

*Shit.*

Georgiy removed the false cover again and walked it over to his truck, setting it in the bed. He closed the tailgate and returned to the Crestliner, slamming the trunk hatch in disgust. He checked his watch. It was 12:50. He had ten minutes. Seconds later, he was heading toward the main gate. If they looked in his trunk, it was over. And they would surely do that. They always looked in the trunk.

The main gate at the Nevada Test Site was a constant reminder to workers of the importance of security. As he approached it, Georgiy's eyes caught the back of the sign incoming personnel were faced with every day. He knew the words by heart:

ATTENTION

ENTRANCE BEYOND THIS POINT

CONSTITUTES CONSENT TO SEARCH

OF VEHICLES ENTERING, LEAVING,

AND WHILE WITHIN THE

NEVADA TEST SITE

The normal procedure for personnel exiting the site was to pull up to the gate and present your identification to one of the guards, while the other inspected and searched your vehicle. At 1:00 A.M. there were no cars in front of him, and Georgiy gave some consideration to simply running the gate, but there were too many miles of highway to go before he would meet William. They would catch him in no time. He pulled the Crestliner to a stop under the bright lights and extended his ID through the window.

"Freddie, me lad," bellowed Tom O'Hara in his finest Irish brogue when he saw who it was. "Jesus, we heard about Dr. Ellison. Horrible thing."

The other guard was a man Georgiy did not know, and he began running the parabolic mirror slowly under the car. "Yeah, I was with him, Tom. It was bad. Probably a heart attack. I'm headed to Vegas to get his daughter. She's going to be my fiancée."

"Serious?"

Georgiy nodded. He was visibly sweating through his uniform shirt now, watching the other guard with one eye in the rearview as he approached the back of the car. "Yep, I just hope the doctor is going to make it. I'm afraid this news is really going to shake Kitty."

O'Hara handed him back his identification. "Sounds like he'll be okay," O'Hara said. "You know they took him to the hospital in town. Left about fifteen minutes ago."

Georgiy's right foot began an incremental slide from the brake to the gas pedal. "Christ, I gotta get moving then." His right hand moved slowly to the .38 Special riding on his hip. If he had to, he would shoot them both.

O'Hara could see the fright on Georgiy's face as the guard in the back released the trunk latch. "Step on it, Miller," he yelled. "I got a man in a hurry here."

Miller shined his flashlight inside the trunk, and Georgiy could see him moving a few things around. "Boss?"

O'Hara glanced at Georgiy apologetically and then walked to the rear of the car. Georgiy slipped the .38 from its holster and laid it next to his right thigh. Panting like a dog on a hot day, he watched as the more senior guard returned to his side. "Sorry, Freddie. Teaching the lad here the ropes. What's in the blanket? Something heavy, I see. You got a body in there?"

"Worse," Georgiy said, winking. "Nuclear bomb."

O'Hara laughed. "Really? I pictured them being a lot bigger."

Georgiy laughed back. "This one is a mock-up some of the engineers put together for Dr. Ellison. They were going to put some firecrackers on top of it and set them off after the shot. Strange sense of humor. But I guess that's going to have to wait now."

The guard stared at him for a long moment, and Georgiy's fingers tensed around the revolver's grip. "Well, God Almighty," he said, "why didn't they just make the man a cake? Get outta here, Freddie. We'll be praying for the doc."

A moment later, the gate was up and Georgiy drove off the

grounds of the Nevada Test Site for the last time, turning left onto the Widowmaker highway. He couldn't believe it. He was alive, no one had been killed, and he had a warhead full of deadly plutonium in his trunk. If he could make it to Indian Springs, he might just survive the night.

They would be looking for him now, if only to determine why he had left Building 11 and not rotated to his next post in Area 13 or returned to CP-1 in Area 6. In a very short time, Georgiy knew, they would alert the entire site, and the guards at the main gate would report his departure at 1:00 A.M. As he pulled into the darkened Thunderbird station, he knew it wouldn't be long until someone checked inside Building 11 and realized they were missing the device for their top-secret project.

Pulling around to the back of the gas station, Georgiy watched as William, in coveralls and a knit hat, motioned him to drive up a ramp into the back of a long moving van. It was red and white and had a North American Van Lines logo emblazoned on the side. "Why?" Georgiy yelled.

William approached his door, his coveralls bearing the same emblem. "Do you have it?"

Georgiy wiped the sweat from his brow with a handkerchief. "I do."

"Then they will be looking for your car. Now drive up the ramp."

It was a tight fit on the sides, and once in the back of the trailer, Georgiy engaged the parking brake and crawled out of the window. He helped William stow the ramp behind the Crestliner, and a minute later they were driving south.

"Where are we going?"

"You'll see," said William. "It won't be long."

Georgiy lit a cigarette and blew the smoke out the open window, his nerves finally starting to calm.

William seemed ebullient and clapped Georgiy on the chest. "You did it, Comrade Captain. No problems?"

Georgiy looked over at the man, bewildered. "Problems? Not for you. In an hour, every law enforcement officer in the country will be looking for me."

William handed him a thermos. "Vodka. Calm your nerves. It's American and tastes like shit, but it will do the job. We'll drink the real stuff when we get home. Heroes!"

He needed the drink. "How are you getting me back to Moscow, William? What is the plan for that?"

Keeping his eyes on the winding road, William related the steps. "Once we've set the warhead in motion, we will drive to a warehouse we have rented. It contains furniture, appliances, enough to fill this truck. We are a moving company after all."

"And?"

"And we will drive to San Diego, California, where we will charter a deep-sea fishing boat that will take us into Mexican waters."

Georgiy was unconvinced. "What then?"

William glared at him. "When we get there, Captain, you'll know."

Georgiy had no doubt that was true. If he actually made it to the waters off Mexico, William might just shoot him and throw him overboard. It didn't make sense—Georgiy would be a treasure trove of intelligence his masters in Moscow could pick through—but in his gut he didn't trust William to keep him alive.

As the drink took effect and the adrenaline in his veins subsided, Georgiy allowed his exhaustion to take him. He was jarred from the slumber more than an hour later when William turned onto a narrow dirt road well outside of Las Vegas that led west through the desert toward the Sierra Nevada mountains. Georgiy checked his watch. It was almost 3:30 A.M. To the south and east, he could see the bright neon lights of the Las Vegas Strip. Surrounding those lights were fifty-five thousand inhabitants, Kitty included.

*Kitty.*

Did William actually have someone watching her, or was that a bluff? Georgiy looked over at his superior as he steered carefully around the larger rocks on the trail, the big wheel vibrating in his hands.

"Anything on the radio yet?" Georgiy asked.

"Just bad music. No alerts about a missing warhead, if that's what you mean. This will be the biggest scandal the American nuclear program has ever encountered, Comrade. They won't be broadcasting their embarrassment on civilian radio."

"They must know it's gone by now."

"Yes, but they will be unsure of what to do. They will put up roadblocks. They will be looking for your car but won't find it. They will go to your apartment. You won't be there. By the time all that happens, it will be over, and they will have something else to worry about."

"Are we close?"

"Twenty minutes." It was actually thirty, at the speed the moving van could manage over the bumpy trail, when William turned due south and stopped next to a smaller pickup in the empty desert. "We transfer here," he told Georgiy.

After removing the warhead from the trunk of the Crestliner, both men lifted it down from the moving van and set it gently in the bed of the gray pickup. "Why the blanket?" William asked.

Georgiy shook his head. There were a million things that had been done to get him to where he was today, and William would appreciate none of them. "It doesn't matter now."

William shrugged. "Bring the vodka. This desert makes me thirsty."

Georgiy returned a minute later with the thermos and poured William a cup. "To success," the KGB man said raising his glass and noting Georgiy wasn't drinking. "None for you?"

"I'll drink more when we get to Mexico."

At just about half past four, they arrived behind a small, lone mountain west of town. In fact, it was called Lone Mountain. On the west side of the mountain, though, the city was invisible, and the Russians were completely concealed. Before they even came to a stop, Georgiy got the answer to how William planned to deliver the warhead to Las Vegas: below them in a trough in the road three men were already inflating a giant balloon, just like the ones Georgiy had photographed months earlier.

They had several lanterns surrounding them, enough to illuminate their tools and the immediate space they needed to inflate the balloon, and as Georgiy climbed out of the truck, he could feel the wind hitting his back, blowing from the northwest. His heart sank. Once it crested the mountain, the balloon would float over the heart of town just a few short miles away. For the first time, he could see how this "accident" would happen. When the balloon was over the city, the explosion would be triggered remotely. There would be no huge fireball, no mushroom cloud like what the town's residents had witnessed from their rooftops countless times. No, this detonation would be tiny by comparison but sufficient enough to crack the plutonium core and spew perhaps the most deadly element on earth across the valley below, an invisible mist spreading through the open air, poisoning thousands as they unwittingly inhaled the radioactive particles into their lungs, killing them in miserable ways over the next weeks and months and making the area uninhabitable for the rest of man's time on earth.

William started down the hill, flashlight in hand, motioning for Georgiy to follow. Two of the men were the Spetsnaz apes Georgiy had seen several times at the Thunderbird, but the third man was bespectacled, much thinner, with gray hair. William introduced him as Dr. Volkov. *The scientist,* Georgiy said to himself. *Here to manage the bomb.* The man was adjusting a valve on a large tank attached to the inflating balloon by a long hose. Several cables extended from the fabric of the balloon and were tethered to the ground around it.

William instructed the Spetnaz soldiers to retrieve the warhead from his truck. "Be careful. It is heavy."

"Why the balloon?" Georgiy asked. "Why not just drive it into the city?"

"Because it's an accident, remember? We need people to see the balloon before we detonate the device. That way, the Americans will not be able to blame this on us. By the time the balloon is over the city, it will be daylight, and there will be many witnesses."

"If they survive," muttered Georgiy. "What kind of gas are you using?"

Volkov turned. "Hydrogen."

The breath caught in Georgiy's throat. "Hydrogen? Are you insane?"

"Relax," said the man, adjusting his glasses. "We're not creating the *Hindenburg* here. And all the better that it's more flammable. We actually need that for the accident."

William stepped up to check the gauge on the cylinder. "We couldn't get helium. And hydrogen is actually lighter. More lift."

"Twice as light, actually," said Georgiy, stepping closer to the balloon where a large square platform stood in the dirt. It was black, about four feet high by three feet wide. "You're going to suspend the device from this."

"Precisely," said Volkov, opening a flap on the platform. "And it will be wired to this explosive."

Georgiy took a closer look at the explosive material. It was about eight inches long and looked like a tube of clay. It was wrapped in paper and said "Composition C-4." Georgiy asked what it was.

"The very latest from the U.S. Army," William answered. "We have sympathizers within their ranks, as you know."

The two larger men walked the unwrapped warhead down the hill slowly, one of them tripping as they neared the bottom. "Be careful, you idiot!" William shouted. "We have not come all this way for you to kill us all."

"Bring it here," said Volkov. "And gently lay it on the platform so I can wire it to the explosive."

William touched Georgiy on the shoulder. "Let's let them finish up their preparations, shall we?" He started up the hill to the pickup. "I could use another drink."

They walked toward Lone Mountain with William leading the way in the predawn darkness, and Georgiy followed at an uncertain pace, at one point noticing they were completely out of sight of the other men now. He could just see the top of the balloon rising above the trough in the road. When he turned back around, William was pointing a gun down at him. A long cylindrical silencer was affixed to the barrel.

"Why?" was all Georgiy could think to say.

"Your sidearm, please. In the dirt. Slowly." Georgiy removed the .38 from its holster and tossed it on the ground next to William. "Even if we could get you back home, Comrade, what we do here today must remain with the fewest people possible. I have my orders. I am sorry, if that means anything. You did well. And you will die a hero."

"So, the exfiltration plan—"

"Is for me," William said.

"The others?"

William shrugged. "The others are like you. Loose lips potentially, as the Americans say. You especially, Georgiy."

Georgiy stuffed his hands inside his trouser pockets, somewhat consigned to his fate. "Me especially?"

William took two steps down the hill, glowering. "It's that moral superiority of yours, that ethical angel that whispers in your ear. We can't have you walking around with a guilty conscience about what needs to be done."

"And you, William—what is your real name, anyway? Will you have no guilt about the deaths you will cause today, the lives you will take on this hill and down there in the city?"

William switched to Russian. "Very well, my name is Miroslav. But everyone calls me Slavko. And no, I will not lose sleep over what I do today. Duty is duty, Comrade Captain."

Georgiy's head came up. "Doesn't the fact that I did go through with it tell you that I can be trusted?"

"I'm afraid we are out of time, my—"

William froze. Georgiy had seen the expression before, just a few hours earlier when he watched Dr. Ellison grab his chest. William's body reacted involuntarily, the sides of his face scrunching up in the middle as the pain stabbed into his heart, his free hand coming up to support the other with the gun. "Bastard," he squeaked.

Georgiy had given him ten drops, almost twice the amount he had given Ellison, and since William was far smaller, they had done their work in half the time. Before William could fire, Georgiy slapped his hands away. The shot sounded almost like the popping of a champagne cork, and the bullet struck the dirt somewhere behind Georgiy. But somehow, William was still on his feet. Georgiy bull-rushed him, his shoulder catching the spy just above the waist, landing him on top. William's arms flew above his head, as did the semiautomatic pistol. The crushing weight squeezing his heart had just increased by another two hundred pounds.

Georgiy could feel the life ebbing out of the man, his breath coming in great gasps now, his eyes bulging from their sockets. "Die, you miserable shit," he whispered, his nose pressed hard into William's. "Die."

He did not see the knife coming up. It struck him on the right side of the face, angling up from his cheekbone toward his eye. It was the pain that saved him, forcing him to roll off William to the left into the dirt and clutching at the jagged tear in his skin. He could feel the blood bubbling up between his fingers. He rolled again to gain some distance and watched as William took a final, blind swipe into the air with the knife again. A moment later, the knife came slowly down and rested on his chest. Georgiy heard one last rush of air escape William's lungs.

*Move or die,* Georgiy told himself, half-blind from the blood. *Move or die.*

It took him minutes to get his breath back after William had taken his last. Struggling to his feet, Georgiy could see the skin hanging from his own cheek like a slab of meat. Gravity pulled at the muscle, sending a searing pain to his brain, and he had to clamp the wound together with his hand to keep from fainting. He was bleeding profusely. A hundred yards away, he could see the top of the balloon rising above the hill like a huge onion in the sky, which meant that he had little time.

After stopping the bleeding by tying a sock around his face as tightly as he could bear, Georgiy dragged William down the hill. Then he traded clothes with him. Finally, he set him just far enough away from the truck so that the men on the other side could not see and walked down the dip in the road, gun in hand.

Volkov saw the man in the Thunderbird coveralls and knit hat coming toward him. "It is done," he said to the two brutes attaching the platform to the bottom of the balloon. "Poor chap." But in the darkness, it wasn't until he was almost upon them that Volkov saw the gray sock wrapped tightly around the face and realized it wasn't William. By the time it registered in his brain and he was able to yell, Georgiy had advanced another three steps.

"No!" Volkov screamed just before Georgiy fired a bullet into his forehead.

The Spetsnaz men were strong but slow. They turned simultaneously and froze for an instant, just long enough for Georgiy to shoot the man on the left in the chest. The one on the right threw up his hands. "Don't shoot," he pleaded in Russian.

Georgiy shot him in the face. In the span of ten minutes, he had killed four men. They were his countrymen, men who had survived the Nazi invasion, the great purges, the starvation. The cold. They had shared a common purpose, to defeat the American imperialists and free the slaves of capitalism around the world. But now Georgiy's purpose had changed, and he could never go home again. He had betrayed his country.

A minute later, the balloon and its empty cargo shot into the sky and immediately caught the stiff wind and headed southeast. It rose quickly but not enough to avoid slamming into the mountain in front of it, where it bounced and rattled around before finally climbing several hundred feet and over the crest. Where it would eventually crash, Georgiy did not have a clue and cared even less. He only cared that the warhead was not on board.

There was just one last thing to do before he left the scene, and that was to make it appear he never left it. With William now dressed in Georgiy's security uniform, Georgiy carefully drove the truck down the hill to where the three bodies lay. He placed his identification and test site badge several feet away in the dirt. The gash in his cheek feeling like a hot iron, Georgiy lifted William into the driver's seat. Then he took his .38 Special and placed the muzzle against William's right temple. The explosion of gunpower echoed off the mountain walls, but there was no one around to hear it. He let the revolver tumble out of his hand onto the floor of the pickup.

Carefully, he took the end of the hose that had been used to fill the balloon with hydrogen and placed it in the passenger window, securing it in place by rolling up the window. Then he walked back to the tank and turned on the valve. The invisible gas began to fill the truck's cab. Uncertain of what to do with the warhead but certain it was in too close proximity to the hydrogen, Georgiy wrapped it in the blanket again, and dragged it over the next rise in the road. He didn't like the idea of leaving it unsecured, but he was confident the Americans would find it in short order. Exhausted and racked with pain, he walked back to the site, taking a position a good twenty yards behind the pickup. He withdrew William's pistol from his belt and fired a round through the rear window. The first explosion was the hydrogen igniting. It lifted the truck off the ground, and knocked Georgiy off his feet. He had just glimpsed the huge fireball rising into the sky when the hydrogen cylinder next to the balloon exploded. The blast felt like he had just stepped into the sun, the sound crashing through his eardrums, and in that moment he was certain that nuclear detonations, a million times hotter, had no place in this world. The flames and the sound would bring people running, but he stayed a minute to be sure that all physical traces of Frederick Meyer would burn to a crisp, everything except his badge which now reflected the firelight in the pre-dawn sky.

How he ran so far so fast, Georgiy would never be sure. With every step came white-hot pain and thousands of reminders that if he somehow survived, he would carry a scar on his face that would likely terrify any woman or child that gave him a passing glance, leaving him to face the world alone. Perhaps that would be better since his life would be lived on the lam. His only hope was that the KGB and the Americans would believe that he had perished in a botched "nuclear accident" along with the others Moscow had sent.

He covered the distance in just under an hour.

The Ellison home was a hundred yards to the east and faced south, and like nearly all of the houses on the upper-class block, there were still no lights on inside. He had expected the opposite. The quiet house meant either Kitty had already been taken to the hospital to be with her father or they had not bothered with her yet because of the confusion that must have ensued after discovering the warhead was missing. From his position in a large hedge down the street, he waited and watched, and after a few minutes, the first rays of sun shooting over Sunrise Mountain, he was just a moment away from slinking away. But then his eye caught a spark of light coming from the inside of a black Chevy Styleline parked about seventy-five yards away. It was the flame from a cigarette lighter.

Was this the man William had watching Kitty in case Georgiy failed to access Building 11 and the warhead? Or was this the CIA or FBI waiting and watching for him? He quickly discounted the latter scenario. If the manhunt was on and the authorities wanted to talk to Kitty Ellison, they would not sit patiently outside her home until she got out of bed. No, this was a KGB man, a man who had not yet heard from his boss, a man who was waiting for direction.

Georgiy moved slowly and quietly through the vegetation from house to house, careful not to stir the neighborhood dogs. That lasted until they started howling at the police sirens coming in their direction. As the man in the car sat up stiffly in his seat, the commotion gave Georgiy the advantage he needed. When two police cars and a black sedan pulled onto the east end of the street, he had closed to within twenty yards, ducking into a hedge. The men in the cars got out and swarmed the Ellison home.

As he watched Kitty Ellison answer the pounding on her door and the authorities rush in, the man in the Styleline slowly slunk downward in his seat. He would watch and wait. But he was looking forward and, so, did not see the man with the bloody sock tied around his face approach the passenger side of the car.

Georgiy was in the car before he could react, a semiautomatic with silencer leveled at his oversized gut. "You're the man William sent?" he asked in Russian.

"Yes!" the man responded excitedly in Russian. He was older, probably in his fifties. "What's going on? What happened?"

His Russian was perfect, so Georgiy shot him. With so much belly fat, however, it was as if he was having a mild case of heartburn. He reached out with both hands and seized Georgiy's gun hand. His grip was like a vise, and Georgiy could feel the bones in his wrist starting to break. It was his left hand that saved him, his fingers slicing upward into the man's belly right where the blood was now oozing from the bullet wound. When he recoiled, Georgiy shot him in the throat.

That thirty seconds of struggle was all the time it took for the American authorities to remove Kitty Ellison from the house. In her bathrobe, they led her to the black sedan. If any of them looked in Georgiy's direction, he would be seen, as would the blood that seconds earlier sprayed the windshield. He pulled the fat man down across the seat and lay over the top of him, the smell of spent gunpowder and fresh blood filling his nostrils.

His eyes barely above the dash, Georgiy looked at Kitty Ellison one last time. "I'm sorry," he whispered. A minute later, the sirens and lights pulled out of the neighborhood. Georgiy waited. The neighbors were all awake now, many of them looking out their windows or out on the front lawn wondering what all the noise was about so early on a Wednesday morning. Once they withdrew into their respective homes, Georgiy Dudko got behind the wheel and drove inconspicuously away.

# CHAPTER 17

It is 6:00 P.M., and my nemesis the dark night waits outside. I take a call at my desk. It is brief.

"There is a brown Mustang parked just across the highway. Walk Wolverton to it, get in, and drive south. Leave your phone behind. There's one in the car. I'll call you in five minutes."

"Really, Pete? You're jacking cars now?"

No response, just dead air. I had anticipated something like this. Pete is too smart to allow me to take my own vehicle or to bring my phone. This way, he controls the means of transportation and communication. I pull the Kevlar vest over my head, strapping it tightly to my torso, and take my favorite flannel-lined Duluth jacket off the door hook. I walk out of my office for what I know could very well be the last time and nod to the folks. "It's on. Arshal, you're in charge. I'll see you when I see you."

They look at me, knowing that is very wishful thinking. I remove the holster strapped to my thigh and set the Glock down on Tuffy's desk, along with the two spare clips attached to the back of my belt.

Tuffy steps toward me. "Boss."

I shake my head. "No, Tuff. I've got something he wants. He'll trade." I look over to the waiting area where my father is sitting. "All of you are to stay here. If you don't hear from me in three hours, all bets are off. Do what you think best."

It seems inconceivable to them that I am willing to risk my father's life like this, to pass him off as a Soviet spy from the 1950s, even though he is exactly that. This is news I haven't shared with my deputies and which they would never believe, especially Arshal and Tuffy. The man who hired them both, who trained them, who knew their families and friends. I would have told them if the information would have been useful, but in this case all it does is put their lives in more danger.

The air is chilly and the sky all but black, the half-moon just now rising in the east. It took no convincing on my part to get Pop to come along with me on this. He demanded it, unwilling to risk another life for his. I walk him slowly across the street from the office, as much to pass him off as a partially disabled Chuck Wolverton as to allow me to focus on my narrowing field of vision. Pop does his part, bending over Wolverton's walker, his winter hat pulled down low over his forehead, the portable oxygen tank slung over his shoulder. I see the brown Mustang immediately on the corner, and a minute later we are in.

"Why am I driving?" Pop asks.

"Humor me." I tell him to take a right onto the highway. The burner phone on the seat rings.

"I'm here," I say, hitting the speaker button as Pop quickly accelerates. I motion for him to bring the speed down as my eyes adjust to the spray of the headlights. Pop throws on the high beams, which widens my peripheral vision a few feet on either side.

"So far, so good, Sheriff. A few ground rules before we begin: I have eyes on you, obviously. Not me specifically, mind you. It's important you follow my directions as soon as I relay them to you."

About what I figured so far. No doubt Pete has a device under the car that tracks its location so that he and any helpers will know our location at all times. This way he can relay his directions a piece at a time, and I won't know where Pop and I are going to end up.

"Second," says Pete. "It should go without saying that the woman dies if you try anything stupid. That includes drones overhead, helicopters, other vehicles. If I get paranoid, she dies."

I look over at Pop. "Check, no high-tech toys that will make Pete paranoid."

"Third, I know your history, Colonel. You are not a man who likes to lose. You have lost a lot already. Atterbury, Pollack, that imbecile Wardell, and you're about to lose Wolverton. If your pride tempts you to try to even the score, you will lose again. And you will never find Agent Locke."

That confirms what I've suspected: Sana is being held in a separate location. If I have a chance at getting her back, it won't be until I have surrendered my father to the Russians. And I doubt very much this is going turn into one of those Checkpoint Charlie scenes from the movies where I send Pop down the road while they send Sana toward me. This won't be a one-for-one exchange. "Seems pretty clear to me," I say.

"I'll call you back," Pete says. The line goes dead again.

I look over at the man who has shattered my reality. "Pop, you understand what we're doing, right?"

He raises his chin, a look of shame on his face.

"I'm serious. I need you to repeat it to me."

"The guy thinks Wolverton is the illegal. He's never seen me, at least as far as we know, so we let it play as long as we can. When he starts asking me questions, I answer."

Actually, Pete has probably seen Pop fifty times in his two months on the job. My office has his picture on the wall. The question is, will he recognize him in person and in the dark?

"Thing I don't understand," Pop says, "is why you didn't tell the crew who I really am."

I can feel my face getting hot again. "Oh, I may tell them. I may have to. Because whatever happens out here tonight, you are not going anywhere. Are we clear? You remember what to do if it comes to that?"

Pop's head falls forward. "You don't worry about me. I'll do my part."

We drive another minute, and I have Pop keep the Mustang close to thirty-five. "What are we doing all the way out here?" he suddenly asks, a blank look on his face. I know that tone.

My jaw drops. It's not wise to have him driving right now, given his dementia, but right now his disability pales in comparison to mine. "Pop, are you with me? Don't go away on me now."

Pop turns to me. "Porter, this isn't the way home. Take me home. I'm hungry."

*Shit*. "Pop," I say, and then slowly in Russian, "Georgiy, remember where you are. We are going to meet the man who has been hunting you. Do you remember?"

It takes a few seconds, but I see my words registering on his face. "Da," he says, "ya pora domoy." *Yes, it is time to go home.*

I have to look away. "Hearing you speak Russian upends my entire universe, Pop. Maybe we try putting that genie back in the bottle."

He laughs, continuing in his native tongue. "Ah, but it feels so good to say the words out loud. For sixty years, I've only said them inside my head."

"Jesus, please stop." Thankfully, the burner rings again, and I press the green icon on the screen.

"Why are you driving so slow, Sheriff?" Pete asks.

So, he's tracking us but has no idea Pop is driving. "Well," I say,

"Mr. Wolverton is not in very good shape, and he had to spit up a little. But I think we're good now."

"That's good to hear because you're coming up on your exit. In half a mile, take the turn for Cathedral Gorge."

"You're the boss." It is a place of staggering beauty in the daylight, a two-hundred-acre narrow stretch of volcanic ash and bentonite clay formed millions of years ago, carved by erosion into the most spectacular sand-colored spires, some of them as tall and grand as cathedrals. It has been a home to various groups of Anasazi and, most recently, the Southern Paiutes, and as I came to know early in life, is the perfect place to play hide-and-seek.

I motion to Pop to make the turn into the main entrance of the park, more from memory than sight, the car's headlights doing little to help me. "Park at the trailhead," Pete says. Moments later, Pop brings the truck to a stop at the Eagle Point Trailhead.

"Hey, Pete?"

"Yes, Sheriff."

"I have to ask. Why did you take out your own guy at Big Rocks the other day?"

It takes a moment for him to respond. "From the blood, I knew you had wounded him badly. There was no way for me to get him out, and I couldn't risk you interrogating him. It was . . . unfortunate."

"Gosh," I say, using my finest sarcastic tone. "I'm sorry about that. I hope he wasn't a friend of yours."

I can hear the hate simmering in Pete's voice. "Both of you get out of the vehicle. Take the stairs to the canyon floor and walk south on the trail until I tell you to stop. We're watching."

I drop my chin to my chest. "Is it just me, Pete, or is this an odd place for a handoff? Can't we do this up here? Mr. Wolverton here is pushing ninety, and that's a lot of steps to walk down."

"Do it," Pete replies, and I motion Pop to get out of the car.

The moon is a bit higher now, but looking down from the top of the gorge, I can barely see the stairs in front of me. Month by month, my disease is getting worse. If I make it out of here tonight, I will have to reevaluate a number of things, including available treatments, maybe a friendly Chihuahua who can guide me around at night. I've simply put too many lives at risk, Pop's included now. I listen, but there is only the slight wind and the sound of desert crickets that carries on the air. Clicking on my flashlight, I support my father by the arm, and we precariously descend the metal stairs to each of many landings. It takes forever. Finally, we reach the desert floor and begin walking south.

A few hundred yards in, I hear Pete's voice on the still-open line. "Up ahead to your left is a UTV. Get on and take the trail south. Do that until I tell you to stop. It will be noisy so keep the phone to your ear."

I nod, wondering if he's close enough to see me. "I'm impressed, Pete. You know your way around here. Beautiful place during the day. Nothing like this back home, though, right?"

There is no answer. My light finds the vehicle a minute later. It's a nice rig, a Polaris RZR, one of the really expensive ones, and I wonder who Pete ripped off to get it.

"Thank God," Pop says, yelling toward the phone and climbing in. "I'm on oxygen, you know?" I wink at him for playing the part well.

For better or worse, I'll have to take the wheel this time. Pop drives these things like he's riding a rocket, the faster the better. In this canyon, with cliffs and sharp edges, we'll be dead inside two minutes. Thankfully, the headlights help a lot, and we drive slowly down the narrow, bumpy trail that meanders through the many ancient megaliths. Pete has planned well and obviously has called in additional help. The RZR will be how he takes his prisoner out of the canyon, leaving me on foot and too far behind to try to impede his escape. If I'm alive.

"Drive faster," Pete says into my ear.

"Listen, asshole, it's dark out here." I don't speed up because I'm buying time. Passing the Juniper Draw Loop, we come upon the old adobe-style water tower built in the 1930s by the Civilian Conservation Corps.

As we take the bend in the road, I hear Pete say, "Keep going, you're almost there."

That tells me everything I need to know. I reach into my coat pocket and touch a button on a little metal cube the size of a ring box. Then I pull it out and let it fall from my hand into the dirt. A minute later, Pete commands me to pull off the road into the area that fronts the Moon Caves, possibly the most majestic part of the park. Here the volcanic spires stretch highest into the sky, and sheer walls of clay and ash descend more than fifty feet in some places. Some of the interconnecting passages are barely wide enough to hold a human body.

"Stop there. Bring the key with you. Get off the buggy and walk straight. There's a slot canyon to the left. Take it."

Pop and I proceed on foot and enter a narrow crevasse between two massive walls of hardened ash.

"Stay behind me," I tell Pop, pointing the light ahead. In a few minutes, I know, the moon will be high enough to light up these tunnels. Please hurry, I tell the moon.

"Don't have much choice," Pop says, turning sideways to squeeze through the tight space.

After a minute or so, we emerge into a grotto, a huge semicircular end of the road as it were. Pete is waiting twenty feet ahead. With my flashlight, I can just make out that he is wearing his night vision goggles and has a handgun with a silencer pointed in my direction.

"Douse the light, Beck. I can see you just fine." I kill the flashlight. "In the dirt, both of you."

I help Pop to his knees and then drop onto the hard ground. "Wish I could say it's nice to see you, Pete."

"Remove your coat, Sheriff. Slowly. And toss it to me."

I comply, tossing the jacket just a few feet and making Pete come in for it. When he does, I can see him going through the pockets. He's found the key to the four-wheeler. Then some handcuffs land between my knees. "Put them on. Behind you, if you please."

"I gotta say, Pete. Your English is better than most Americans. Kudos to your instructors."

He laughs. "Please. No more Pete. My real name is Drusan. Drusan Prostakov. My father was a diplomat. I spent three years in Washington when I was a boy."

Not a good sign for me. If he's telling me his name, he's going to kill me for sure. "Ah, a diplomat," I say, hoping I can buy another minute. "Hey, Drusan. You ever hear that joke about Russia sending a secret message over diplomatic cable to Syria?"

"No, Beck. I've never heard that one. Please tell me."

"Love to. The message said 'If we attack Turkey from the rear, do you think Greece would help?'"

He actually chuckles. "Funny. I'll pass that one along when I get home." I click the handcuffs into place behind me. "Show me," he says. I swivel on my knees, my back to the Russian now—the young one, not the old one. Prostakov steps over to us.

I ask, "Where is Agent Locke, Drusan? Did you forget to bring her?"

"She's close by." Prostakov kicks me in the back, sending me sprawling onto my chest and face. "Stay there." He moves quickly to the old man on his knees, grabbing him by the chin. "Mr. Wolverton, I presume?"

Pop spits at him. "Get on with it, shithead. I'm ready."

I know that even with night vision, it will be almost impossible for Prostakov to clearly see the face in front of him, so Pop simply has to act the part.

"Is it really you?" Prostakov asks. "I wonder. Do you remember your Russian name, old man?"

"Georgiy Dudko," Pop replies.

"Really? Not Chuck Wolverton?" Prostakov switches to Russian now. "Where were you born, Georgiy Dudko?"

"Odessa, 1930."

My face flinches in the dirt. In addition to realizing for the very first time that I am half Russian, I believed my father was in his early eighties, but it appears now that he is eighty-seven. Good genes, I guess. *What else don't I know?*

"What was your code name?

I see his face go blank. "I don't remember," he says. Prostakov slaps the top of Pop's head, and that seems to do the trick. "Uh . . . Lisa. My code name was Lisa. The fox."

"When were you last in Russia, Lisa?

Pop thinks for a moment. "September . . . no, August 1954."

"Your assignment in America?"

"Look," I say, interrupting and wriggling to my knees again. "Is there some other old man in this county who you think has this information who also speaks Russian? Can we get on with the exchange, please? I brought you your agent, now where is Agent Locke?"

Prostakov squats down in the dirt next to me. "You know, I was this close to killing you that night in Moscow five years ago. That was you, wasn't it, running like a scared rabbit through the zoo and back to your embassy?" I stay silent. "Of course, killing diplomats, even spies, on Russian soil is a tricky thing. Your operation didn't go very well, did it, Colonel?"

"I never went to the zoo when I was there, Ivan. Every Russian citizen lives in a cage, so there wasn't any need."

Prostakov strikes me across the bridge of the nose with his gun, and I hit the dirt hard. "Rudenko was another traitor. You seem to have surrounded yourself with them, Sheriff. I have to tell you it was a bonus when we received intelligence that this old man was still alive and that he was living here, and then we found out *you* were the local police. I volunteered for the assignment immediately."

"Jesus," I say, spitting blood. "You could use some serious counseling." In truth, I need to pull whatever anger I can out of him right now. Making cracks about his countrymen seems to do the trick.

Prostakov turns to the man he has come halfway around the world to find, my father, putting the gun to his temple. "You are a traitor, sir."

Pop's laugh is loud and unrestrained, the sound carrying through the tunnel and bouncing off the sides. "To what, exactly? To a country that wanted to kill thousands and blame it on their enemy?"

"You are also a murderer."

Pop's blood is up, which is not smart right now, but I'm not inclined to stop him. "You have no idea what you're talking about, you ignorant shit. I only killed men who were going to kill me, and I was defending my country by killing Germans forty years before you were an itch in your daddy's pants. Spare me the lecture about murder."

I'm transfixed, hearing him speak with a fluency that even I do not possess and defend a life I never heard of, a life I know nothing about.

Enraged, Prostakov strips off his goggles and grabs Pop by his long silver hair. "Do you know who you murdered, old man? Do you have any idea?"

"I do," I say in English. "And I'll tell you something you didn't plan on, Drusan. I have his remains."

"That is not possible."

"But true nevertheless. I had to do some research, but this whole thing was just way too personal. I mean it's not like it's still the Cold War. For your government to send you over here to find an illegal from sixty years in the past, well, that is not something undertaken lightly. It's just too much risk. That kind of thing can only be approved by your president who—let's face it—has to sign off every time you SVR guys take a crap. So why would he do it? It had to be personal to him. I knew about Miroslav Zhilin, his older brother, knew he supposedly died in a training accident in the Urals. But when I saw the date again, all the pieces fell into place. Spring of 1957."

I can't see much right now, but I can just picture Prostakov's thick, Slavic brow rising into an arch. "Bravo, Sheriff. You continue to amaze me. But it changes nothing."

I tilt my head to one side. "I'm not so sure. But you're the guy with the gun, Drusan. If you want to take that gamble and risk leaving the remains of Maxim's brother behind, that's certainly your call. If I were him, of course, I would want my brother's final resting place to be back home in Kharkiv."

"I checked those graves a week ago, Sheriff. There was nothing in them."

*Just a little more time, pal. That's all I need.* "No, there wasn't. That's because an industrious, slightly whacked-out journalist beat you to it. About three years ago. He was chasing a story on Project 57."

Prostakov takes a big sniff of the night air. "Bullshit." But I know the seed of doubt I just planted is already taking root in his brain. I hear the uncertainty in his next words. "And where are these remains?"

"In a secure place," I answer. "Call your minions and tell them to let Agent Locke go. When I get confirmation of that, I'll tell you where they are."

He hasn't planned on this development, and every second he considers my offer works to my benefit. Finally, he says, "No, I'm leaving now, with the traitor. I will release Agent Locke when I'm clear and am certain we are not being followed. You can keep the remains."

*He isn't going to kill me.* The realization is both a relief and a painful confirmation of what I've been half suspecting all day. I manage to get to my feet, looking Prostakov straight in the eyes. "Yeah, that's just not going to happen tonight."

Prostakov takes two quick steps and hammers his fist into my side, doubling me over but giving me a chance to create more room between me and Pop by falling to my left. "And why is that, Sheriff. Why is that not going to happen tonight?"

"Because," Pop says, "I have this." He thrusts out his tongue, where a pea-size gray oval capsule lay in the center. Before leaving my office tonight, he showed it to me, and I was sure he was bluffing. Upon closer examination and listening to him talk about it, though, I'm now convinced it's the real deal. The outside is surrounded by a thin ampoule covered in rubber, and I know from my studies of Russian intelligence operations, this layer was designed to protect against accidental breakage, since the interior was a concentrated solution of potassium cyanide. He's been ready to take it, to end his life if necessary, for sixty years.

Prostakov pulls his own flashlight from his belt and shines it on Pop's face. "What is that?"

"It's the capsule I was given before the warhead was to be stolen, in case I was caught."

"You expect me to believe that's a suicide pill? You kept it all this time? As what, a keepsake?"

Pop slowly withdraws his tongue. "As a reminder of who I was and what I did, and in case you ever found me. Now here's the deal, you let the woman go, and I will go with you. If you don't, I'll bite into this right now. I'll cheat the hangman, and you go home empty-handed."

"I'll take your corpse with me," Prostakov says with a mocking laugh. "That's hardly empty-handed. And then I kill the sheriff. Now spit it out."

I know I'm out of time. As lucid as my father seems to be at the moment, he could sunset at any moment, actually forgetting what we are all doing here or that he has a cyanide capsule in his mouth. "No," I say. "You release Sana now, or Georgiy here starts foaming at the mouth. Do it my way, and you get a bonus. I'll FedEx you Zhilin's remains."

Prostakov points the gun at Pop's head. "Fine, I'll just kill him."

"Go ahead," Pop says. "I've lived my life. The bullet or the pill, makes no difference to me."

My body tenses as Prostakov presses the muzzle to Pop's forehead. "Hey, Drusan?"

"What?"

"It's funny you picked this particular place to meet."

The assassin gnashes his teeth. "Funny how, Beck?"

"I used to play here as a boy."

"Fascinating."

"And I figured you would end up at Cathedral Gorge after we discovered who you were. We really didn't leave you any other place to hide when we're checking every building."

Prostakov removes his finger from the trigger. "Tremendous powers of deduction, Sheriff. Once again, congratulations. So what?"

"So, you think this passageway only has one way in, but you're wrong about that. There's actually a back way."

Instinctively, Prostakov turns, pulling his night vision goggles back over his eyes and examining the grotto behind him. The bullet catches him center mass, taking him off his feet and launching him behind Pop and me.

I see the muzzle flash, and though I can't see her, I know who fired the shot. From the ground, Prostakov fires back blindly, his goggles in the dirt now. I see him grabbing at his chest with his free hand, his vest taking the round, but also knocking all the air out of him. He climbs to his feet, I swivel on my butt and whip-kick him behind the ankles, somersaulting him backward, the bullets spraying from his handgun into the towering pillars around us and the Milky Way above. Unfortunately for me, I'm squarely between Prostakov and my backup. On my feet now, I lash out with a foot again, catching him square on the jaw, the kick sending me into a roll and landing next to Pop.

"Move now," Brinley yells, and an eruption of bullets follow. I can just make her out, dressed like a ninja and slipping down a sandy slide from above.

"Go, Pop," I say, pushing him to his feet with my shoulder.

As we move in Brinley's direction, I turn back and see Prostakov snap into a shooter's crouch, returning fire. Another round slams into his shoulder, spinning him back into a crease in the walls of ash and clay. He is gone.

But he is going the wrong way.

Brinley keeps firing as she approaches, knowing that the Russian is outgunned and wanting to keep him from coming out of his hole. She's on level ground now and pulls Pop behind a rock.

"Move," she screams at me, still firing. In a moment, I collapse in the dirt next to them.

"Thanks for coming, Brin," I say, trying to catch my breath.

"Thanks for asking me," she says, spinning me around and seeing the cuffs around my wrists.

"Key is in my back pocket." But then I feel something dripping on me. It's warm and liquid, and I think for a moment I've been hit. "What the—"

"It's me," Brinley squeaks. "Caught one in the biceps." She takes the flashlight from her belt and shines it on her arm.

The bullet has split the polyester fabric of her black shirt, and I tear the sleeve off her arm as gently as I can. Blood is oozing from the wound. "Shit, Brin." I use the torn cloth as a field dressing, wrapping it tightly around the arm. She winces but doesn't make a sound. "Through and through, no artery." In the glow of the flashlight, I can see her getting woozy from the initial shock.

"Bad luck," she says. "Now let's go kill him." She unslings the H&K MP-5 off her other shoulder and hands it to me, along with the two magazines in her vest. From a holster on her leg, Brinley pulls out a Sig .380.

"You sure?"

"He took the wrong slot, Beck. No easy way back to the four-wheeler from there."

I nod. "Pop, you stay here. If we're not back in ten, you go right back out this slot, the same one we came through." I turn to Brinley. "You can't climb with that arm, so I'll go high."

"Okay," she says and is gone into the crack Prostakov took a minute earlier.

I scramble up the rock face Brinley came down, thankful for the dim light of the half-moon in the eastern sky and for my memory, which has recorded every hand and foothold up these steep faces since I was old enough to walk. Moon Caves are a labyrinth of passages, many of them dead ends, and that gives us the advantage now. Prostakov has been hit twice, one that might have cracked a rib and another in the shoulder. The loss of blood from Brin's 9x19mm Parabellum rounds might not prove lethal, but it will slow him down.

I work my way up the spires. Before I can get Sana—I'm certain now where she is—I need to kill Prostakov. I really need to kill him.

# CHAPTER 18

I know the Moon Caves like a mouse knows a maze. I'd been in every hole, crack, groove, and notch as a boy and memorized the outcome of every path. And just like one can see the way out when viewing the maze from above, I know how tough that can be on the ground floor with tight walls and umpteen turns to the left and right, the majority of them ending in a solid wall. It can be quite unnerving for a first-timer. Crawling carefully around the top requires an equal amount of experience, especially in the dark, lest one fall the equivalent of a five-story building to one's death, so I work slowly over the uneven towers, seeing the map in my head, listening for movement below. My turn to be one step ahead.

Brinley has spent at least as much time here as me. It is the perfect playground, and on any given summer day you can find half the kids within a twenty-mile radius skittering through its hallways and across the great rooms of Moon Caves. On summer nights, the teens of Lincoln County come for other adventures. On some of those nights long ago, Brinley would spy on me and my girlfriends from above. Tonight though, in the middle of February, she slips silently over the soft ground beneath me with a handgun, playing for keeps with a Russian assassin. My money is on Brin.

Her size is an advantage, and I know her well enough to know she will stop every few feet and listen for her target, his larger square shoulders scraping against the walls of the narrow tunnels. I follow the sounds, too, and by the series of turns Prostakov is taking, I know he's heading into a section the locals call the Rabbit Hole, another seeming dead end but with a small opening cut into the rock that opens into another chamber. Pausing, I think I hear a voice. It's low, maybe an expletive uttered under the breath. He has reached what he thinks is the end and will have to come back now, toward me. I sling the MP-5 around my neck and slowly lower my body into the slot canyon, my hands and feet digging into the walls of ash and clay to support my weight. I picture Brinley slithering on her belly along the floor of the tunnel like a snake to the next bend and then the next. In the confines of the Moon Caves, better to present a smaller target.

The moon is overhead now, casting its light down through the slit in the mountain carved by wind and water over a million years. I hear the footfalls approaching, rounding sharp corners, coming toward me, freezing me, a sitting duck high up on a wall, the sweat beading on my forehead, my arm and leg muscles beginning to cramp. If I reach for the rifle, I fall.

From farther down the winding channel, I hear something brush against the wall just enough to disturb the otherwise silent air. Prostakov fires repeatedly, the sound deafening and filling the tapering space. I see the muzzle flashes from the other end and the distinct sound of Brinley's Sig returning fire. The rounds have nowhere to go but into flesh and dirt, and huge clouds of pulverized ash erupt into the air, concealing the space below me. When she stops to reload, I know Prostakov has already done so. Through the rising particles of dirt, I catch movement to my right and see him advancing on Brinley's position, firing again. When he passes below me, there is no time to think. I let go, my bare hands the only thing guiding my descent down the steep walls. Hearing something above him, or more probably noting a shadow appearing beside him, Prostakov suddenly realizes what is about to happen. When he looks up, he sees me, halfway up the wall and coming down like bag of cement.

There is something called a Splat Calculator that tells you how fast and how hard something will fall from a certain height. For my weight and the height I'm falling from, I'm moving at just over thirty miles per hour in about a second, so when the Russian's gun comes up too late, my boots catch him square on the collarbones, exploding them. The collision sends us both crashing to the cavern floor. I roll off Prostakov and to my feet between him and Brinley.

"It's over, Pete," I say, the submachine gun firmly set in my bleeding hands.

In agony, Prostakov staggers to his feet, gun in hand but unable to use his arms. "I still have your agent, Sheriff. Kill me and she dies."

I shoot him in the abdomen, just under his body armor, sending him backward another few feet, jamming his shoulders between the walls and preventing him from falling. "That's for Agent Atterbury, Guy Pollack, and Wardell Spann."

Prostakov coughs a lungful of blood out through his mouth and manages to laugh. "I lied. She's already dead."

I shoot him again in the thigh. His leg buckles and he slides to his knees. "That's for terrorizing poor Michaela Edwards."

Prostakov spits out more blood, his eyes red and glowing in the moonlight. "We will . . . send . . . more—"

I take a last step forward. "And this is for my friend, Anatoly Rudenko." I let loose a burst into the Russian's chest, where several rounds penetrate the Kevlar and enter his heart.

As the smoke from the machine gun's barrel rises into the sky, taking Drusan Prostakov's evil spirit with it, I feel Brinley's arms slip under my arms and around my chest.

"Hey, brother," she says. "You good?"

I spin around and see her covered in ash and dirt. "Never better. You?"

She nods. I see something protruding from Prostakov's coat pocket. When I remove it, I know instantly what it is. I recognize the unit and know its manufacture all too well. In a few minutes, we're out in front of the Moon Caves, where Pop is waiting by the RZR.

I drop the key in his hand. "Pop, get Brin to the hospital and get that arm looked after."

"Jesus," Brin gasps. "Your hands."

They're shredded. "I'm good," I say.

"Where are you going?"

"After Sana," I say, ramming a fresh magazine into the MP-5 and slinging it over my head.

"He said she was dead, Porter."

"He was lying. I know where she is. Now go."

# CHAPTER 19

The Lincoln County Airport is very small, not like an airport at all and really more like the many tiny airstrips that my father the Soviet spy must have seen a million times when he worked at the test site. It has a single runway, a few outbuildings, and a pilot's lounge. It is also within the Desert MOA, or Military Operations Area of Nellis Air Force Base, which begins at 1,500 feet above the airfield, meaning anything above that altitude is technically military air space. The U.S. Government also uses the airfield occasionally, but none of us civilians are allowed to know why, which is fine by me. Most importantly, the airfield is located only a mile from where I left Drusan Prostakov in the Moon Caves. How convenient.

I have Prostakov's night vision goggles, but I take my time approaching anyway and see a single plane parked on the dark runway. As I get closer, the aircraft takes shape. It's a sleek white Gulfstream 5, a favorite of the clandestine services of the United States. The interior of the plane is lighted and the door is open, its short ladder extending to the tarmac. I see no guards outside and so proceed up the steps holding Brinley's machine gun in front of me. I really like this gun, and it kind of pisses me off that her armory is better than mine.

Entering the plane, I peek into the cockpit where two uniformed pilots are chatting. Looking down the fuselage, I'm not surprised to see the high-backed white leather chairs and couch arranged in an L shape. Facing me is a man in his forties with short black hair with too much gel and wearing a white dress shirt with too much starch, a blue tie, and a pair of pretentious suspenders to hold up his pin-striped slacks. He's talking to someone in front of him that I cannot see. I don't have to see. I know who it is. As I close the distance, the man looks up and sees a stranger advancing on him with a short-barreled automatic rifle. He freezes in midsentence.

Slowly, Sana Locke rises from her chair and turns, looking just as nice as the day we met and wearing a smart gray business suit and white blouse. Her hair is washed and perfectly styled, curling predominately over her right shoulder. With her large circular earrings, she looks like she could be heading to a cocktail party or a Security Council meeting at the U.N. "Beck," she says, her breath catching in her throat, "I'm . . . so happy it's you."

"Uh-huh," I say. The man in the suit gets to his feet, but I level the MP-5 at his head. "You the person in charge of this operation?"

Hesitantly, he nods. "I am."

On the small side table next to him, I see a twin to the radio I took off Prostakov, along with some other electronic devices, trackers by the look of them. "Then I'm guessing this belongs to you." I toss him the radio, and when he lifts his hands to catch it, I take one step forward and slam the heel of my hand up under his nose, right in the septum. Before his head even bounces off the bulkhead behind him, he's raining blood all over his nice white shirt. He'll need surgery to repair that. "That's for putting my people in harm's way."

"Beck, please!" Sana yells. "This isn't necessary."

Suspender man manages to right himself and pulls a nice white handkerchief from his pocket to stanch the blood flow. "Off the plane, asshole," I tell him. "Take the pilots with you."

Sana turns back to the man. "It's okay, Jeff. He won't hurt me."

Slowly, the man approaches, his hands in the air. As he passes, I throw him against the couch and pat him down for weapons. Finding none, I grab him by the collar and toss him toward the front of the plane. Moments later, he exits with the two pilots. Now it's just Sana and me, and I motion her to sit.

"You clean up very well, Sana," I say, unslinging the MP-5 and wiping the sweat from my forehead as I plop down on the pristine couch. "I see the CIA is still sparing no expense on its aircraft." I nod toward the rear of the plane. "Full shower?"

Sana smiles and leans toward me. "It's not what you think, Beck."

"Sit back, please," I say softly but seriously.

Slowly, Sana rocks back into her seat, looking me over. "My God, what happened to you?"

There are some nice white cloth napkins on the table in front of me, so I take one and wipe my bloody hands on it.

She asks, "I take it our Russian friend is not coming?"

I reach to the table again where three glasses and a bottle of eighteen-year-old Macallan are set up. Examining the bottle and approving, I pour myself two fingers. I pass the glass briefly under my nose and take a long sip. "If you mean Mr. Prostakov, no, he will not be joining us this evening."

"He told you his name?" she asks, her eyes on stalks.

I drain the rest of the glass. "Well, at the time, I'm sure he thought it was going to be him sitting here sipping scotch instead of me."

Sana folds her hands together in her lap, which draws her blouse tighter into her very alluring cleavage and, inevitably, my attention. "And Mr. Wolverton? Is he . . ."

"Alive?"

Sana nods.

"Yes, he is," I answer. "But sadly for all of us, he is not the illegal. I was really hoping he was." Her expression tells me she's skeptical. "I led Prostakov to believe he was because I thought I needed to make a trade for you. But Wolverton is just an old Army deserter."

"Are you making that up, Beck?"

I hold up three shredded fingers. "Scout's honor. I can prove it if need be, but I don't think that's necessary at this juncture."

"And why is that?"

I pour myself another scotch. "Because Prostakov is dead, and I'm angry enough to kill as many Russians . . . or CIA agents as I need to. I'm pretty sure this ends now, Sana."

There is no surprise in her expression, just the slightest lifting of one eyebrow. "When did you know I wasn't FBI?"

I sit back and stretch my arms along the top of the couch, my bloody hands stroking and smearing the white leather. "I had my doubts when you showed up in my office. Your badge looked like it had never been opened. Too shiny, too new."

The right side of Sana's mouth pulls upward, making a slurping noise. "I told them it wouldn't hold up. We were pressed for time."

"What is it you do exactly, for the CIA?"

"I guess you would say I'm a facilitator of sorts."

*Of course you are.* "Facilitator. That's a five-dollar word."

She laughs. "It is. So, was that it, just the badge?"

"There were the little things, like your lack of familiarity with crime scenes and autopsies. Plus, you recognized the thallium we found at Atterbury's for what it was, though you did your best to hide it. An FBI agent would not have made the connection to KGB work."

"Very astute observations."

"Thank you. And then there was the way you parceled out the details of what happened in the desert that night in 1957."

"That was true, Beck."

I nod. "Yeah, I believe you. But an FBI agent would never have shared that with me. They don't trust local cops with national security stuff. You did, because you were thinking I could find the illegal for you before Prostakov got to him. Did he really take you at Wolverton's, or was that all planned for my benefit?"

"I'm embarrassed to say he did. I never saw him coming. He darted me as I understand he did you. And you saw me strung up in his basement. That was all too real, I assure you."

"Uh-huh." She may be lying again, I don't know, and while I think about it, I pick some dirt out of the tread on my boot and flick it on the Gulfstream's otherwise spotless carpet. "You don't seem too angry about it now."

Sana fiddles with an earring. "Oh, trust me, I would have loved to have killed him myself, but, well, then it seemed prudent to make the deal."

I look up, the revelation hitting me full in the face. "So, you go free and the CIA makes sure Zhilin gets the guy who killed his brother."

"That was the agreement, yes."

"And you assumed I would just hand over the illegal to Prostakov, trade him straight up for you."

She shrugs her beautifully toned shoulders. "That was the hope. I told our people I didn't think you would, that you were too principled."

I wonder now what I would have done if the illegal had turned out to be somebody other than Pop. "So, Prostakov had the green light to take him from me if I didn't play along."

"High-stakes international diplomacy, Beck. You've been there. You know." I do. I point to her glass. She nods, and I pour her a drink. "How did you figure out it was Zhilin's brother?" she asks.

Before I can answer, suspender man pokes his head around the bulkhead, and I fire a burst from the MP-5 above his head, the rounds tearing into the beautiful wood paneling and scaring him back. Sana never flinches as the smoke settles around us. "Boyfriend?" I ask.

She laughs. "Jeff is my boss, so please don't shoot him."

I set the gun down on the sofa again. "As I told you earlier, this whole thing was just way too personal. I knew it had to be someone high up. I had done a bio on Maximum—that's what we called Maxim when I was in Moscow. I knew about his brother. The rest was just math."

Sana raises her glass and clinks it against mine. "I read that bio. You certainly captured the man." She takes a sip and then swirls the scotch provocatively with a finger. "How did Prostakov die?"

"Badly," I say dispassionately. "He shot Brinley. She'll be okay, but that was sort of the icing on the cake for me."

She looks like she just lost a big pot in a poker game. "I'm sorry, Beck. I hope you believe that. We had to agree to let Prostakov finish this and take his illegal home with him."

My lips purse. "Zhilin gets his brother's killer, the U.S. has one less Russian spy in the country, and the CIA gets its valuable agent back and some concessions to be named later."

She nods. "We had an opportunity, and you know what those are worth in my world."

I don't respond for a moment, mostly so I don't have the urge to fire this gun again. "Your opportunity was not worth my deputy's life. It wasn't worth Guy Pollack's life."

Sana empties her glass. "Don't be naïve."

She has a worldview I will never agree with. It's disappointing but not unexpected. "So, if he were still alive, you would have given Zhilin the illegal even though he prevented a nuclear catastrophe and saved thousands of people?"

She plays with the ends of her hair. "Is he still alive? I wonder. My people, and Zhilin's people will think he might be."

I bring the MP-5 up and rest it across my lap, my eyes narrowing. "You should dissuade them of that notion, Sana." I wait for her to answer my previous question, but she clearly doesn't want to. "I just want to be clear. We wouldn't protect him is what you're saying?"

"These things are complicated, Beck. Nothing is black and white in intelligence, you know that. The illegal's value to us is . . . negligible at this point."

Negligible. It's the kind of arm's-length word people with no moral compass use to describe a person's value. I fold my arms across my chest. "And me? Was I an expendable piece on the board as well?"

Sana scoots over next to me on the couch. "You were expressly *off* the board. That was an essential part of the deal."

I believe her. Prostakov clearly had no intention of killing me, so I add one bonus point to Sana's score.

"Please understand," she continues, "we couldn't bring in a bunch of agents to get Prostakov. The CIA isn't supposed to operate on U.S. soil. We had to go to the president to get authorization to just get me here. And after spending some time with you, I was confident you would find the illegal. Your talents are that extraordinary."

I flash back on when Pop told me his real name. "But I didn't find him, so what now?"

She stares at me, searching my eyes for the truth. "Well, Zhilin is wanting something out of this, and we want to give it to him. Having a chit we can use in the future is everything in our world, as you know."

"You mean in the world of spooks and dark alleys and lies."

She chuckles. "I do. But you killing Prostakov doesn't help us, I'm afraid. In fact, I'd have to say it's a bit of a setback."

I stare into the dark orbits of her eyes. *Does she know about Pop?* "I'll tell you what, Sana. I'm going to give you your chit. It's not what you were hoping for, but I have a feeling it's worth a lot more."

She's shocked, genuinely and for the first time since I met her, I think. "What do you have, Beck?"

"If you'd like to take a ride with me, I'll show you. And it's going to cost."

Two hours later, Agent Locke and I climb out of the Grey Wolf helicopter Sana's boss has ordered up. We have flown seventy miles, landing on a baseball field a hundred yards away from an L-shaped building that serves as the Alamo substation of the Lincoln County Sheriff's Department. I've given Sana my Duluth jacket since her CIA business suit is insufficient protection against the cold. Together we walk into center field, our breath visible white wisps. I take her hand in one of my now-bandaged hands, leading her over the brown winter grass and across the blacktop to the station, a large Air Force flashlight shining the way.

Inside, Arshal has somehow beaten us here, having made the trek south in his vehicle. "Nice ride," he says, with a head bob out the window toward the government helo.

"I'm thinking of getting one," I say. "Arshal, you remember Agent Locke?"

"Good evening, Deputy," Sana says.

Arshal strokes his mustache. "For some, ma'am. For some."

"You pick up my package, Arshal?"

"Yeah. Over in the boot."

The boot is what we call the gun locker. I take Sana around the corner of the building and open the door with a combination. On the floor are four long gunnysacks. I reach down and lift the end of one, its contents loose and shifting inside the bag.

"Is that what I think it is?" she asks.

I nod. "For Maxim, with my compliments. He'll have to determine which of the four is his brother Miroslav, of course. He's big on family, so he might even be willing to hand over the name of your mole to get Miroslav back."

She crouches down to more closely examine her treasure. "Where did you—"

"I think we're done sharing secrets, don't you?"

Sana pulls herself up on my arm, squeezing lightly. "If this is the genuine article, I think this will do the trick, Beck, and I'm very grateful."

I'm sure she knows we're only a short distance from the home of my good buddy, X-Files, and that's he's the only logical source for what's in front of her now, but she's being polite and pretending. I put my hands on my waist so they won't wander anywhere else. "I suppose this is where you tell me that none of this ever happened, and that you were never here."

Closing the door, she leans in to kiss me on the mouth. My hand gently intercedes before our lips connect, and she settles for a handshake. "None of this ever happened, and I was never here."

I kick one of the gunnysacks lightly with my boot, rattling the remains inside. "Meanwhile, several people are dead, my little sister was almost killed, and a completely innocent young woman was traumatized."

There is nothing she can say that will change any of that, so she doesn't. Instead, she offers something else. "Beck, when I learned about what happened in Moscow five years ago, I had my people go back through the material we knew had been sold to the Russians."

My eyes stay focused on hers, revealing nothing, I hope.

"The leaker has been giving them information for a dozen years. That's how they knew about Rudenko. It wasn't anything you did."

I open the door again. "I appreciate you sharing that with me. But I was supposed to protect him."

We stand in silence while Sana calls her guys and they come and collect the remains. I see her to the front door of the building. When I don't follow her out, she looks back. "Aren't you coming? I'm happy to give you a lift. Nice and quick, no more of this horrible driving."

"No thanks," I say. "Now that you have what you need, I'd be afraid of falling out of your nice helicopter. Or maybe that Jeff guy would push me. A long drive suits me just fine right about now. Good luck, Sana."

# CHAPTER 20

When I arrive at the hospital, it is already past midnight, and the twenty-bed facility seems as much asleep as the rest of the county. I find Tuffy sitting inside the tiny waiting area of the emergency room speaking to Dr. Hadji Bishara, the wispy chief medical officer. I plop down beside them, and Hadji cleans and rebandages my hands while they fill me in, first on the collection of Wardell's body and then on Michaela Edwards's condition.

"No signs of sexual assault," said Hadji in his thick Turkish accent. "She was very clear that he never did that, so it's more a matter of care and counseling now. She was a bit banged up, as you saw, but mainly bruises, some rope burns. We'll release her tomorrow probably."

"Thanks, Hadji. Appreciate you looking after her." I look over at Tuffy. One thing we have our share of in Lincoln County is sexual assaults. She knows what I'm going to ask, so I don't.

"I think Michaela is telling the truth," she tells me. "She says Pete fed her, took her to the bathroom whenever he was home. He just kept her locked up. But even without rape, the psychological trauma of being kidnapped and held in a cage will take some time, but we'll get there. She'll be okay."

Tuffy is not only my best investigator, she exudes a warmth toward other women that makes her easy to trust. Michaela is in good hands. I ask, "And Clem?"

"He blames us," she replies. "But I imagine that might wear off over time."

My eyes turn to Hadji. "Brinley?"

The doctor looks at Tuffy and then back to me. "Yes, she took a bullet in the left biceps as you know, and while it thankfully avoided the brachial artery, it significantly tore through much of the muscle. She lost a little blood, and I transfused two units into her. I repaired the biceps surgically. In fact, we just ended a half hour ago."

"Recovery?"

"Six to eight weeks in a sling. Physical therapy. She's extremely strong, this girl. At her fitness level, she might be back to normal in a few months."

My expression softens with relief. I need to crash, maybe in one of Hadji's beds for a week or so. "Thanks, Hadji. I'll make sure she does the therapy."

Tuffy scratches her nose. "The old man is in the room with her. He wouldn't leave."

"Yeah, she's everything to him." I find them both down the hall in the surgical recovery suite, Brinley still asleep from the anesthesia, and Pop asleep in the armchair next to the bed. I gaze down on my father, a man five years older than I thought, a man with a different name and a history I know little about. *My whole life is not what I thought it was.*

I take Brinley's hand, running my fingers through hers. Her left arm is heavily bandaged and already in a sling. Two IV bags hang above and behind her, dripping antibiotics and painkiller into her veins.

"Hey," she whispers, her green eyes coming alive.

"Hey, sis. You should be asleep."

"Did you get Sana back?"

I smile and pull some strands of hair away from her face. "I did, but not how you might think. I'll fill you in later."

"Don't let her get away, Porter. You're not getting any younger."

That shocks me. "I didn't think you liked her."

"I don't. But you do."

Time to change the subject. "You saved our lives, Brin. Pop and me both."

She reaches up with her good arm and strokes my face. "Then you saved me."

I wipe a tear out of my eye. "I almost got you killed."

"I would die for you or Pop anytime, Porter."

I bend down and pull her gently into my arms, her head into my neck. "I'm going to work a little harder to make sure that never has to happen, okay?"

We hold each other until she releases me and lies back down. "He's still Pop. He might have been someone else, too, but he's still Pop. You know that, right?"

As she falls back to sleep, I realize I don't know the answer to that question.

# CHAPTER 21

We bury Wardell Spann three days later out at the Bullion-ville Cemetery, a place I have always likened to Boot Hill in Tombstone, Arizona, where old cowboys were once laid to rest at the edge of a mining town long since abandoned and covered by sand carried in the desert wind. It's actually a historic marker now, and I had requested and received special dispensation by the governor to inter Wardell at Bullionville since his ancestors helped start the town's first mills in the mid-1850s. Some of the grave sites are no longer marked, eroded by time and weather, but Wardell will have a nice stone over his resting place. The staff at the Lincoln County Sheriff's Department has seen to that.

It's a nice late winter day in the high desert. The sun has already ticked past forty degrees, warm by our standards, and the snow on the ground is as scarce as the vegetation. Wardell's two sons have come in from Utah, though his ex-wife has not, and the entire Sheriff's Department circles the plot with some neighbors and townspeople as the pastor reads a few verses. And although he is certainly entitled to it, there is no twenty-one-gun salute. Everyone has heard enough gunfire for a while.

Clem Edwards and his wives attend as well, including Michaela, since they view Wardell as having died while trying to save her. I will never argue the point, as it's possible he went there with that idea somewhere in his mind. More likely, he went to spite me and prove me wrong that he had hired an agent of the Russian Foreign Intelligence Service. Amon Jessup shows up too, and stands with his brother, Arshal, a sight I am happy to see. As the casket is lowered, my mind turns to a vision of what another burial sixty years ago might have looked like, when four Russians were unceremoniously covered with dirt. Four men killed by another Russian.

With Brinley by my side, I say goodbye to everyone and drive home to Lost Meadows. It is Sunday after all, and Sunday is always dinner with Pop. We find him out in the back pasture with his pet sheep. He has already forgotten that Wardell is dead, a man he worked closely with for many years, so I didn't see any point in bringing him to the graveside service. It would have upset him greatly, and for all I know he would have blurted out his real identity to everyone in attendance. I couldn't risk that. Better to let sleeping dogs lie. Both of them, I think.

"Go easy on him," Brinley says. "He might remember a lot of the stuff from the past but still has trouble with right now."

Before I can respond, Pop's head swivels around, and he waves to us. When he makes his way to the back porch, he looks at Brinley, her arm in a sling. "What the hell happened to you?"

She looks up at me. "See?"

"She got shot, Pop," I say. "Do you remember that?"

"Shot? By who?"

I put my arm around him. "How about a beer, Pop? I could use a beer."

We take a seat, and Brinley fetches us each a Corona. "I can leave if you'd like," she says softly to me.

I shake my head. "He's as much your dad as he is mine, Brin.

Stay." She nods and sits down on the porch swing next to the man named Joe Beck.

"What did you do to your arm this time, girl?" Pop asks again. It's a question she will get over and over again for the next few weeks.

"Pop," I say, "tell us about your life growing up . . . in Russia."

It takes a moment, as he first appears confused and then, either in fear or shame or perhaps the realization of what he has lost, covers his face with his hands.

Brin puts her good arm around him. "It's okay, Pop. We just want to know."

I have never seen my father cry, and my gut seizes when he begins sobbing. "You know about that? I told you?"

"You did," I say. "And it's all right."

"We love you, Pop," Brin reassures him. "Tell us about Georgiy."

Pop wipes the water from his eyes and squeezes her hand. He loves her more than me, but that's okay. She was marooned in the desert just like he was, and that makes them kindred spirits. "Georgiy Dudko was my name, yes. I was born in Odessa in the Ukraine, a part of the Soviet Union, in 1930."

Brinley chuckles. "So, you're an older coot than you previously let on."

Pop removes his hat and scratches his head. "Am I? How old did I say I was?"

"It's not important. We stopped counting a while back."

His head bobs a few times. "Right, well the Germans invaded on June 22, 1941. I guess I was ten or eleven then. My parents and my sister were killed by the bombs on the first day while I was at school."

Brinley pulls back. "What were their names, Pop?"

I have never been happier to have Brinley here. She has a level of empathy far beyond mine, and she has already recognized this as a catharsis for the only father figure she has ever known. She catches my smile, thinking it's for Pop, but it's not. We may not share blood, but our bond is the most important thing in my life.

Pop continues, "My father was Dmitry. He worked in a factory. My mother, too. Her name was Irina. My sister was Nadezhda. She was two years older than me and the prettiest girl I ever saw." He tears up again, his hands squeezing his cheeks together. "Sometimes, I can see their faces."

I take a pull on my beer to keep my own waterworks at bay. "What happened during the war? I've been there, but I can't imagine how it must have been."

Pop raises his beer bottle and points it at me. "No, you can't." His eyes close and then clamp shut even tighter, and Brin and I exchange worried glances. "We had nothing once the Nazis came. We retreated into the forests, wherever we could hide and find food, and then one day they gave me a rifle, and I started killing." His eyes open again. "When is it Sunday again? I like our Sunday dinners."

Brinley rubs his arm. "Today, Pop. I have a roast in the oven."

"And potatoes?"

"Cut thin, just like you like them," she says.

I lean forward in my seat. "What happened after the war, Pop?"

It takes him a second to find the 1940s again in his mind, and his eyes brighten at the memory. "I went to university to study physics!"

Physics? I've known the man for forty-five years, and he never so much as hinted at an interest in Newton or Einstein or the laws of the universe. The only laws he seemed to care about were the ones that governed how people treated each other. That said, I guess my middle name makes more sense to me now. I'm not saying if it's Newton or Einstein, as both are equally disastrous.

"Yes, physics," he says, seeing the shock on my face. "I loved the stars and was interested in rockets. And then the KGB found me." His tone turns morose. "They sent me to school, trained me to spy, asked me to come to America. Do you know they sent me here to get a job at the Proving Ground?"

I nod. "Where you became Freddie Meyer."

He laughs. "Yes, Freddie Meyer. That was me. I was hired as a security guard there. I saw everything." His jaw clenches for a moment, making the scar on his face stand out even more. "I saw what the bombs were doing, the fallout to the people and the animals downwind. I didn't like it."

I lean back into the wooden rocker, pushing it back with my feet. "Do you remember Project 57, Pop?"

He puts his arm around Brinley. "What happened to that arm again?"

"The Russian shot me, Pop. Remember?" I roll my eyes and Brinley gives me a stern warning with hers.

"Oh, that's right. That's my fault, Brin." He kisses the top of her head.

"Nobody's fault, Pop," I reply. "You saved a lot of lives that night in 1957, and the Russians never forgave you for it. But I have to ask, why did you even take the bomb if you weren't going to let them use it?"

He looks up, searching through the fog. "Kitty," he finally says.

Brinley and I look at each other, both wondering if this is just another episode where he imagines things. "Who is Kitty?"

And he tells us the story, all of it. It takes the better part of an hour, and we listen with fascination as he recounts his mission, his fears, his role in a war that brought the world close to annihilation, and how he really got that scar on his face preventing what would have later become known as the first *dirty bomb* from being unleashed on a civilian population, none of which he views as heroic at all. When he is done, Brinley tries her best to hide her tears and says she needs to check the roast. I get up and sit down next to Pop.

"I upset her," he says.

"No, Pop. She loves you, that's all. She's proud of you."

"What about you, Porter? What do you think of your old man?"

I think for a moment. "I don't know what to say, Pop. I guess I don't really know you."

He nods. "It was my cross to bear. I almost told you when you were taking Russian classes, and I almost told you again when you were leaving for the Army. But I didn't have the courage. It was just easy to be dead, I guess. At least for Georgiy Dudko to be dead."

I shake my head. "I don't know if I would have had the courage to do what you did. I've been a soldier. I know what it's like. But you gave up everything for a greater good."

He nods. "I knew I couldn't live with myself if I'd gone through with it. It doesn't take a lot of guts to make that call."

"But why did you come back here? You could have hidden anywhere in this country, and you had to know they were looking for you."

Little Joe ambles over and Pop dives his hands into the animal's furry mane. "Believe me, I did know. I tried to stay away. Did, in fact, for five or six years. Took odd jobs under different names. It wasn't hard. I had been trained how to create new identities, forge papers, be someone else. But I came back, I guess, because I felt partly responsible."

"For?"

"For what was happening here. I knew people were suffering. I knew all that contamination had destroyed people's lives. The government had moved the testing underground by that time, and I actually went to a few of those antinuke protests when I first got back. I wanted to tell people the truth."

"But you couldn't."

He shakes his head. "Nope. I didn't want to go to prison, and I knew that would happen if they caught me, so I came up here to Lincoln County and took a job making leather goods for your grandfather."

"And Mom?"

"Bravest woman I ever met," he says, fighting back the tears. "Couldn't believe she would even look at me with this big, ugly scar on my face, but she did. I didn't deserve her. She had three miscarriages before you, did you know that?"

The question makes me rub my eyes. "I did not. I'm sorry." It makes sense to me now, how he doted on my mom as if she were the only thing that mattered in this world. Having lost through deceit a love already, he would never let himself be the cause of losing another. His overprotection of her, his decision to become a cop. All of it was about saving the world in his own way.

He puts a hand on my leg. "So many had miscarriages then. Birth defects, too. God, it was a tough time. Do you remember when you were a kid and the government would come around and test our milk every month?"

The memory makes me laugh. "And they would come to the school and check our thyroid glands every year."

Pop's head rocks back. "They rewrote people's DNA with all those tests, son. Most of them, good God-fearing people like your mom who were loyal Americans and would never question the government. All of that radiation sitting there in the dirt all around them."

He's right. I think about all the people I have known over the years who have gotten sick or died of some form of cancer. There are so many. Sacrificed for what, I wonder. "How did you end up at the sheriff's department then? Weren't you afraid they would find out who you really were?"

"Oh, by then I had already started passing information to the FBI, and I was living as Joe Beck. I was used to carrying a gun and using it when I needed to, and I found out the department didn't fingerprint you when you applied, not like a big police force. If they had, I would have been caught right away. But it was the job I was made for, I guess."

I notice Brinley watching from behind the screen door now. "Regrets, Pop?"

He thinks for a minute, sadness clouding his features. "For a long time, I regretted having to kill those five men. I think that bugged me more than anything else."

My mouth falls open. "Five? You mean four, don't you?"

"No, it was five. There was the four in the desert and then the guy waiting outside Kitty's house."

I understand immediately. "She was their insurance you would go through with it."

"Yeah," Pop says, looking away.

"Did you love her, Pop? Kitty, I mean?"

He looks back at me. "God help me, son, I did."

# CHAPTER 22

Winter is like a bad cold here, and on Monday morning, a heavy snow returns to Lincoln County. Down in Vegas, it's going to be eighty degrees today, but I'm happy to be right where I am. I return to my office looking forward to hearing about the everyday crimes of the county: a bar fight perhaps, maybe some petty theft. Even the discovery of a new heroin connection threatening the community. But as soon as Tuffy sees me enter the building, she nods toward my office. Knocking my boots together to remove the snow, I grab my favorite mug and pour some coffee. I peek sheepishly around the corner. CIA agent Sana Locke is sitting in my chair, her knee-high boots resting on my desk.

I curse under my breath, mostly because seeing her again causes that contempt I have been clinging to for the last few days to fade. "Thought you had gone back to the factory where they make gorgeous women spies."

"I missed you," Sana says, pulling her feet down. "And . . . the Agency was curious as to how you were going to write all this up."

My flesh tingles as her eyes burrow into my soul, and I take a seat across the desk, hiding my obvious pleasure. "All this?"

"Yes, well apparently, there is still some concern about national security, as you might expect."

Sipping my coffee, I say, "You mean the stuff about most of old Las Vegas having a half-life of 24,000 years and Russian assassins?"

She sweeps her beautiful hair back with both hands. "Those are the things causing the most concern, yes."

I love it when we play like this. "Well, I was thinking I would have to explain it as a newly hired cop was mentally unstable and killed a few people and took a woman hostage before he was caught and killed."

Sana nods appreciatively. "We realize the position this puts you in, Beck."

"Yeah, my own officer going haywire doesn't exactly look good for me. Thankfully, the next election is three years away, and I doubt they'll recall me over this. A couple of the commissioners might want me gone, but Wardell was their guy to begin with, and he's the one that hired the guy we called Pete—Mr. Prostakov to you. Right now, it looks like Wardell went to confront him about his false résumé and Pete went berserk. I should be okay, but thanks for caring, Sana."

She leans across the desk. "I do, you know, care."

I'm not sure she does. She's a good spy, and in my experience, spies have trouble caring about anyone but themselves. "So, we're good?"

"What about your deputies? They are now privy to information, some of which not even the president of the United States has ever seen."

My jaw tightens. "We should be clear with the language we use here, Sana. My people did not ask for any of this. I will have a conversation with them about information of a classified nature, and that will be it. Do we understand each other?"

Sana's eyes blink affirmatively, and then she points to a paper on the desk in front of her. "We do. But we will feel much better if everyone signs this."

I know what it is without even looking at it. I have signed many such forms in my career and understand the legal consequences of revealing anything that violates the conditions set therein. "I will do this, Sana, but I need you to do something for me."

"Anything," she says, biting her lip seductively. "Anything at all."

A month and a day later, I follow the GPS directions and turn the rented Jeep Cherokee onto North Sedgwick Road in the Lincoln Park area of Chicago, my father in the seat next to me and Brinley, sans sling and recovering ahead of schedule, in the back. An early spring drizzle has just ended.

"What's the number?" Brinley asks.

"It's 1176. Should be right . . . here." I come to a slow stop along the curb and point across the street to a nice redbrick colonial with a perfect flower garden in front. We sit and look at it for a minute, and I shut down the engine. The neighborhood is modest, well-kept but older, definitely upper middle class. The air smells like wet road. All the streets are paved, I realize, not like where we come from. It smells like a city, and it's a smell I miss only occasionally now.

Coming here has been a journey for me just as much as for Pop, I think. It's only been a month since I found out about his past and the man that he once was. I was willing to trade him for Sana Locke, my own father, because I was angry and felt betrayed. If things had gone another way, if Brin hadn't been there, he would be in Russia now and dead for sure. After saving thousands. After preventing Las Vegas from becoming a radioactive ghost town forever. Dead for sure.

I also realize bringing him here may be an act of extreme cruelty. Despite all the good he has done in his manufactured existence, Pop understands better than anyone those that he hurt as Freddie Meyer, Kitty Ellison chief among them. For a man who is fighting to remember and forget at the same time, seeing her again may be more than he can take. But this is his call, and I know now that he's earned it. We will, both of us, live with the aftermath. Either way, he is my father and I love him.

"That's it?" he asks, the emotion choking his words. "That's where she lives?"

I nod. "Yeah, Pop. That's the house."

It took Sana more than a week to get back to me, but when she did, there was caution in her words. "She can't know, Beck. You can't tell her. More importantly, he can't tell her. I can't believe you even told me. I shouldn't know this."

I was in my office, so I spoke quietly into the phone. "I came for you that night, Sana. I killed a man for you, and I gave you something much more important than what you came for." There was a long pause on the line, and then she gave me the address. She also filled me in on what transpired in the lives of Kitty and Roger Ellison after that night in the desert outside Las Vegas in April 1957. Records of the interviews conducted by the FBI indicate it was a tough couple of weeks for them both, considering their respective relationships with Freddie Meyer, who perished in a fire after stealing the warhead. Dr. Ellison recovered from his heart episode but not from the shame of letting a Russian spy into his home. "Sloppy with secrets" was the determination of the investigation, and it cost the scientist his security clearance. He drank excessively but managed to live until he was eighty.

Kitty Ellison was less affected professionally, having not started her career in teaching until after Project 57 was done and forgotten by all but a few key people in the United States government. The interviews conducted with her by the FBI were equally thorough, but not even J. Edgar Hoover's men believed she was a Soviet sympathizer. She was bereaved at the loss of a man she loved, refusing to believe he was a spy.

"You're wrong about him," she told each of the agents who questioned her. "I loved Freddie. He was a good man. He cared about peace in the world. He cared about me. If he did anything, he stopped them from doing something *horrible*."

Ironically, Pop had used the same word more than fifty years later when he called the Russian embassy in Washington, D.C. "But you were asking me to do something horrible," he had said. Kitty Ellison had known his truer nature. She had known he would never hurt the innocent.

I shared this with Pop after my call with Sana, and his face came to life like nothing I had ever seen. Sitting outside this house in Chicago now, I think that was the right call.

"What do we do?" Pop asks.

I turn and look at them both. "Well, we can wait and see if she comes out, but she's about the same age as you, Pop. It might be a while. Might be never."

Pop stares at the house. "A physics professor, you say?"

"University of Chicago. Forty years and one of the best, as I understand it. And she became an ardent antinuclear activist, apparently."

I can see him picturing her in his mind. "She was so smart. Married?"

He has asked the question three times since we landed at Midway Airport. "Since '61," I reply. "Three children, twin girls and a boy. Her husband passed away a long time ago, but she has a passel of grandkids. Lives here with one of her daughters."

"Good for her. So, what do we do?"

I look back to Brin. "Well," I say, "we thought Brin could go up and knock on the door, say she was looking for directions or something. That way you might get a look at her, if only for a minute."

Pop unbuckles his seat belt and reaches for the door handle. "Hell, let's just go up there."

Brinley tugs on the back of his coat. "We can't do that, Pop. Remember? We talked about this."

Dejected, Pop rights himself in the seat again. "Oh yeah. National security. Isn't that some bullshit?"

I touch him on the shoulder. "What do you say, Pop. Shall we give it a try?"

He lifts his chin. "Please."

A minute later, the front door opens and a woman of about fifty looks out at the younger woman in front of her, a deadly ninja with curly brown hair swallowed in a smart leather jacket. Inside the car, Pop gasps. "Kitty."

"No, Pop," I say. "She's too young. Must be the daughter."

"Damn," he says. "She's the spitting image."

This will be enough, I think. But then another woman appears at the door, and this time there can be no question. "Pop, look."

He does, and weeps. I have never been prouder to be his son.

# ACKNOWLEDGMENTS

This book would have remained just a wild hair of an idea if I had been a rational human being and kept it to myself. Because I didn't, you got sucked into this strange journey with me, and for that I owe you. So, thanks. To Janet Reid (JetReid Literary), for rolling the dice and agreeing to represent, befriend, and counsel me. You are the student-loan debt I will probably never pay off. To Keith Kahla, Kelley Ragland, Alice Pfeifer, and the marvelous team at St. Martin's Press and Minotaur Books, I am thrilled to be in your fine stable and hope we make a lot of hay together. To Kristen Weber, none of this would have happened if it hadn't been for your exceptional editing skills. This is entirely your fault. To those I constantly strain the bonds of friendship with by pestering you for your expertise and to read and improve my work, Steve Hampton, LtC, USAF, Ret.; Katie Hampton; Lt. Col. Wayne Mason, US Army, Ret.; Jamie Woodard; Milan Njegomir; Ed Camhi; and Dr. William Gallus, Professor of Meteorology, Iowa State University. I will never let any of you leave my dungeon. Sorry. Special thanks to Sheriff Kerry Lee of the Lincoln County Sheriff's Department; Jocelyn Maldonado, Senior Crime

Scene Analyst (retired), Las Vegas Metropolitan Police Department; Michael Hall, Executive Director of the National Atomic Testing Museum; and Suzanne Becker, Ph.D., University of Nevada, Las Vegas. Thanks for pointing me in all the right directions and keeping me on course. My greatest thanks to Pam Borgos, my wife and oldest friend. When I told you in the second grade this was going to happen, you didn't believe me, did you?